CASH BRADDOCK

What Reviewers Say About Ashley Bartlett's Work

Dirty Sex

"A young, new author, Ashley Bartlett definitely should be on your radar. She's a really fresh, unique voice in a sea of good authors. …I found [*Dirty Sex*] to be flawless. The characters are deep and the action fast-paced. The romance feels real, not contrived. There are no fat, padded scenes, but no skimpy ones either. It's told in a strong first-person voice that speaks of the author's and her character's youth, but serves up surprisingly mature revelations."—*Out in Print*

Dirty Money

"Bartlett has exquisite taste when it comes to selecting the right detail. And no matter how much plot she has to get through, she never rushes the game. Her writing is so well-paced and so self-assured, she should be twice as old as she really is. That self-assuredness also mirrors through to her characters, who are fully realized and totally believable."—*Out in Print*

"Bartlett has succeeded in giving us a mad-cap story that will keep the reader turning page after page to see what happens next."
—*Lambda Literary*

Dirty Power

"Bartlett's talents are many. She knows her way around an action scene, she writes *memorably* hot sex, her plots are seamless, and her characters are true and deep. And if that wasn't enough, Coop's voice is so genuine, so world-weary, jaded, and outrageously sarcastic that if Bartlett had none of the aforementioned attributes, the read would still be entertaining enough to stretch over three books."
—*Out in Print*

Visit us at www.boldstrokesbooks.com

By the Author

Sex & Skateboards

Dirty Trilogy

Dirty Sex

Dirty Money

Dirty Power

Cash Braddock Series

Cash Braddock

CASH BRADDOCK

by

Ashley Bartlett

2016

This Trade Paperback Original Is Published By
Bold Strokes Books, Inc.
P.O. Box 249
Valley Falls, NY 12185

First Edition: November 2016

CREDITS
Editor: Cindy Cresap
Production Design: Susan Ramundo
Cover Design By Megan Tillman

Acknowledgments

I'm still probably not a grown-up. But maybe I'm getting closer. Cash Braddock is totally a grown-up. She just happens to be a drug dealer. But Cash and I have one big trait in common. We are done with social niceties.

My mother always said that the only thing she wanted was for me to be healthy and happy. I spent the better part of my twenties cultivating personal health and happiness. It went well. But now I realize that the external, the social, the constructs are relevant. I have always disregarded the rules, but I also let it slide when other people followed them. Even when the rules were wrong or hateful or built on lies. This book is my first salvo. I don't always agree with Cash. She may have given up on too many rules. But maybe the rest of us can be a little less abiding.

As always, I couldn't have finished this book without some help. A massive thank you to Sydney Stigerts for the gift of legitimacy. You answered some very strange questions in intricate detail. And you frequently did so at all hours of the night.

Carsen Taite, you have been many things to me: pal, mentor, bro, cheerleader, mother? But you have consistently been my hero. Thanks again for guiding me through the last month of blind panic that comes with finishing a novel.

Everyone at Bold Strokes Books, but especially Radclyffe and Sandy Lowe for never shutting me down. Even when they probably should. And thanks to Cindy Cresap for always shutting me down. Like a champ.

Finally, thanks to you, my readers. Without an audience this would be another exercise in arrogance. It still probably is, but I appreciate the indulgence anyway. I hope you will stick around for the rest of the series. Cash and I are just getting started.

Dedication

For my wife.
If I ever go to jail,
I know you'll be right there with me.

CHAPTER ONE

There were two wedding invitations in my mailbox. That was when I realized I was getting old. It wasn't the way my back hurt when I got up at noon. Or my mutual funds maturing. Hell, it wasn't even the way that teenagers looked liked children. It was the fucking wedding invitations. Three this week.

I had to blame Prop 8 and DOMA a little. Most of my buddies from college had been married for years. They were just making it official. But half of them were terrified back in the summer of '08 when their significant others started eyeing wedding bands. Prop 8 was pretty much a relief. Not that they—in their queer activist twenties—would admit it. And now it was legal for real. Even the non-activist kids were signing up.

But it wasn't even the gaymos. It was the straight kids too. Not that I knew a lot of straight people. Still, my little cousin was marrying her boyfriend. And my old roommate was marrying his girlfriend. I couldn't even feign insult anymore at being sent invitations when I wasn't allowed the privilege of marriage. That trick had gotten me out of quite a few weddings.

I fucking hated weddings. Not for some sad, lonely reason. And not because of the expense or the pain in my ass that it was to attend. I just didn't like pretending I gave a fuck. I didn't mind dressing up. I didn't enjoy it, but I didn't mind it. I simply didn't want to bother filling out the damn R.S.V.P. and putting it in the mail. I didn't want to show up and smile and tell people they looked pretty or handsome or happy or lucky. I didn't begrudge my friends their happiness. But sitting there and watching a ceremony that I was supposed to be emotionally invested in was draining. I didn't do well with shit that was socially obligatory.

Maybe my uncle was right and I really was a cynical asshole.

The rest of my mail was crap. I tossed it all on the table inside my front door and hoped the invitations would miraculously fall and disappear. I stretched out on my couch, thanked myself for remembering the AC before I left the house earlier, and picked up the book I was reading.

I woke up to the obnoxious chirp of my cell phone and my cat kneading my stomach. Her claws went right through the cotton of my T-shirt and into my skin.

"That hurts." Nickels seemed okay with it. I disentangled the cat's claws and looked at my phone. I had three new deliveries in addition to the six already on my schedule. The last was a party, which was probably good, but also sucked. Damn social niceties. Even college boys had social standards. I hated playing into them.

I sorted through the fresh cut herbs stored in my pantry. I arranged a couple bunches in two low, flat boxes. They looked a little sparse so I added a few organic tomatoes into a corner of each box. They were passable. I pulled the basil back out, tucked a bag of white pills into one, light orange into the other. None of my other deliveries required me to keep up appearances.

As I was leaving, I glanced in the mirror by the door. My accidental nap had done terrible things to my hair. I set the boxes back on the kitchen table and went into the bathroom. It took five minutes of careful straight iron application to make my pompadour stand up the way it was supposed to. I smoothed the sides and part with paste. It would do. I went back out to the kitchen. Nickels was staring at the boxes like she knew I was abandoning her.

"I'm sorry," I said. She was unmoved. "I'll be back later." She meowed. "Yeah, I love you too."

I grabbed my keys and bag, glared at the wedding invitations, and took off. My first two deliveries were easy. Fab Forties. I turned off Folsom Boulevard and marveled at the way the trees dropped the temp a couple degrees. Wealth had its perks. Even nature helped with the imbalance. At the first house, I parked on the street. Visibility was one of my greatest services. Brant opened the door about two seconds after slight bells echoed through the house.

"Honey, you're just in time. I'm doing a lime cilantro vinaigrette, and it needs time for the flavors to fully absorb."

If he was bothering to tell me what he was cooking, that meant he had company. I glanced at the garage. No luxury sedan visible through the leaded glass. The husband wasn't home. That meant one of Brant's walking friends.

"Then you're lucky I brought lime leaves. I'm almost out this week."

"No." Brant looked shocked.

"One of my customers decided they were divine in cocktails. She cleaned me out. But I saved some for you," I said.

"That's tragic. Why would anyone do that to a cocktail? Come inside. You have to see the new curtains."

As if I gave a fuck about curtains. "The ones you were telling me about? I thought they wouldn't be here until next week."

Brant winked. He knew how painful this conversation was for me. "You'll love them." He spun and led me through the house. We stopped on the way to the kitchen so I could admire the curtains in the white room. I didn't think people called them that anymore. Maybe people never called them that. But I had too many friends growing up with mothers who maintained a perfect room that no one was allowed in. White couches weren't meant for dirty teenagers. Brant had chosen a rich cream for the curtains. Something warm enough to lighten the room without being too heavy for a Sacramento summer. I said appropriate things.

"Have you met Janice? She's Chuck's baby sister," Brant said as we stepped into the kitchen. "Janice, this is Cash."

Janice looked up at me from the breakfast nook. She took in my worn designer jeans, plain white T-shirt, and dirty Converse. She smiled at me. The smile was strained in the way that was reserved for the help. I guess I wasn't hiding my status well enough. What a shame.

"Pleased to meet you." I gave her the smile she was expecting. The one that said I respect that your husband's bank account is bigger than mine.

"Yes," she said.

Wasn't it my fucking honor.

"Let me take that." Brant held out his hands. I gave him the box. He took it into the oversized pantry and unloaded a few items. The bag of pills went into a container of rice. He was lucky I knew to double bag for him. Janice didn't look up from her iPhone.

I took out my phone. It was the same generation as hers. Brant watched me punch in items arbitrarily until we reached the magic number. He handed me his credit card. I swiped it through the reader and handed the phone to him for a signature.

"You're a lifesaver." Brant winked at me. His stash must have been low. Boy was abusing the product. I'd have to watch his intake. An overdose led to a lot of nasty questions.

"I bet you say that to all the boys," I said.

Brant laughed. Janice scowled. Queers weren't supposed to be so casually queer. Even when your brother was in the club. Though Chuck did very well at the whole gender conformity thing.

"Only the dirty farm boys," Brant said. "Janice, I'd let you use Cash too, but her supplies are regulated. I can't have you cutting into my source of organics."

Janice's curiosity won over her disdain. "Is that really your name?"

"Only since infancy," I said. She looked skeptical. "I think my mother was high when she named me."

Brant laughed. Everyone always did. It was a great joke. Except for the part where it was true.

"Thanks for the produce, honey." We walked back to the front door.

"Of course. I'll see you next week?"

Brant nodded. "I'll text you with my order."

The rest of my afternoon was easy. Peggy, the straight version of Brant plus twenty years, didn't have company. I gave her the box of produce and swiped her card.

Four of my deliveries were in the various apartment complexes around Sacramento State University. Most of my business at the college dropped off in May, but there were still a few stragglers. Plus, summer session kept the campus limping along.

One of my deliveries was in Land Park. It was another housewife, but she didn't bother hiding from her husband. No sweating, wasted produce there. The final kid was a City dropout. He enrolled in classes twice a year, collected financial aid, then dropped all the classes. The school or the government was going to catch on at some point, but until then he enjoyed Oxy and I enjoyed money.

The college boys having a party texted to up their order so I called Nate, my weekend help, and enlisted him. He agreed to meet at my place at nine, which left enough time for me to inhale a burrito and a beer. Not bad for a Friday.

I was two bites of salsa and a swig of beer in when there was a knock on my door. Nate wasn't the type to be early. I swung the door open and leaned against the jamb.

"You ever heard of Natasha Lyonne? She's that dyke chick on *Orange is the New Black*. Like hot, but in a real way." My fifteen-year-old neighbor pushed past me and went straight to the DVD shelf.

"I have a pulse, tiger."

"What's that mean?" Andy flipped her honey brown hair out of her face. She was rocking an Ellen Page post coming out cut. This week.

"She's hot. Yes, I know who she is. Does your mother know you're over here?"

Andy traced her fingertips along the shelves and mouthed the alphabet. Nickels decided to grace us with her presence. She must have heard Andy's voice. "Hey, Nick, Nick, Nickie." Andy picked her up and continued with the alphabet. The cat started to purr. "Mom's working. I texted. But I'm not staying."

"I hope not. You haven't been invited to stay." I almost managed arch, but then I remembered I didn't have quite enough class to be arch.

"So Nicky, Lyonne, whatever, is in this cheerleading movie. I'm totally into her right now."

"Top shelf. *But I'm a Cheerleader*. Grab *Girl, Interrupted* too. Once you watch *But I'm a Cheerleader*, you're going to be madly in love with Clea Duvall. Trust me. She's a freak show in *Girl, Interrupted*, but a hot freak show."

"How do you have so many old movies?"

"If you keep making cracks about how old I am, you won't have access any more."

Andy looked up from her task. She managed to look confused and guilty all at once. "I didn't…I'm not saying…Sorry."

"I'm giving you shit."

"I just mean, your collection is like better than Netflix sometimes."

"Netflix has the worst lesbian movies. And they were all made the year you were born. And the lesbians are represented by thin metaphors instead of actual lesbians."

"I think that was an insult. Pretty sure, actually. But you like Netflix so shut your face. Also, I like Netflix so shut your face. I'm just saying, you've got better lesbian movies than they do." For her generation, that was a huge compliment. I think.

She tucked both DVDs under her arm. Nickels batted at them.

"Your mom leave dinner?"

"Yeah. She'll be back at midnight. I'll be fine."

I nodded. "*But I'm a Cheerleader* is R because of a sex scene, but it's a homophobic rating." Andy tilted her head. "Lesbian sex will destroy the children. You'll survive. But *Girl, Interrupted* has some tough spots. It takes place in a mental institution. If it's too much, turn it off, 'kay?"

"Yeah. Fine." So much sincerity.

"There's a chick in there who's institutionalized 'cause she's a dyke. Keep an eye." I grinned.

"Are you going to give me another history lecture?" Andy sighed and set the cat down.

"Always. Now, get out of here. I have to work tonight. Got to finish my dinner."

"Thanks." She headed out the door. "I'll text if I light the place on fire."

"If you light the place on fire, call the fire department. Then text," I shouted. The door was already closed, but I could hear her laughing. Nickels climbed back in her bed. "Oh, I see how it is." She closed her eyes.

CHAPTER TWO

Nate showed up as I was rinsing my bottle. We counted out a full rainbow of pills and stuffed the small baggies into our messenger bags. Nate was good with numbers so I trusted him to keep track without taking notes. Parties were terrible for tracking inventory. His ability to rattle off numbers at the end of the night was one of his best qualities. That and nearly six feet of muscle. Very few people were dumb enough to argue with Nathan Xiao.

I followed Nate to a house off 65th. He knew the neighborhoods around the colleges better than I did. I had my dignity so I made it a point to not know college neighborhoods. We parked a block away from each other. Neither of us had ever articulated an escape plan, but we both had a vague understanding that we didn't want to be there if the cops broke up a party full of drunk twenty-year-olds. If we parked in opposite directions, it increased our chances of driving away.

A hipster kid opened the door. He would have been a prep-type in my day, but ten years of trends had done nothing good for his style. Too tight button-down, too tight jeans, haircut reminiscent of the Victorian era. I knew the kid. He was the one who had texted me an invite, but I could never remember his name. Something woefully nineties and forgettable. Pacey? Bailey? Television was never good for baby names.

"Cash! Nate! You made it!"

As if we were friends.

I shook his hand. "Hey." He nodded and dismissed me.

"Hey, Dawson." Nate shook his hand just hard enough to show who was stronger. "You always have great whiskey. How could we pass it up?"

I managed not to roll my eyes. This was Nate's other talent. Talking to douchey guys in their own language.

The kid nearly jumped in excitement. "We were just going to do a tasting. You want in?"

"Later, definitely. Got to unload our pockets first, you know?" Nate nodded at his messenger bag.

"Totally. Well, come on in."

Dawson melted away in the direction of his cheap whiskey tasting and we moved into the living room. I was constantly amazed that kids still had house parties. But they were good for business, and this one was packed. By unspoken agreement, Nate found a wall to post up on while I made my way to the back of the house. In the backyard, I found a keg and more drunk college kids. A girl approached as soon as she saw me.

"Hey, you're Cash, right?"

"That's me."

"I heard you got Adderall." Her eyes shone. Youthful. Dumb. Yes, for her I definitely had Adderall.

We negotiated to a price twenty percent higher than I charged my regulars. She gave me some cash from her cleavage—I should have gone for thirty percent—and I gave her a bag of blue pills.

Parties were nice because I didn't have to be nearly as discreet. In fact, blatant tended to earn higher revenue. It made me more approachable. And at a party like this I didn't need to worry about cops. The kids were all so young that anyone older than twenty-five was as obvious as, well, me.

After I had done the backyard for an hour, Nate and I swapped. I wandered through the kitchen and was thankful I wasn't drinking. Nothing looked clean.

The wad of cash in my chest pocket had grown to a decent size. I'd gone through about half of what I was carrying and overcharged nearly everyone. I didn't feel bad about upping the price at parties.

Hell, they expected it. Plus, Nate was the party guy. His tolerance was higher. I was much better at peddling subpar organic produce with a side of OxyContin or Xanax. Housewives loved me.

I followed an intoxicated couple toward the front of the house. He tripped and she pushed him upright. He grabbed her ass. For balance, I'm sure. Her heel caught on the perfectly restored hardwood and they stumbled into a wall.

Alcohol was not an attractive drug.

Across the living room, I caught sight of a woman who very much did not belong. She was my age, maybe a couple of years older. Her dark hair caught the glow of the dull lights placed throughout the room. She disappeared behind a group of wrestling boys, then reappeared in the mouth of the hallway leading to the back of the house. With a final glance around the room, she melted away. She was looking for someone. I wanted to be that someone.

I ducked into the hallway. She wasn't there. Not in the rooms off the hallway either. When I got to the backyard, Nate started to approach me, but I waved him off. She was sitting on the retaining wall holding up the long dead garden. Weren't hipsters supposed to be into gardening?

She had her feet stretched out on the cracked patio. She was wearing boots and comfortably tight jeans. Her hair was long by my standards, cropped between her ears and chin.

"You look as lost as I feel." I sat next to her.

"That obvious, huh?" She smiled and I was ready to send out one of those damn invitations myself. "My baby sis and I were supposed to hang out tonight. She brought me here and ditched me." She tugged at the collar of her checked shirt, loosened her tie more. "Which she has done one thousand million times. So, really, I should have seen it coming."

"She sounds like a peach," I said.

"She's much more charming when she's not present. Trust me."

"I'm Cash Braddock." I held out my hand and she took it.

"Laurel Collins."

About four seconds after the appropriate time to let go, I released her hand.

"So, Cash, how did you end up at this sad affair?"

"Wingman meets third wheel. I've been ditched and now I think I need better friends."

"May I suggest friends who don't date twenty-year-olds?"

I laughed. "Noted. Any chance I could interest you in a drink? Somewhere legal where we don't get a lecture on home brewing." Also, somewhere no one would come up and ask me for drugs. That was more second date material.

"You're reading my mind here." Laurel stood. "Do you need to tell your friend that you're leaving?"

"As tempted as I am to abandon him, yeah, I should probably give him a heads-up. You?"

"You know, I think this will be an excellent lesson for my sister. She can walk home."

I laughed. She was kind of a dick. I liked it.

"Are you driving?" I asked.

"Yeah. I'm a couple blocks away."

"Me too. Do you know The Depot?"

"Little place next to Badlands?" she asked.

"That's the one. Meet you there in twenty?"

"I look forward to it." Her mouth twitched like she was fighting a grin.

I watched her walk away. She had a fantastic walk. Like she knew where she was going. I wished I had that knowledge.

Nate was finishing a sale when I found him again. I hovered far enough away so his customers wouldn't feel crowded. When he was done, he turned to me.

"Please tell me you're taking that chick out."

"You don't mind?"

"Hell no. You need a life. And that woman is totally your type."

"You know my type?"

"Gorgeous dykes. You're simple like that. Even I could get a read on her. She's got that whole chick who could kick your ass look."

"You're crazy."

Nate grinned. "Let me guess, up close she's kinda buff, but tone not muscle. Strong jawline. Pretty eyes. Full lips—"

"No, just the bottom one," I interrupted.

He laughed. "And she was annoyed by everyone at the party except you."

"I don't like this game."

"Get out of here, man." He pushed me toward the door.

"Yeah, yeah I'm going."

"I'll follow you out. How much product you got left?"

"About half. You really don't mind?"

"You ask again, I'll punch you," he said.

We stopped by my car. I dug the remaining pills out of my bag and gave them to Nate. We bundled the cash we had made so far, and I stashed it in the locked compartment in the back of my SUV. No point carrying it around. He told me he'd be by my place in the morning to count out and get paid.

Fifteen minutes later, I snagged parking on 20th Street. I realized I was nervous. Carrying a trunkful of drugs and illicit cash, smuggling pills across the border, selling product for a dirty cop, none of that scared me. But this was unfamiliar territory. What if she wasn't there? What if she was boring? What if she thought I was boring?

I pushed open the door to The Depot and waited for my eyes to adjust to the dim lighting. This was the only quiet gay bar I'd ever found. It was probably the only quiet gay bar in America. Maybe the world. That was its appeal. I felt movement to my right and turned in time to see Laurel push off the wall.

"Hey." I managed not to grin. Had to be cool.

"Hey. I don't think I've ever been inside this place. Only walked past."

"Yeah? It's never crowded."

"Big plus."

We moved to the bar. Laurel leaned over and made eye contact with the bartender. He took his time making his way over. They didn't mind women here, but we weren't their intended clientele.

"What can I get you?" he asked.

"Anchor Steam for me." I looked at Laurel.

"Any chance it's on tap?" she asked both of us.

"Yep," the bartender said.

"Two then."

"IDs?" He pulled glasses from under the bar while he waited.

I thumbed out my ID and some cash. Laurel took the ID and handed hers over with mine.

Getting ID'd was obnoxious, but I knew I'd be even more irritated the day they stopped asking. The bartender handed back our licenses and started to fill our glasses. Laurel handed my ID back.

"Your name's actually Cash?"

"Long story."

She nodded. I put some money on the bar and we grabbed our glasses.

"Best seats are out back," I said. She nodded and followed me. Out back was actually caged in, but the air was fresher than in the bar and it was far enough from the pool tables to escape the noise. We settled on bar stools.

"So you gonna share?" Laurel asked.

"What?"

"The long story."

"Oh. That." She nodded. "My mom was broke so this way she always had cash."

Laurel looked skeptical. "Can't say she never did."

"Oh, that's good. I think I'll add that to the cheap explanation."

Almost got a smile. "And the real story?"

"My mother is an addict. She managed to stay sober until I was born, but as soon as she had me…" I shrugged. "Decision-making—like baby names—wasn't her strong suit."

"That's rough."

"Not really. My uncle Clive, her brother, raised me. Last time I saw her, I was six years old. She wasn't really a parent. Kind of like a crazy aunt. My uncle is cool though."

"He live in Sac?"

"Up the hill. He has a little organic farm. Well, I guess we both do. I'm a partner."

"You're a farmer?" She smiled and pushed her hair up out of her eyes. It stayed for half a second before falling back across her cheek. Swoon. I had to replay the conversation and remove my head from my ass before I answered.

"Not really. He farms, I deliver his produce. It's very glamorous. What about you?"

"Am I a farmer?"

I grinned. "No. Although, yes, are you a farmer? And if not, then why? You got something against farmers?"

"I can't say I've always been a fan of farmers, but I recently met this super hot farmer chick, and she is making me reevaluate my prejudice."

Christ, the girl was smooth. I used to be smooth.

"That's good. You're so open-minded. I've always appreciated that about you."

"I do my best."

"If not farming, then how do you disappoint your parents?" I asked.

She scoffed. "Please. I'm so good at disappointing my parents." She took a long drink of Anchor Steam. Nodded in appreciation. Set the glass down. "I was a double major. Criminal justice and English. And I've now managed to avoid law school for about a decade."

"Impressive."

"It's a talent."

One of many. I was sure.

"Sibs? Baby sis any good at being a disappointment?"

She laughed. "She makes me look like an amateur. I'm the oldest of four. I've been told they will mature. I'm still waiting."

"How old?"

"Four or five years between all of us. Youngest is eighteen. She's at Sac State, obviously, but I'm thinking studying hasn't been a priority."

I laughed. If sis was going to the parties I was invited to, then no, studying was not a priority. Except maybe the week before finals when I would sell out of Adderall.

Laurel told me a bit more about the family, one of her brothers hadn't escaped law school. She asked some questions about my uncle's farm. She was easy to talk to. Easier to look at. Nathan was right. She was exactly my type. Dangerous.

CHAPTER THREE

When I got home just after two, I noticed that the light out back was still on. I glanced out and found Andy sprawled on the bench on her side of the porch, the glow of her phone illuminated her face. She was asleep. The phone finished vibrating its message, then went dark. I let myself outside.

"Andy, hey, Anderson." I shook her foot. "Wake up, tiger."

"Huh?"

"What are you doing out here? Your mom home yet?"

Andy sat up and rubbed her face. "She got stuck at the hospital. It's nice out. Fell asleep." She swiped her phone and grinned.

I sat next to her. "Hot text date?"

"This is why I think you're old. What the hell is a text date?" She tapped her phone, then locked it.

"Sorry. Snapchat date."

She sighed. "Yeah. Snapchat date. That's a thing."

"You're an ass."

"One of us has to talk to chicks. You're not stepping up." Andy leaned her head back against the side of the house and closed her eyes. "I can't help that women want me."

I did my best not to laugh at her. "I will have you know that I just shut down a bar with a chick."

"Uh-huh. Me too. I way just shut down a bar with a chick."

"Do you have any idea what that means?" I asked.

"Of course." She opened her eyes. "It's like you…shut down a bar…with a chick?"

"It means we were there so long, the bar shut down."

"Wait. For real. You went on an actual date? With an actual chick?" I nodded. "That's dope." She shoved my shoulder.

High praise.

"It's late. I'm going to bed. So should you." I stood.

"Yeah, sure." She made no move.

"At least go inside. I haven't fixed the lock on the gate yet." The neighborhood was safe enough, but I didn't like her being out alone this late. Neither would her mother.

"I thought you were going to last week?"

"Bought the lock. Haven't installed it."

She perked up. "Can we tomorrow? I can help."

Kid just wanted to wear my tool belt. "Sure. If you go inside now."

"Fine." Andy stood.

"Good night."

"'Night."

I opened my door and waited until she was inside before heading in. I heard her locks click, then footsteps to the front door. She slid the deadbolt and hit the lights. She'd be asleep on the couch in two minutes.

❖

I woke up to my phone vibrating. It was a text from Robin thanking me for making Andy go to bed the night before and inviting me to dinner. Another text from Henry telling me to call him. Who used phones to make calls any more? Boy was so twentieth century. And paranoid. He was a deputy sheriff. I doubted the sheriff's department was interested in investigating its own members. I hit call.

"Cash. Hey."

"What's up?" I rolled out of bed and pulled on yesterday's jeans.

"Big bust last night. I collected evidence."

"Yeah?"

"And I've been doing a lot of paperwork. Needing to check evidence in and out. You know how it goes."

"Meet me tonight? My place." I had no desire to see Henry, but he always delivered good shit.

"I get off at eleven."

"Cool. See you after?"

"Yep." He hung up. No phone etiquette. You gotta at least say good-bye. Let the other person know. Henry was a lost cause. I made a note to give Andy a talk about phone etiquette.

By the time Nate showed up at ten, I had managed to brush my teeth and put on a T-shirt. I opened the door to a cup of coffee. Which made Nate perfect in every way. We sat at the kitchen table and sorted out how much we had sold and for what price. I took some shorthand notes, then counted out his cut. He double-checked it.

"You're giving me too much." He started to count again.

"No. You worked longer and covered me. It's fair."

"But that's not what we agreed."

"You complaining?"

He laughed. "Okay, no. I guess not."

"Besides, I know summer is tight. I need to keep you around."

"And I need to pay tuition." Nate was a grad student at Davis. He was studying something having to do with brain chemistry. He'd tried to explain it to me once, but I didn't do well beyond monosyllabic words. "Thanks. Do you still want me to make deliveries in West Sac this weekend?"

"Yeah. What do you need?"

We counted out the leftover pills from the night before and separated what he would need for the weekend. I added some hydrocodone to his mix and he was good to go. I was running low on Xanax. Nate didn't need it, so no big. Xanax was my territory.

"Hey, how did it go with the chick last night?" He grinned knowingly. Obnoxious.

"Good."

"That's it? Good? She was smoking and you say it was good?" He scoffed and went back to stowing baggies in the Thermos he used to hide drugs.

"We talked until the bar closed. It was good."

"You didn't get any? She was cruising you hard. Come on."

"She was not. Get your head out of your ass." I started putting away the detritus of our negotiations. Pills in the pantry. High shelf above Andy's head. That kid was too curious. Money in the empty flour tin. I'd put it away properly later.

"Cash, she watched you from the moment you walked outside. She's got it bad."

"You think?" Man, I hoped he was right. "Should I text her?"

"And I'm the one with my head up my ass? You're an idiot."

"Whatever." I knew right then that I was going to text her later. But he didn't have to know that.

Nate shook his head. "Good luck. I'll catch you later." He clapped his hand on my shoulder and headed out the door. I locked it behind him.

I took the cup of coffee Nate had brought into my study. While I waited for my laptop to boot, I glanced over our notes. The revenue from the party had been entirely cash. No one used their credit card to buy drugs at a party. I entered the numbers into a spreadsheet. It tracked the sales as produce, which kept Braddock Farm's accountant happy. When everything was entered, I shredded the handwritten notes. It didn't matter than I was a low-level dealer. There was no need to be stupid about this sort of shit.

I went back to the kitchen and pulled the money out of the flour tin. I trusted Nate, but that didn't mean I had to be naïve. I moved half the shit out of my freezer and pulled out the box of taquitos from the back. I shoved the stack of cash underneath the taquitos. As I was replacing everything in the freezer, there was a knock on my back door.

"Come in," I shouted. Only Robin or Andy used the back door.

"Sounded like you were up. Can we fix the lock on the fence now?" Andy rounded the corner into the kitchen.

"Sure. Just a sec." I put the coffee pot together. Nickels followed Andy into the kitchen and meowed at her.

"Nick, Nickels." Andy sat on the floor. Nickels head butted her.

I hit the button to grind the coffee and Nickels ran out of the room. Coffee grinding was rude. Andy waited not so patiently.

"Your mom still sleeping?" I asked.

"Yeah. Figured I'd let her." Andy got up off the floor.

"How big of you."

I pushed aside the curtain under my sink and hauled out my toolbox. Andy leaned in past me and grabbed my tool belt. I tore into the lock packaging while she wrestled with the buckle on the belt. She stashed the screws I handed her in one of the tool belt pockets.

Andy followed me outside. And she only ran into one wall while adjusting the contents of her belt. I went to the gate. Andy huffed while I spaced out where I wanted to put the lock and marked the wood with a pencil. I handed Andy my drill.

"So I just put the screws in?"

"That's generally how they work."

Andy sighed disapprovingly and placed her first screw. I had one of those panic moments where I wondered if I should have given her safety goggles. But then I remembered that I didn't have safety goggles. And if I had goggles, Andy still wouldn't wear them. By the time I had figured all that out, Andy was done installing all four screws in the latch.

"Now what?"

"Now we install the bolt on the other side." Again, I marked the placement. Andy fished the rest of the screws out of her belt and installed the bolt. When she was done, I swung the gate open and closed. The latch did its thing.

"That's it?" Andy asked.

"Too anticlimactic?"

"I guess. It just seemed like it would be more complicated."

"I'll try and break something this week, okay? Maybe something involving a motor."

"But you don't know anything about motors," Andy said.

"Neither do you."

"So what's the point?"

"I was kidding. I'm not breaking something just so you can fix it."

"Oh. Asshole." Andy handed back the drill.

Yep, that broke my heart.

I went back inside to put away my drill. Andy followed to put away the very necessary tool belt. I poured myself a cup of coffee. Andy stared at it longingly.

"Would you like a cup of coffee?"

"Oh. Okay. I guess. If you're having one."

One day, I planned on not indulging her. One day.

We took our coffee outside. Andy told me about the three girls she'd been flirting with. One lived on the East Coast, and Andy only knew her online, so she didn't count. But I didn't tell Andy that. The other two were from Sac. One went to McClatchy High with Andy. The other was a private school kid. I managed to gather absolutely no detail about any of the girls. Probably because I missed their names and that made it a bit hard to follow. Also, Andy wasn't great with specifics. One of them played water polo and another was into art and one of those two had big tits. I didn't bother reprimanding the use of tits because I was reasonably certain that I'd taught her the word when she was far too young to talk about tits. Her mother was clearly a tolerant woman.

"So what are you doing today?" Andy asked when she realized I wasn't listening. Perceptive.

"Drinking coffee. Then I might text the chick from last night and agonize for the rest of the day about why she isn't texting me back."

"Agonize?"

"It means—"

"I know what it means. I just like it. Agonize. You always use random words."

I had no fucking clue if she was being sincere. "Thanks?"

"So get on it."

"On what?"

"Text her. What's her name? Why wouldn't she text you back?"

"I can't just text her. It's only been like nine hours," I said.

"You're a pussy."

"Dude." I glared.

"What? You are."

"No. Don't say 'pussy.' It's degrading to women."

Andy laughed. Hard. "Okay. I won't say pussy. You're a pansy. Now text the chick."

"Her name is Laurel. And I'll text when I'm ready."

"You know I'm gonna steal your phone and do it if you don't, right?"

"You do and I'll tell your mom."

"Tell me what?" Robin asked from the doorway behind us. She opened the door and sat in the big Adirondack across from us.

"The usual. Andy is a bad seed. And," I lowered my voice to a whisper, "I think she might be a lesbian."

Robin laughed. "It's good you told me. I've got to nip that right in the bud."

"Cash met a chick," Andy said.

"Well done, Cash." Robin nodded at me.

"But she's too much of a pansy to text her." Andy put way too much emphasis on pansy.

I decided to ignore Andy. "Robin, you want some coffee?"

"Thanks. I've already got some brewing."

"Cool. I'm just going to go top mine off." I went into my side of the duplex. As soon as I was in the kitchen, I pulled out my phone and texted Laurel.

CHAPTER FOUR

The restaurant was crowded as hell. Saturday night in the early days of summer. Not surprising. I leaned against a wall and tried to look cool while waiting. Not sure if I pulled off cool, but Laurel seemed happy to see me when she showed up. The host put us at a little table on the back corner of the patio. Just far enough away from the crowded interior that we could hear each other speak. She handed us menus and left.

"I didn't expect you to text me this morning." Laurel leaned back in her chair and grinned.

I smiled back. "I wasn't planning on it, honestly. I was going to be cool and wait a couple of days."

"So what changed your mind?"

"Shame."

"Shame?"

"And fear," I said.

"Shame and fear?"

"I have this neighbor. Fifteen-year-old. When I got home last night she was out back texting her girlfriends."

"Girlfriends like girl friends? Or like girlfriends?"

"The second one. I'm pretty sure she's dating like three other baby dykes."

Laurel laughed. "Three? So you got shown up by a teenager?"

"There's that, but no. I bragged a little that I had been on a date. This morning she threatened to text you if I didn't."

"So that wasn't you who texted to say I was hot as fuck?"

I had a moment of panic before I figured out she was screwing with me. "I don't think she has figured out the passcode on my phone yet. I'm sure she will soon enough."

"So maybe we should come up with a codeword."

"Totally. Like, if you think I sound weird, ask me something only adults would know."

"Like who is president?"

"No, she's smart. But if you ask her what political party Al Gore belongs to, she won't know," I said.

"She could Wikipedia that."

Damn, she was right. "Good point. Ask about The Cranberries. She thinks music started about five years ago."

"She doesn't know who The Cranberries are? That's wrong. You have to educate her."

"I'm doing my best." I held up my hands in surrender.

"That's admirable. So. Very important question." She gave me a look that suggested she was serious.

"Yes?"

"Favorite Cranberries song?"

"No way. You can't pick a favorite Cranberries song. It's like picking a favorite book. You need like a multi-tiered system."

Laurel laughed. "Okay, books at the top of your multi-tiered system?"

"I'm assuming you are talking like desert island scenario here."

She pursed her lips. Which was hot. "No, top twentieth century poets."

"Sylvia Plath and Ani DiFranco."

She nodded. Also hot. "Playwrights?"

"Does it have to be twentieth century? Because Wilde, obviously."

"Modernist? Literature, not art."

"Djuna Barnes, but I've only read *Nightwood*. Modernist for you, but art not literature."

"I see your point about narrowing. Art is too broad." Laurel pushed her hair off her forehead again. Yep, just as enticing as it was the night before.

"Painter, then," I said.

"Picasso, but only because he's the only one I can think of right now. I had an art history class junior year. Did spectacularly bad. Lowest grade I got in college, but the professor was obsessed with Picasso and she was absolutely brilliant."

"Are you a fan by default then?"

"Totally. Of course, I only have opinions on the pieces we discussed in class."

I laughed. I didn't know if it was the honesty or the self-deprecation, but it was working for her. "Okay, I'll admit that I just like to say Djuna Barnes. Great mouthfeel. I had to read *Nightwood* like twenty times to get it and I'm still not sure I do."

"I'm impressed you got through it. It was assigned in queer lit, but I couldn't bother to finish it."

"I'd tell you it's worth it, but I'm not really sure."

"Except for the mouthfeel of saying Djuna Barnes," she said.

"Well, yeah. Except for that."

The waitress arrived, but we had to send her packing. Christ, we hadn't even ordered drinks yet and had covered art, literature, and music. This chick was fantastic.

I walked home from the restaurant. It was later than I'd planned, but Laurel didn't seem in any hurry so I'd figured it was smart to follow her example. We hadn't talked about anything, really. Or anything of substance. No, that wasn't right either. We had talked about everything of substance except for ourselves. Maybe that was my fault. I'd avoided anything that might force me to lie. Most of the time, I liked what I did. It suited me. But somehow I didn't want Laurel to think less of me. Maybe that was why I let her veer so sharply from anything personal that couldn't be found online.

Now, in the retrospect of twenty minutes, I realized how distant she had actually been when it came to herself. I knew what kind of beer she drank and that she wore vintage ties. I didn't know what made her get out of bed in the morning. I did know that she had eyes the color of the sky at dusk. There was a scar on her left hand that she traced when she was nervous. She liked to read. Maybe that was all I needed to know.

I knew I wanted to call her. I knew that was a terrifying thought.

When I got home, Henry's newest Mustang was parked out front. This one was electric blue. Very discreet. I wasn't sure if the flashy car or the fact that he got a new one every year was worse.

Henry was on my front porch. He was splayed on the stairs projecting an air of cool, but I knew he was pissed. He didn't like to be kept waiting, and he definitely didn't like to be kept waiting on the porch of a drug dealer. Not that he would ever say anything. He had a whole good guy thing going on. Perfect smile with perfect teeth, perfect mustache on his perfect face. Perfectly blond hair combed into place even after a twelve-hour shift in a sheriff car. He knew the perfect thing to say to charm anyone at anytime. Women loved him. Old ladies especially. Basically, a Boy Scout. The surface looked good, but underneath was a whole lot of fear that someone might notice that he was a petulant little boy.

"Sorry to keep you waiting, man."

"Hey, no worries. I just got here." It was nearly one. I was willing to bet that he'd been waiting for twenty minutes. He took his time standing. Nope, nothing untoward going on here. Just a couple of high school buddies hanging out.

"Cool. Come inside. You want a beer?"

"Sure. That would be awesome."

If I'd offered him Tang, he would have said it was awesome. I once saw him graciously accept a bologna sandwich from an elderly woman as payment for helping clear her yard. And he was a vegetarian. But then, Henry was polite. I had never mastered that skill. Or wanted to, for that matter.

We went into the kitchen. I opened two beer bottles and set them on the table. Henry proceeded to unpack an assortment of pills from his designer backpack. Elongated yellow pills. Round, white Tylenol #3. Thick beige circles mixed in with shockingly white pills.

"Ambien, Codeine, Xanax, and—I know you don't usually have a market for it, but—Molly."

I pulled out a chair and dropped into it. "You know I can't sell that." Can't was relative. Clive would be pissed, but I'd lied about the business to him plenty of times. Which Henry was well aware of. He was also quite aware that ecstasy wasn't my territory.

"I know you don't usually, but we busted a rave last night. It's so pretty. Look at it. You should have seen the kid I stripped them off. It looked like *The Craft* and *Can't Hardly Wait* had an awkward child. Did you know the nineties are the new eighties?"

"I'm aware." That was why I hated the party scene. Street drugs—and the people who consumed them—were so crass. "But that doesn't mean I can sell Molly."

"You can and you will." It was an order. Henry didn't have the weight to enforce it, though. "Summer is starting. Ecstasy will be a big seller. I know it's not our agreement, but I'll take a ten percent cut on my profit."

"What if I sell them for half price?" It was a bluff.

"Your call. Your risk."

I had an unsettling feeling that he wasn't talking about my risk on the street. "Fine. But don't pull this shit again. I don't care how many raves you bust."

"Cash, man. You don't get it. Raves are cool again. Nineties, hello?"

"Here's the deal. I'll sell this batch, but never again. Or, I can not sell this batch and also never sell Molly." Nate could unload it in Yolo. Somewhere far enough away that no one would notice. Probably.

Henry sighed. "Fine. Just this batch. But promise me one thing."

"What?"

"If it goes well, be open to it in the future. That's all I ask." He put his hands up in surrender.

If I wasn't so set on shielding Nate from Henry, I would make him take these meetings.

"If it sells easy, I'll tell you." Not if it sold for a grand a pill.

"That's my boy." Henry leaned back and sipped his beer. "You hear the reunion is coming up?"

"Reunion?"

"High school? That place we graduated from ten years ago."

"Oh. That. I think I blocked out most of it." I drank my beer and pretended I was catching up with a buddy.

"Come on. You had a great time in high school. The cheerleading squad was never the same when you were done with them." He raised a sculpted eyebrow.

"I never slept with a cheerleader." Student body president, yes. Cheerleader, no.

"Right. I forgot. Never touched 'em." Henry grinned.

I really didn't want to relive my teenage years. "So you can see why I don't want to go meet the husbands of all the chicks who broke my heart."

"Hey, I heard Amy Becker came out. So she won't have a husband."

"She came out two weeks after graduation. We dated the entire summer before I went to college."

"Oh."

"Sorry. You're lacking on the queer kid gossip."

"Damn. I thought that was a good one." He turned the bottle in his hands. "Jessie Chandler."

"Ran into her at Faces." I thought back and tried to situate it in time. I was really into cuffed pants that summer. "About eight years ago."

"Skylar…umm…James?"

"Jamison. I went to her wedding last year," I said.

"Fuck me. You win." No shit. "What about you? Anything exciting happening?"

I searched desperately for something to tell him that couldn't be used as leverage. Andy was off limits. So were my uncle and Nate. "I went on a date tonight."

"No."

"Yes."

"She hot?"

"Totally. Met her at a party. Followed her around until she agreed to leave with me."

"That's my boy. Never give up. So how'd it go? Pretend I care about more than her bra size."

I mustered every ounce of the douche bag teen I had been. "Her name is Laurel. She's got a body that—actually, she doesn't. Not your type."

"Too gay?" he asked. I nodded. "So she's got a body that would make you blow your wad? But mine's safe?"

I laughed because he expected it. "Exactly. But I don't know. She's kinda standoffish. We'll see. You know?"

"Ahhh, classic Cash." There was no classic Cash. "Let me guess. She doesn't know you're a drug dealer. And she's got some job that makes you clench when you think about telling her. You're not going to call her."

I realized that I had no idea what Laurel did. I'd avoided the subject for my sake. "It's not like that. I just don't know if I'm gonna call her." I almost believed it.

"She didn't put out? Poor kid." Henry drained his beer. "I'm going to take off. Thanks for the beer."

"No problem."

"Let me know if the chick puts out."

Sure. Henry would be the first person I'd call. "Right, man. I'll see you later."

He left. I heard the door close. I waited until his car started up, then went to turn the lock. I could never quite place what I didn't like about Henry. He was fun. Charming when he wanted to be. Great for looking at girls with. Total dick, but I never felt threatened by it. It was more like, under the surface, he was a misogynist. I'd never seen overt evidence. It was just that most women weren't really people to him. Somehow my looking like a boy was enough to escape his misogyny though.

I rinsed out our bottles and tossed them in the recycling. Then I stashed the pills he had brought. At least he was good for free drugs.

Chapter Five

"What are you doing tonight?" Andy dropped into the chair next to me.

"Ice skating." I didn't look up from my book.

"It's June."

"And?" I asked.

"It's sunny."

"That would explain why I'm wearing sunglasses."

"And this is California. Nobody ice skates," she said.

"All valid points. You neglected to mention that I don't know how to ice skate."

"You don't know how to ice skate?"

"Does this shock you? Do I seem the ice skating type?"

"You're not going ice skating, are you?"

"Thank God you're pretty." I set down my book.

"Why do you bitch about me being sarcastic? It's a learned behavior." She had a point.

"Were you leading somewhere with your questions?"

"Huh?"

"Tonight?" I asked.

"Oh, yeah. I didn't know if you were like going out with that chick again or anything." She studied her shoes intently.

Smooth. "It's not on the schedule."

"Oh, okay. 'Cause it's been a couple days since you went out. I didn't know, if like, you had plans."

"Why are you trying to manage my social calendar?"

"Tonight's open mic. At Fox and Goose. Mom said I can't go solo because they serve alcohol. So I asked if I could go with Cassie, but since Cassie is fifteen, Mom vetoed that too."

"So I'm your third choice?" I asked.

"Only in the most respectful sort of way. I didn't want to go with Cassie. She's like clingy. I think I'm over her."

"Be still, my beating heart."

"You have a heart?"

"Don't you have school?"

"School's out. Remember last week when I got home and I was like 'school's out' and you started singing some song and I was confused?"

I grinned. "Alice Cooper. Good times."

Andy stared blankly at me. "Does this mean you'll come?"

"If they take requests, you're required to ask them to play that song."

"Okay."

"And don't ask me to buy you beer." Andy had never asked me to buy her beer.

"That'll be tough."

"If we accidentally run into your friends and you ditch me, I'll be pissed." I put air quotes around accidentally.

"I told you, I'm over Cassie."

"And I have to speak with your mother."

"Mom," Andy shouted. "Cash said she'll go."

"You lack decorum," I said.

"Mom, what's decorum?" Andy shouted.

"Something you lack," Robin shouted back.

"Hey, you guys agree." Andy nudged me.

"Shocking."

"Leave at eight?"

"Sure."

"Dope. You're the best." Andy ran back in the house.

Great. I always wanted to be the best.

❖

I was waiting in line at the bar for a beer and trying to keep an eye on Andy at the same time. Thankfully, Andy was staying stationary. The line for beer, sadly, was stationary too. The music was terrible. Not that I was expecting a lot from an open mic, but I could be an optimist. Sometimes.

By the time I got back to our table, the act had changed. Some girl was on stage failing at an Ani attempt. The only thing going for her was a buzzed head. Delightfully retro.

"This is an experience," I said.

"Shut your face. You don't know how to have fun." Andy sipped the soda I'd brought her. "Thanks."

"You're welcome."

A group of people migrated to stand in front of our table. Andy strained to see over them. After a minute, most of them moved on. Except for one chick.

"This sucks," Andy said.

"Sorry, kid."

"I'm gonna be tall like you one day."

She was already close to passing me. "It's good that you have aspirations."

"Big words." Andy nodded.

"Excuse me," I called to the body blocking us. "Hey, you mind?"

She turned. It was Laurel. In that moment, I regretted not calling her. Mostly because her eyes flashed the sexiest shade of blue I'd ever seen. It was like the ocean at nighttime. When the ocean was pretty. And her hair was falling into those blue eyes. It was all fantastic. Christ, I should have called her.

"Laurel?"

"Cash? Hey."

Andy looked at me and mouthed "Laurel?" in the most obvious way possible.

"Hey, what are you doing here?" I asked in all of my intelligent glory.

"Suffering through open mic with no seats. You?"

"Just suffering." Andy coughed. Subtle. "Why don't you sit with us?" I grabbed Andy's backpack and shoved it into her lap, then pulled out the remaining seat at the table for Laurel.

"No, I don't want to intrude." But she stepped forward like she wanted to.

"I'm Andy Ward." Andy reached across the table to shake Laurel's hand.

"Laurel. You must be the neighbor."

"Yes, ma'am. I, of course, have no idea who you are. Nope. Not a clue," Andy said.

"So you're not the one who threatened to text if Cash refused to?" Laurel sat down.

Andy turned an impressive shade of pink, but she managed to keep rolling. "Tragically, Cash is a pansy. But I'm not, so I figured I could help her out."

"That's kind of you."

"Yep. That's me. Benevolent."

"Big word," I said.

"I downloaded a dictionary."

"I'm proud."

"So I guess I've gotta pee. Or something. I'll be back." Andy stood.

"If I find you making out with Cassie, there will be hell to pay," I said.

"Got it. If I make out with any girls in line for the bathroom, I'll make sure none of them are named Cassie." Andy saluted.

"Go get 'em, tiger."

"She's a pistol," Laurel said as soon as Andy was out of earshot.

"Noticed that, did you?"

"I'm very observant."

"You know, you're not required to sit here. I mean, the teenage charmer can get a bit obnoxious."

"Totally. And if you guys don't want me cramping your style, just let me know."

"Done."

"Cool."

Suddenly, I missed Andy. She was good at being a buffer.

Laurel leaned back in her seat and studied the stage. I looked to see if it had gotten interesting. Nope. Same old Fox and Goose. They were going for a pub thing. And they'd been around since the last time pubs were cool, so there was a certain nostalgia to the place. The open mic, however, was still subpar.

Laurel was not subpar. Her V-neck was just low enough to show me a slice of tanned skin. It was distracting. Actually, all of her skin was distracting. The hint of muscle in her arms, the flash of ankle below her pant cuffs, the smooth plane of her neck. I had a disturbing desire to trace my fingertips from her ear down to the loose neck of her shirt. I was pretty sure that would be a bad idea. Kind of creepy. She pushed her hair back from her face in that way she did, and I almost lost it.

Thankfully, Andy decided to come back. Or maybe that was a bad thing. I wasn't sure. I feigned interest in the stage. Laurel was seemingly fascinated by the terrible musicians. Andy was fascinated by her phone. At that moment, my phone started vibrating with a text. I pulled it out and glanced at the screen. Andy. It was Andy texting me from one seat over.

Shud I get gone?

I gave her a withering look. She shrugged.

"No," I said.

"Your call." Andy turned to the stage.

I leaned back in my seat. Just enough so that Laurel wouldn't see me staring at her. Why wasn't I going to call her? Oh, yeah. She was distant and detached. And if she stopped being distant, I was afraid to tell her what I did. Why was that a problem? I wasn't looking for a marriage and two point five of my own. Andy was enough of a handful and we only shared a building, not an address. Who could it hurt if I got Laurel naked and never ended up cohabiting? No one. That's who it would hurt. I didn't need emotionally available. We didn't need honesty.

I leaned closer to that tantalizing neck. She smelled really good. Like cedar and the musky bite of hair product.

"You want another beer?" I asked.

She glanced at the glass in her hand. It was almost empty. "Sure. Arrogant Bastard." The beer, not me.

"Done. Andy? You want anything else?"

"Nope. Thanks."

I scooted back and maneuvered out from between their chairs. The line at the bar had dwindled. I caught the bartender's attention.

"Two Arrogant Bastards, please."

He glanced at me. "ID."

I handed it over. He checked it, looked at my face again, looked back at the ID. It was the name. And the haircut. I'd had stoner hair to my ears in high school, and my lovely ID still had the same photo. Now, with the sides nearly shaved and the top combed with pomade, it was surprisingly different from the kid I'd been. Every time I renewed my license, I meant to get a new photo, but then I remembered I'd have to go to the DMV, and that was unappealing. So the shot of me at seventeen stuck.

The bartender set two glasses on the bar and took my money. I went back to our table and squeezed back into my seat, careful not to brush Laurel in the process. Had her seat moved closer?

Andy was still on her phone. She was typing, but watching the stage. From the look of the screen, she was on Snapchat. I didn't get it.

Laurel took the glass I set in front of her and nodded her thanks.

It was kinda nice sitting there. Okay, it was filled with tension. From me mostly. Laurel was cool as fuck about the whole sitting a foot away thing. Andy was seemingly unaware. So that just left me. Sitting, vibrating, pretending that I was interested in a kid playing Simon and Garfunkel on the ukulele. Tragically, his set ended and the next band started to set up.

Next to me, Andy went electric, then slumped lower than humanly possible on a bar stool.

"What's up?"

"It's her," Andy whispered.

"Who?"

"Bailey." Andy groaned and sunk lower.

"Bailey? The girl from homecoming."

"The girl from homecoming." More groaning.

Laurel leaned over. "What's up?"

"Andy's not feeling well."

Laurel looked confused. "That's too bad. What happened?"

"Her ex-girlfriend is in the band."

Andy tried to hide behind me.

"With the new boyfriend," Andy whispered. "Don't forget the new boyfriend."

"With the ex-girlfriend's new boyfriend," I told Laurel.

"Got it." Laurel glanced around. "So we're gonna need to get her out of here, right?"

Andy stopped groaning.

"I think that would be good," I said.

"Okay, but she doesn't want them to see her. That door is too close to the stage. Won't work." Laurel turned around and looked behind us. "We can head for the door back that way, but we have about fifteen feet of open space. You think we can shield her? I'm thinking if we stay shoulder to shoulder, keep the pace even, this will be totally doable."

For some reason, I found her focus very sexy. "I'm in. How do we get up?"

"You stand first, let Andy get behind you. Start walking, then I'll close in."

"You got that?" I asked Andy.

"Got it."

I stood and tried to be taller and wider than I was. Andy practically fell out of her chair. Laurel leaned across the table for Andy's bag, which blocked us long enough for me to turn around. I nudged Andy forward. We started walking. Laurel pressed in against my right side. When Andy veered too far to the side, Laurel took her elbow and directed her between us. There was a tricky moment when I tried to open the door, but then we were outside free and clear.

"Oh, my God. I think I almost died." Andy collapsed against the railing ringing the sidewalk.

"Here's your bag." Laurel handed over the backpack.

"Thanks for getting me out of there. That was awesome. I could have died, you know? Holy shit." Andy clutched the backpack to her chest and did some deep breathing.

"That was very impressive," I said.

"Well, yes. It was. I mean, at any time we could have been seen. The world might have ended. But we kept it together." Laurel managed utter sincerity when she said it. She put her hand on Andy's shoulder. "You okay?"

"I think I'll pull through. It was touch-and-go there for a minute, but…" Another deep breath. "Yeah, I think I might make it through the night."

"At the very least."

"You'll have to check my vitals in the morning," Andy said.

"Probably two or three times throughout the night. Four-hour intervals should do it," Laurel said.

Andy started to laugh. "If you think that's often enough."

"Maybe we should consult a medical professional."

"It's okay. My mom's a nurse."

Laurel nodded. "Good. That's good. But I think you need proper medication."

"There's medication for this?"

"Ice cream. It's standard. Five to ten ounces. With hot fudge."

Andy glanced at me. I smiled.

"What about whipped cream? Is whipped cream standard?" Andy asked.

"I didn't think I needed to mention it. I just assumed you knew," Laurel said.

"I'm young. I'm still learning."

"That's allowed." Laurel started walking. Andy and I hustled to keep up. "So this girl?"

"Asshole," Andy said.

"I gathered."

"She broke up with me at homecoming."

"Interesting. I didn't take you for a sports fan."

Andy scoffed. "No. Like at homecoming. The dance. I'm there in my fancy shirt and tie. I'm wearing suspenders. I've even got a fedora. And we're dancing. It's nice. I leave the floor for two minutes and when I get back, there's Bailey making out with Bailey."

"I don't understand."

"They're both named Bailey. The ex-girlfriend and the new boyfriend," I said. "Remember *Party of Five?*"

"No way. What parent would do that to their child?" Laurel asked.

"What's *Party of Five?*"

I patted Andy's head. "Shhhh, honey."

"Don't patronize me."

"That dictionary app is doing wonderful things for you."

"You were so right." Andy dropped her plastic spoon into the melted remains of her sundae.

"We are older and wiser," I said.

"You're definitely older." Andy grinned.

"Hey," Laurel said.

"You can be wiser. Cash is just old."

"And that wraps up our evening," I said.

"Awww, Cash. Come on. I was kidding."

"Yeah, I know. But it's late and I promised your mom."

"Square," Andy said. I shrugged. "It's summer. My curfew isn't until eleven."

"Yeah, but you have a dentist appointment in the morning."

Andy rolled her eyes at me and sighed.

"Yes, your mother and I do communicate on occasion."

"Glad we just gave her so much ice cream," Laurel said.

"She'll survive. And she'll brush her teeth extra good. Won't you, tiger?" I used my most condescending tone.

"Yes, ma'am. And I'll floss."

"You floss?" Laurel asked.

"Starting tonight, I do."

"That's admirable," I said.

"I do my best." Andy collected our trash and tossed it in the bin. "Let's go, buzzkill."

It was my turn to roll my eyes.

Our duplex was only about five blocks from the ice cream shop. Andy wandered ahead of us, her head snapping up and down as she looked between her phone and the sidewalk.

"That's impressive." Laurel nodded at Andy.

"Walking and texting? Yeah, I'm in awe."

"Not so much?"

"She almost never walks into poles now," I said.

"So she has goals. I like that."

More than once, Laurel bumped into me as we made room for other pedestrians. I held firm like it wasn't a big deal, but she seemed to stay closer every time someone passed. By the time we got home, we were walking shoulder to shoulder. As Andy turned up the walkway, she glanced back and grinned.

"Honey, I'm home," Andy called into the open doorway. "Later, guys. Thanks for the ice cream."

"Don't forget to have those vitals checked," Laurel said.

"On it." Andy pulled open the screen door and disappeared inside.

"So, this is your place?" Laurel followed me up the steps. I'd forgotten the porch light, but the ambient light of the city made her glow faintly.

"Yep." I shoved my hands in my pockets.

"Very cool. Looks older."

"Built in 1903." Yep, I was playing it cool.

"I'd ask to come in, but I'm not that kind of girl."

Damn. "Obviously." I nodded.

"I mean. You didn't even call me."

"Noted." I took out my phone, swiped to Laurel's name, and hit dial. Laurel's phone started vibrating. She grinned at me. The voice mail kicked in. "Hey, Laurel. This is Cash. I had a really great time with you—"

"A great time?" Laurel asked.

"I had a super awesome, fantastic time with you." Laurel nodded. "And I'd love to go out again. Call me. I'll be waiting by the phone. Counting the minutes. Just hoping—" The voice mail cut me off.

"Hoping?"

"Your voice mail doesn't really allow for monologue."

"Ahh, got it."

"I had a speech planned."

"You did?"

"Totally. I can't remember it now, but it was a good speech."

Laurel grinned and took a step closer. "I'll take that into consideration."

She was definitely in my space now. I waited, afraid to move or speak or breathe. She leaned closer. Her face was inches from mine.

"Good night, Cash."

"You're killing me here."

"Yeah?"

"Yeah."

"Good." She kissed my cheek, spun, and walked away. "Call me."

"Girl, I'm calling you right now."

She laughed and disappeared into the dark.

CHAPTER SIX

"Girl, I'm calling you right now?" Andy collapsed into the lounge next to me, squinted into the morning sun, and dropped her sunglasses into place with a scowl.

"Eavesdropping?"

"I'd think you were spitting mad game, but you didn't even get a kiss."

"The rest of us just don't have your charms."

"Please. Chicks fall all over you. Oh, shit." Andy sat up straight and gave me a hard stare. Or it looked hard. The glasses obscured too much. "You actually like this woman."

"Why do you say that?"

"You're in it for the long game."

"No, I'm not. Stop trying to analyze me with your Psychology 101."

"Are you suggesting that freshman psychology did not make me an expert? 'Cause that hurts. And it was Psych A."

I was getting ready to mount a rebuttal when Robin stuck her head out the door. "Train is leaving, bud."

"Where's the train going?" I asked.

"Grandma's," Andy said.

"Oh, shit. That's tonight?" My monthly date with Robin was Second Saturday. One of these days, I was going to remember before she told me.

Robin came outside and leaned against the porch rail. "If you bail on me, I'll be hurt."

"Wouldn't dream of it. Are we eating in or out?"

"Cash Braddock, I am not a cheap date." Robin crossed her arms.

"Thai place?"

Robin laughed and shook her head. "Yeah, I'll be back in an hour."

"When do I get to go out on Second Saturday?" Andy asked.

"When you ask a girl out on the second Saturday of the month. Bonus points if she's an artist," I said.

"No, when do I get to go out with you guys?"

"Never," Robin and I said simultaneously.

Andy gave us a sigh of epic proportions and went inside.

Robin and I laughed at her antics.

"There's a new gallery on Nineteenth. It's in that white cinderblock building," Robin said.

"Oh, that place that was a tattoo parlor?"

"And before that it was that barbershop. And before that—"

"Shut up. It was that little gallery we loved." How had I missed that?

"Smash? Lush?"

"Lather? Something that sounded like a bar on *The L Word*."

"Yes." Robin laughed. "They had that textile show."

"Badass. So, first stop?"

"After dinner."

"Yeah, yeah. You ain't cheap."

Robin nodded and went inside to gather her offspring.

Ten minutes after they left, I started unpacking drugs. I was almost finished when there was a knock on my door. Nate. His punctuality was enviable. I led him into the kitchen. He sorted through the drugs, pulling out what he needed. Until he got to the mixed bag.

"What's this?" He held it up.

I sighed. "Ecstasy."

"You're not serious." Nate dropped the baggie on the table.

"If you don't want to sell it, no pressure."

"I can sell it. People keep asking for it. It's just…weird."

"I know."

"You've never had Molly before."

"I know."

"I mean, our thing is prescription, not just pills all willy-nilly." He waved his hand back and forth.

"Really? You're going with willy-nilly?"

"You heard me. How exactly—"

"You really want to know?" I asked.

"That cop who steals drugs from the evidence locker."

"Yeah. He busted a rave and forgot to log some evidence."

Nate shook his head. "He's getting ballsy."

Not surprising, really. Henry tended to get excited in summer. It was great for my inventory. Once fall hit, he'd tone it down again.

"I really don't mind if you don't want it."

"I'll give it a shot." He opened an empty bag and started counting pills into it.

"Take it all. I don't want it."

"There's like a hundred pills here."

"I know. I'm sorry. But I'll give you an extra twenty percent."

Nate stopped and stared at me. "You won't make shit."

"I told him I didn't want it. He offered an extra ten percent. I'm giving you ten on top of that for the risk."

"Okay." He nodded. "I assume you won't be getting any more."

"Not a chance in hell."

"Then I'll spread it out. I don't want anyone to expect it in the future."

"Good plan."

Nate packed the baggies he was taking. He shook his head at the X, but tossed it in as well. When he was done, he handed me a stack of cash. I put it in the flour tin.

"Anything new from that chick at the party?"

I almost smiled, then stopped myself. "We've been out a couple of times."

"She figure out what you do yet?"

"She thinks I'm a farmer."

Nate laughed. "It will work until she realizes farming doesn't exactly pay the bills."

"I'm aware."

"So what are you going to do?"

"The usual, I guess."

He shook his head. "Tell her you were a weed dealer in college and see how she takes it?"

"Yep, basically." It had never been a great move before. I didn't have a damn clue why I thought it would work this time.

"Good. You should have someone."

"Says the boy who sends all his money to Mama Xiao."

"Shut up. My brother made varsity track. He needs better shoes." I smiled a little. "I wish you'd been my big brother."

"Right. Don't go soft on me, Braddock." Nate grabbed his bag and held out his hand. I shook it. "Later."

Robin and I walked from the restaurant to the first gallery on our list. I'd briefly looked at the gallery online. They had two shows this month. A sculptor and a painter who created three-dimensional pieces. Nothing particularly stood out, but that wasn't the point. Second Saturdays let me indulge my desire to wander around art galleries and gave Robin the opportunity to be around adults. Which just helped drive home my whole lack of desire to have children.

The gallery was in a squat little building. From the outside it looked cramped, but inside it was surprisingly open. Wide windows showed the street and a small wooded courtyard out back. The bright lights were hung to accentuate the art rather than the less than attractive crowd. It felt intimate, not close.

We made our way around the inside perimeter. Robin vacillated between musings about the art pieces and updates about her life. I relaxed and listened. Robin was comforting in all the right ways. She let me have my silent moods. She knew when to let me speak.

We were studying a found object piece when Robin decided to exercise her ability to make me talk about my feelings.

"So what's the deal with this woman you're seeing?"

"Huh?" I liked to really use my college degree.

"Andy says she's funny and gorgeous."

"Andy talks a lot."

"Then I shouldn't tell you that Andy also says you're really into her?"

"Andy is an imaginative fifteen-year-old," I said. Robin gave me a mom look. "Okay, she may be right."

"Tell me about her."

"I don't know much," I said. Robin waited. "She's quick. She can keep up with me."

"You tell her yet?" she asked. I shook my head. "It will be harder the longer you wait."

"I know."

"Libby was a fluke," Robin said. She was chiding me.

"Libby threw things at me."

"Libby was crazy."

"I lied to Libby," I said.

"True. But she was crazy before that. Normal people don't throw things when they are lied to."

I laughed. "What about the girl who stole my inventory?"

"Oh, the girl you picked up while you were working and gave free drugs to? The one who stayed the night and didn't leave for a month? That girl?" Robin's voice climbed in pitch, but not volume with each question. By the end only dogs could hear her.

"I don't think I like this brutally honest thing we do."

She smiled and shook her head. "We didn't even get to talking about feelings yet."

"Gee, that's real disappointing."

Robin leaned into my shoulder and laughed. "You want to hit up Oak Park Brewing when we're done?"

"Yes. That's a question I like," I said. Robin shook her head. "Sorry, I feel good about that question. Oak Park Brewing makes me feel happy."

"You're getting good at this feelings business."

"I know. I've been practicing."

❖

Got your message. I guess we could go out tonight.

I'd always prided myself on my ability to throw shade, but Laurel took it to the next level. Shade and a date. All in ten words.

I'm in Davis. Give me time to get back? Nate and I had only been working this bar for an hour, but I was sure he wouldn't mind taking off.

Shady Lady at 9? she asked.

Hipster.

You want to be the pot or the kettle?

I grinned at my phone. Which probably made me look super cool. *Kettle. See you there.*

I had a date. A fourth date. Not that I was counting. I pocketed my phone and looked around for Nate. He was across the room talking to a guy who was just a little too old to be in a college bar. I stood to get a better look and realized I recognized him. Take away the beard and a few years, and he was a dead ringer for a cop who had busted a buddy of mine for dealing in college. Fuck. I dialed Nate's number. He didn't pick up. I was going to have to intervene.

I slid through a group of drunk grad students who were failing spectacularly at shouting each other down. Past that was a circle of girls attempting to start a dance floor where there was no dance floor. That asshole was closing the deal, and I still had fifteen feet of intoxicated students ahead of me. I hated the post finals partying. The undercover cop palmed a soft wad of cash and held it out to Nate. I interrupted a game of darts. Didn't get nicked and managed to gain five feet from the open floor. The line for the bar spilled ahead of me and I had to weave around it. Nate reached into his bag. When he pulled his hand out, I could see the sheen of plastic. Six feet and I was close enough to shout.

"Nathan." Nate didn't respond. Five feet. "Hey, Nathan, right?" I finally got close enough to stand between them. I spared the narc a glance, then backed up a step as if in apology. "You were in Nineteenth Century Lit with me."

Nate stuck his hand in his pocket. "Yeah, man. I'm really starting to hate Brit Lit."

"Same. I have to take Nineteenth Century B over summer."

"Me too! I'm never going to finish the upper division requirements."

I nodded in sympathy. "They're the worst. Actually, I was wondering if you had notes on De Quincey. I did not get that dude."

Nate laughed, but it was strained. "Yeah, why would you want to romanticize such an ugly subject?"

"Exactly. Give me Shelley any day. Adonais was kinda hot, you know? Oh. Well. Not for you I guess." The narc was listening to the whole conversation, but he looked like we were speaking something other than English.

Nate leaned back against the wall and settled into his borrowed subject. "I can appreciate the appeal of the homoeroticism, but no, not really my scene. The language is brilliant, though. The way he weaves his love of the poet into his love of romanticism and all that it entails." Nate had been studying. Which was good. It lent an air of legitimacy.

"Yeah, but then he flips it with the shifting genders of gods."

"And people."

"Man, where have you been all quarter? My study group was all hung up on incest and I'm like, that's not the point, you know?"

The narc coughed. "Hey, uhhh."

"Oh, yeah, man. Talk to Jerome. He's around here somewhere." Nate made a show of looking around. "I think he went out back. I'll point him out to you. Just give me a second." Nate turned back to me. "Can I give you my number? I'm meeting some Brit Lit people for coffee tomorrow. You're welcome to join."

"That would be great. As long as you bring that *Opium* shit."

The cop looked like he'd been handed a million bucks. "Opium?"

"You know, De Quincey? *Confessions of an English Opium-Eater*? Hey, are you taking Brit Lit too?" I asked.

His face fell. "No."

Nate grinned at me. "Number?"

"Yeah." I gave a halfhearted pat to my pockets. "Shit. My phone is in the car. Walk me out? I'm taking off anyway."

"Sure." Nate glanced back at his botched sale. "Back patio. Five minutes?"

"Okay." He seemed caught. I'd seen it before. The guy was pretty sure he'd lost his mark, but was still holding out hope that Nate would show up.

I led Nate to the front door. We kept up appearances until we got to Nate's car parked at the far, dark corner of the lot. I got in and he drove away at a nice sedate pace.

"You almost got nailed," I said.

"Shit. Yeah, I noticed. Thanks."

"Hey, I can't have your mother coming after me. That woman is terrifying."

Nate nodded a bit too emphatically. "Try coming home hungover and covered in debauchery at seventeen. Now that's a terrifying lecture."

"I believe it."

"Fuck. I'm sorry. That was bad."

"Don't sweat it. I only caught it because I recognized him."

"Either way. You totally saved me." Nate took his first full breath since I'd walked up to him. "I guess that bar is off the list."

"It would be dead in a week anyway."

"But that killed our night."

I shrugged. "I was about to call it anyway." Nate looked at me sharply. I smiled. "Laurel texted. We're meeting in forty-five."

"Shut the fuck up."

"Will not."

"Look at you. Going on a date like a normal human."

"That's me. Normal."

"So normal." Nate started laughing. He thought he was so damn funny.

CHAPTER SEVEN

The Shady Lady was packed. That wasn't very surprising. Weeknights were bad. Weekends were worse. The fact that it was summer just poured gasoline on the whole thing. I scanned the patio as I walked up. Laurel was in the shadows on the edge of the patio, sitting sideways with her feet up on one of the church pew benches. A young couple was subtly glaring at her oxfords and bare ankles as if that would make her give them more than the scant inch of room between them and her. I smiled at her tactic.

"Hey." One of my better opening lines.

"Hey." She swung around so I could sit and handed me a beer. Then she kissed my cheek and everything was right in the world. The young couple glared some more. Laurel was wearing a sports bra under a tank top with the arm holes cut to below her ribs. It afforded me quite a view. I stretched my arm along the bench behind Laurel, tried not to stare down her shirt, and took a swig of beer.

"Waiting long?" I asked.

"Nope. You walk?"

Technically, I had walked from Nate's car four blocks away, but I figured she didn't need that level of detail. "Advantage of living in the heart of Midtown. You?"

"Not everyone has the good apartment karma you have."

"I did have to kill a few orphans and sign a blood oath to get it." She laughed. "That explains it."

"Actually, I just had a really good real estate agent."

"Wait. You own it?"

"Yeah, Robin—Andy's mom—rents the other half from me. It makes the mortgage payments easy."

"Damn. Organic farming pays better than I thought."

I shrugged. If organic farming was lucrative, Clive wouldn't need me. "Clive manages the business well. The first good year, I paid off my student loans. But it took a few years to get a decent down payment." Twice the usual down payment, but she didn't need to know that either.

"I'm still paying my student loans."

"Mine were…low." I waited for the look that suggested she wanted me to elaborate. She complied. "I sold weed in college. It helped with the whole tuition thing."

Laurel started laughing. "Shut up."

"Nope. It was super glamorous."

"Oh, I'm sure. My weed dealer in college was super glamorous too."

"Really?" She was taking this way better than the last chick I had dated, Libby who liked to throw things.

"Yeah. I mean, not a lot of people understood his glamour, what with the not showering and all. But I could see it." She nodded sincerely.

"It's a common misconception among weed dealers. You know, the need to shower. But I feel I moved past that admirably."

"Clearly. You almost never smell like a Snoop Dogg show."

"It's one of my better qualities," I said. She wasn't wrong. My entire senior year, everything smelled like weed. It was worse than fast food. My apartment, my car, my clothes, all reeked. The worst part was everyone assuming I was stoned all the time when I didn't touch the stuff.

"So you outgrew weed with graduation?"

"It was that or the lesbianism, and I'm partial to my queerness."

"Well, that explains it," she said.

"What?"

"Why you keep looking down my tank top." Laurel polished off her beer, the epitome of casual.

I laughed at getting caught. "I am doing no such thing."

"Liar."

"In my defense, you look super hot. You're basically inviting it."

"Solid logic."

"I know." I drank some more beer. Mine was almost gone. I leaned in close to her ear and whispered, "So if I go in for more beer, you think you can keep the junior heteros from taking over the bench?"

Laurel tilted her head back so her mouth was just brushing my neck. "Please. They're terrified of me. The girl spent five minutes angry whispering at him to ask me to move my feet."

I managed to slow my heart rate enough to reply. "You're a badass."

"Hey, you shower, I'm a badass. We all have our winning qualities."

Having her lean in so close was torture. It wasn't just the smell of hair product, which I inexplicably enjoyed. Before, I had noticed the smell of cedar, but it was richer than that. It was leather and the biting sweetness of raw almond.

Her lips were tantalizingly close. Every exhalation danced across my throat. I tilted my head just a little and stared into her eyes. I could have kissed her. She would have let me. I waited. This wasn't the place. Not with the next generation being ignorantly conceived a foot away. Not without telling her the truth about myself.

What a fascinating moment to grow a conscience.

"I'll be right back." I really didn't want to leave. Laurel was radiating heat. If I fantasized any more about touching her warm, bare skin, I might be tempted to take her home with me. We weren't there yet. Well, maybe I was, but she wasn't. She was teasing me and I was enjoying the hell out of it. So I stood, waited for her to put her feet back on to the bench, and took her empty glass.

It was marginally cooler inside the bar, but the press of body heat and sweating hipsters was an unwelcome perversion of Laurel's warm skin. It felt suffocating. I pressed through the crowd toward an open spot at the back of the bar.

One of the bartenders made eye contact, then looked away. He was crafting a series of unnecessarily delicate cocktails. Artisanal, I was sure. I didn't get it. Then again, I didn't generally drink anything stronger than beer. Maybe that was the source of my aversion.

After the second bartender looked at me and proceeded to help someone else, I leaned against the wall. Once more and their tip was going to be crap. I knew it and the bartenders knew it. They would get to me.

I felt someone slide in next to me but stop short of the bar. I glanced over and had to stifle a curse.

Jerome St. Maris, epic fuckwad and shitty street dealer extraordinaire. He smiled at me and turned just enough to block my view of the bartenders. It didn't help that he was well over six feet and solid muscle. Actually, it probably helped him a great deal. It wasn't helping me though.

"Let's talk," he said.

"Nope. I'm busy." I tried to edge around him.

Jerome grabbed my arm and wrestled me into the hallway leading to the bathrooms at the back of the bar. "You always have to make shit difficult, don't you?"

"You could try not being an ass." I crossed my arms over my chest, leaned against the wall, and did my damnedest to look like I wasn't trapped. This was why I brought Nate whenever I had a deal that wasn't one-on-one. I could hold my own, but some people simply responded better to height and muscle. At the moment, my five eight was looking pretty sad.

I hoped Laurel kept defending that bench and didn't come looking for me. I only had a few more minutes before she would notice my absence.

"I just want to talk. You're forcing my hand here." Poor boy.

"Go ahead, then."

"Nate is dealing X," he said.

I scoffed. "Oh, please." This was not good.

"Tell him he's done."

"Sure. I'll get right on that."

"Stop fucking around. He's moving in on my customers. Does that mean prescriptions are fair game?" Jerome smiled. He knew he had me on that one.

"I'll ask him, but he's not dealing X. Someone is lying to you." It was me. I was the one who was lying to him.

"My information is good."

I took a deep breath and made a decision. "Fine. He might be. But it won't happen again. I just had some product to unload."

Jerome relaxed a little and shook his head. "Not good enough. You know that's my territory."

"Yeah, I should have given you a heads-up."

"No, you should have given the pills to me."

"Right." As if I was going to give him quality drugs on a whim. Or give him access to Henry. Not fucking likely.

"I'm not being unreasonable here."

He wasn't, which made him that much more dangerous. Nate and I had broken an unspoken agreement. I never should have given in to Henry. Of course, I wasn't going to tell St. Maris that. I tried to walk past him, but he blocked me. "Get out of my way."

"No, I'm not done talking."

I shoved Jerome aside, and he punched me in the stomach. Which made things like standing and trying to look cool really difficult.

"What the fuck is going here?" Laurel asked. She was standing in the mouth of the hallway. The look she was giving Jerome was terrifying.

"Nothing. Go back to the bar." Jerome took a step toward her.

I forced myself upright so I could try to get between them. There was no way I was going to let her get involved with Jerome in any way.

"Not happening." Laurel moved closer. Jerome blocked my view of her, and I tried to push past him. "Hey, let her go."

"This isn't your business, bitch." Jerome brought his arm up. I don't know if he was going for me or her, but it was my jaw his elbow clipped.

As my head snapped back, I watched Laurel clock him. It was sexy. She hit him hard. Didn't do much damage, but it made him slow down.

"Back the fuck off," Laurel said. "Come on, Cash."

I didn't need to be told twice. Jerome was probing his cheekbone, which was already turning pink. It distracted him enough for me to squeeze past. Laurel and I moved out of the hallway and into the bar.

"We're not done, Cash. Get your boy in line," Jerome shouted as we slipped into the crowd.

Laurel grabbed my hand and led me to the door. We didn't stop until we got to her truck. It was massive and baby blue and about forty years old. I had no clue how she had parallel parked that beast. The door creaked and popped when she opened it for me, but I just stared at her.

"Get in. We need to get out of here." Laurel waved at the open door.

"Where are we going?"

"Away from here."

"Don't you want to know—"

"Not at the moment. Right now, I want to get you home and put some ice on your jaw," she said.

I debated walking away, but my jaw was throbbing, and she had looked really hot defending me. It was enough to help me forget that she wasn't going to stick around once she figured out what had just happened. I got in the truck.

Laurel drove to my place and parked on the street. She followed me up the walkway. I went straight to the kitchen once we were inside. Laurel sat at the table while I filled a baggie with ice.

"I've never hit someone before." She sounded pensive. I turned around. She was holding her hand out for inspection. Her knuckles were rosy and starting to swell. "Like, my brothers and I used to duke it out, but we always pulled our punches."

I grabbed a clean kitchen towel and wrapped it around the ice bag I was holding. "Here. Put this on it."

"Thanks." She arranged the ice over her hand.

I prepped a second bag for myself. I was stalling. This was not going to be a fun conversation. I sat across from her.

"So you're still a drug dealer," Laurel said.

Apparently, we were diving right in. "Yep."

"And I'm guessing that guy is also a drug dealer." She picked at the edge of her towel.

"Yep."

"But you're not friends with him."

"Not so much, no. He peddles street drugs. Party stuff. Acid, X, coke, that kind of thing," I said. This felt far too civilized. She was supposed to get mad.

"So you don't deal those drugs?"

"I stick with prescriptions. Housewives love their Xanax and Vicodin. College kids need their Adderall." I adjusted the ice pack so it conformed to my jaw better.

She pressed her lips together and nodded. "Is that what you were doing at that party when we met?"

"Yep."

"Why not the party drugs then? You know, acid and stuff."

"Street drugs fuck people up. Prescriptions are less ugly." It was a half lie I'd told myself for years. I knew people overdosed on prescriptions just as much as street drugs. But the demise seemed cleaner.

"Got it." She continued her towel inspection. A piece of plastic bag was pushing out of a fold. She poked it in, pulled it out, tucked it back again.

"You can go." I hated myself for saying it. I hated making things easy for her. I wanted her to stay. I wanted her to want to stay. But asking that would be cruel. It was better to let her go.

Laurel looked up sharply. "What? Why?"

I didn't really know how to answer that. It was a sky is blue sort of question. "Because I'm a drug dealer?" I didn't mean for my answer to be a question.

"So?"

"So maybe you don't want to date a drug dealer?" Another question, dammit.

"That doesn't seem like a solid reason."

"Okay, how about you just punched someone for the first time because I dragged you into a fight?" Great. Now, I was convincing her not to date me.

"Technically, you didn't drag me in," she said. I didn't know how to respond to that. "I wanted to cause damage, you know? Plus, this kind of ramps up my badassery."

"So you don't want to leave?"

In response, Laurel stood and came to my side of the table. She sat next to me. "No, I don't want to leave." And she kissed me. Not the cheek this time. A real kiss. Soft lips pressed firmly to mine, a swift intake of breath, a small nibble at my bottom lip. I dropped the ice pack and kissed her back more firmly. I didn't stop until she pressed her fingertips to my cheek and brushed the rapidly growing bruise on my jaw.

"Owww."

"Shit. Sorry."

"Don't apologize. I feel way better." I grinned. Which made my jaw ache more.

"Here." Laurel pressed the ice pack back into place.

"Thanks."

Nickels chose that moment to investigate the strange voice in the kitchen. She stuck her head around the corner and stared at us.

"Hey, Nickels." I put my hand down to coax her forward.

"You have a cat?"

"I don't like people very much." Nickels went around the far edge of the table so she wouldn't have to walk past Laurel to get to me. I scratched her head.

"Yeah, but you're a drug dealer with a cat. Shouldn't you have a pit bull or something?"

"I almost never need protection. Today notwithstanding."

"And her name is Nickels?"

"Yeah, Cash, Nickels. It's a thing." Nickels jumped onto my lap.

"That is oddly adorable." Laurel reached out slowly and petted her. Nickels let her.

"Damn. She's not even drawing blood."

"Why would she draw blood?"

"Nickels hates people as much as I do. It's why we get along. But she's letting you pet her."

Laurel thought that over. Or it looked like she was thinking what with the furrowed brow and all. "I'm thinking this is one of the more exciting dates I've been on."

"Swell. I get you into a fight with a drug dealer and you call it exciting."

"I'm not looking to repeat that particular experience, if you don't mind."

"Noted. Next time we go out we'll bare-knuckle box with someone who isn't a drug dealer." I really emphasized "isn't."

"You sure know how to show a girl a good time."

"Actually, I'm thinking something more civilized. Maybe verbal sparring instead."

Laurel smiled and pushed the hair out of her eyes. "It's a date." I smiled back at her like an idiot. "Shit. The whole farmer thing is a front, isn't it?"

I dropped my gaze to the table. "Maybe."

"Damn. I kind of liked that."

I looked back at her. "If it helps, Clive wanted to be a farmer. The dealing just keeps the farm in the black."

"I guess that helps. So I can still tell my friends I'm dating a farmer?"

"That would certainly help keep my cover intact."

"This is all very strange." Laurel shook her head. "Okay. I'm going to go. But I'm coming back. You owe me a nonviolent date."

"I'll do my best."

Laurel stood. She set her ice pack on the table and flexed her hand. It was still mottled pink, but it hadn't gotten any more swollen. I walked her to the door. Before I could open it, she pushed me against the wall and pressed the entire length of her body to mine. We stayed like that for a moment as she studied my face.

"You, Cash Braddock, are nothing like I expected."

"Is that a good thing?"

"I'm not sure." She leaned in and kissed me again. This time, she was surprisingly chaste, which made it that much sexier. The pressure from her lips seemed to be a promise. Then she stepped away and left. I heard the creak and pop of her door and the big engine starting up.

I stayed against the wall for a long time after the door had closed.

CHAPTER EIGHT

Hello." Nate finally picked up the phone.

"Hey, sorry it's so late."

"No worries. What's up?"

"Jerome interrupted my date to inform me that you're dealing X and he doesn't appreciate it," I said.

"Fuck me. What did you tell him?"

"That it wasn't a big deal and I promised we would never do it again." I readjusted the half-melted ice pack on my face.

Nate scoffed. "I'm sure that went over well."

"Yeah, I really enjoyed the part where he punched me."

"You're fucking kidding." He sounded mad. Which was nice. I would have been mad if someone punched him.

"I didn't even get to the good part yet."

"I hesitate to ask."

"Laurel showed up and punched him in the face," I said. Nate started laughing. "So she knows I'm a dealer now." Nate stopped laughing. "I got her in a fight with another dealer. My face is mangled. And Jerome wants to kick our asses. Yours and mine. Not sure how he feels about hers."

"You're a menace to the lesbian dating scene."

"Thanks. That's exactly what I wanted to hear," I said.

"I'm sorry it didn't work out with her. I know you liked her."

"Didn't work out? Kid, I got game. She kissed me and we have another date. I promised it would be nonviolent."

Nate descended into very manly giggles. "So she's totally cool?"

"A little too cool. She took it really well."

"Don't do that. Get your head out of your ass."

"What?" I asked.

"Don't do that thing where you get all skeptical and think the man's out to get you. She likes you. End of story."

I sighed. "Fine." I realized my hair and the collar of my shirt were damp. I pulled the ice pack away and inspected it. Cold water dribbled down my hand and dripped off my wrist. I tossed the ice pack into the sink.

"You're a piece of work, you know that?"

"Yeah, yeah. Anyway, I wanted to give you a heads-up about Jerome." I grabbed a fresh towel and dried my neck and hand. I tossed that towel in the sink too, then went and stretched out on the couch. Nickels jumped up and settled on my chest.

"What do you want to do about it?"

"Not sure yet. He wants us to give him the drugs."

"That's dumb."

"Right? I'm going up to see Clive and Henry tomorrow. I'll run it by them."

"Works for me. Let me know what they suggest."

"Will do. 'Night."

"'Night, man."

It wasn't even midnight and I was exhausted. I petted the sleeping cat on my chest and closed my eyes. This dealing stuff was hard.

Clive's farm was at the base of the Sierras. The freeway was basically a straight shot from Sacramento, but the last thirty miles gained almost two thousand feet in elevation. The moment I hit hills at the county line, the temperature started to drop. I rolled down the windows, opened the sunroof, and let the wind destroy my hairstyle. It was worth it to feel air movement that wasn't hot.

Just past Placerville, the freeway narrowed to two lanes and stopped resembling a freeway. Massive pines lined the road, miniature neighborhoods spit their traffic directly onto the highway with little more than a stop sign, and fruit stands were erected in precarious turnoffs. Through gaps in the trees, I could see the vibrant green of the apple orchards. Some trees boasted early, reddening apples. Others held fast to their dying pink blossoms.

The sign for Braddock Farm popped up a quarter mile before the nearly invisible turn. Another mile off the freeway, the road curved sharply and ascended. Our fruit stand at the entrance to the farm was open. The teenager inside perked up when they saw my SUV, but settled for a friendly wave when they realized I wasn't stopping.

I parked by the house, just out of view of the road. Henry's Mustang was already parked. I grabbed the grocery bag out of the back and I let myself into the house.

"Cash?" Clive called from the kitchen.

"Hey." I followed the rumble of their voices and found them sitting at the kitchen table. Clive jumped up to hug me, and I was reminded how much taller he was than me. The feeling should have faded sometime in my teen years, but it stuck. The familiarity of his broad shoulders and firm chest, the warmth that seemed to always radiate from him, those things were expected, but his height never stuck in my mind.

I sat at the table and Clive set a cup of coffee in front of me. Even with the breeze from the windows, it was too warm for coffee, but I wrapped my hands around the mug and breathed deeply. Clive's coffee couldn't be duplicated. It was always rich and perfectly balanced. I'd tried imitating it, but I was pretty sure he used magic to brew it.

Clive unpacked the growlers out of the grocery bag I'd brought. He read the tags tied on top with the descriptions, then put them in the fridge.

"How was the drive?" Clive sat across from me and smiled. I smiled back. This was home.

"Good. It's too hot down the hill."

"You said there was some sort of issue?" Henry looked at me earnestly across his own cup of coffee.

"Yeah, Jerome St. Maris."

"He's the boy who sells street drugs?" Clive asked. I managed not to smile when he called Jerome "the boy." Jerome was in his thirties. There was only a scant decade between them.

I nodded. "He's angry that Nate is selling Molly. Says it's his territory."

"So we tell him to back off," Henry said.

"I did, but I don't think he got the message."

"Wait, what is Molly?" Clive asked.

"Ecstasy," I said. Henry studied his coffee mug.

Clive looked at me like I'd said heroin. "We don't sell drugs like that."

"Hey, talk to Henry. He bullied me into it."

Clive looked back and forth between us. "He bullied you into it? You can't make decisions for yourself?" Instead of yelling, his voice got lower and lower. "Are you in fifth grade? He bullied you?" Disappointment dripped from every question. "And, you." He turned to Henry. "Why would you bring her ecstasy? You know we don't do that sort of thing. What the hell were you thinking?"

Henry and I were silent. I was really hoping that he might speak first, but no luck.

"You're right. I should have said no," I said.

"Yeah, I shouldn't have taken ecstasy from the evidence locker. It's just so popular right now." It seemed like Henry was only saying what he thought Clive wanted to hear. Which was fine with me. If Clive could shame him into behaving, more power to him.

Clive shook his head. "Tell me exactly what happened with Jerome and what you think we should do about it."

"I was on a date—"

Clive looked up sharply and grinned. "We are discussing that later."

"Is this the same girl?" Henry asked.

"Henry knew you were dating?" Clive looked hurt.

"We've only been out a few times. You'll like her though."

Clive nodded. "If you like her, I'm sure I will."

"So I was out with Laurel and I went into the bar to get us fresh drinks. Jerome showed up and strong-armed me into talking to him." Clive's jaw tightened, but he didn't say anything. "He said he knew Nate was dealing Molly and asked if prescriptions were fair game. I said no, it was a onetime thing. He suggested that we should have given him the ecstasy. I disagreed. He punched me."

"What?" Clive yelled.

"In the stomach. No big deal. Then Laurel showed up. Jerome elbowed me." I pointed at the faint bruise on my jaw. "Laurel punched him. We left."

"This is a lot of information." Clive spread his hands on the table and studied them. Then he looked up at me. "Why didn't you call me?"

"And tell you what? Hey, come beat up this boy who was mean to me?" I laughed. "There's nothing you could have done."

"I know you can take care of yourself. I just would like to be kept in the loop. That's all."

"Can we go back to your girl punching Jerome?" Henry waggled his eyebrows. "'Cause that's kind of hot."

"She's not my girl," I said. "But it was super hot." I grinned. Henry laughed.

"Are you two finished?" Clive asked. I sighed. Henry nodded. "How would you like to handle this?"

I shot a look at Henry. He wasn't going to like my suggestion. "I think Nate and I should meet with Jerome and offer to sell him the leftover stock at a very reasonable price." Henry made a dissatisfied noise. "We make it clear that there's no more and we won't step on his toes again. It's a show of good faith."

"Okay. That seems workable to me," Clive said.

Henry groaned. "But X is such a good investment right now."

"So is blow, but we don't deal certain drugs." Which is what I should have told him initially. I hated that I felt more comfortable standing up to him with Clive acting as mediator.

"You know that. Don't play around." Clive pointed at Henry.

"But, Clive—"

"Henry Brewer, do not make me have this conversation again. We have been over it too many times," Clive said.

"Fine." Henry wasn't cute when he pouted.

"Good." Clive nodded once. "Now, tell me about your new friend."

❖

I followed Clive through the newest section of greenhouse. When I'd visited last, the pallets held paper cups filled with soil. Now, hopeful leaves spread over the edges of the cups, a wash of delicate green.

"Through here. I've got a surprise for you." Clive waved me ahead of him to a low table of seedlings.

"What is it?"

"Guess." He seemed very exited.

I looked at the plants, which looked identical to the million other seedlings we had just passed. The leaves were vaguely heart shaped, uniform green.

"You know I'm terrible at this game."

Clive shook his head. "Cucumbers."

"Shut up. You're growing pickles for me?"

"I'm growing cucumbers."

"That's what I said. Pickles." I shrugged as if he was missing the point.

Clive sighed. "Yes, I'm growing pickles for you. Shelby is already experimenting with recipes."

"Does this mean I get to sample pickles?"

"You are very strange."

"Says the man who reads poetry to plants."

"I don't need to justify my methods to you." Clive tilted up his chin. I laughed. "Come on. Shelby offered to put out lunch for us. To go with your variety of pickles."

I led the way back out to the private patio behind the house. Through the trees, we were afforded a view of the valley and rolling foothills. I caught sight of Clive's farm manager. Shelby was wearing slightly baggy, artfully torn jeans. The pants were cuffed to boot level, but the boots must have been lost between her car and the patio because she was barefoot. Her long, blond curls tangled in the breeze. When she saw us walking toward her she jumped a little and waved excitedly.

"Cash," Shelby shouted. "Where were you? The greenhouse? Did Clive show you the new plants? He told you about the pickles. Right?" She hugged me, didn't notice or didn't care when I didn't hug her back. She kissed me, didn't notice or didn't care when I didn't kiss her back. "He showed you the pickles. You better be excited because I had to work my ass off to convince him." She squeezed my arm, then dragged me to the table. "I'm working on two varieties to start with. Dill, obviously. And a hot variety. I've got one version with habanero that you're going to love. Oh, my God, it's so good to see you." She hugged me again.

I looked over at Clive, who had stopped walking. He was shaking with silent laughter as he watched Shelby.

"Hi, Shelby," I said.

"Oh no. I'm doing it again, aren't I? I'm sorry."

"It's fine. You're excited. About life. I love that you're so excited about life."

Shelby rolled her eyes, tossed the curls out of her face, and continued with her excitement. I wasn't even sure I needed to be there as a recipient of the excitement.

"I'm using dill and garlic from the herb garden, obviously. But I've worked out a trade with a vendor at Apple Hill to get the rest of the pickling spices. He blends his spices and they are just exquisite. And, oh, my God, he's dreamy." Shelby forced me to sit at the patio table. The entire surface was covered in bite-sized food. Baguettes and cheese. Olives. Cold sausage on a marble slab. She proceeded to hand me various foods. Chewing slowed me down, but not Shelby. "If we start selling pickles, I'll put his name on the label, you know? But right now he is giving them to us at cost."

"Shelby," I interrupted.

"Yes?"

"I'm pouring a beer." I stood to go in the house. "You sit." She did. "Clive, you want a beer?"

"Yeah, let's do the amber ale you brought." Clive slid into a chair next to Shelby. "Shelby, you want one too?" She nodded emphatically.

I stopped myself from asking if she was legal. But I still had to think about it. Her birthday was in spring, which meant she was twenty-one now. Not that it really mattered, but I didn't want to deal with telling her parents that I was the one who let her drink. They were lovely people with a misguided impression of me. They actually thought I was a good person. I wanted to live that lie just a little bit.

I brought three glasses and the growler with amber out to the patio. Shelby started to stand, but I waved her back down. She waited patiently while I poured. I handed her the first glass, but she gave it to Clive. So polite.

"Okay, now that we're civilized, pickle me."

Shelby giggled and handed me a small cutting board with sliced pickles. "These are the dills. The hot ones aren't ready yet. You can try those next time. I did two varieties of the dill, so tell me which you prefer."

"What's the difference?" I asked.

"The darker one has more vinegar in the brine and the spice blend is more balanced. And this one has a more even blend of salt and vinegar. I doubled the dill because the sprigs look so nice in the jar. See?" She held up a very lovely jar of pickles.

"Gorgeous." I tried that one first. It was salty and biting in all the right ways. The garlic rounded out the vinegar with a little kick. "Holy shit. That's amazing. You guys try."

Clive took one of the slices and popped it in his mouth. "Very nice."

"Yes, I win at pickles," Shelby said.

I ate another slice. "Good bite. And I like the hint of peppercorn. That is peppercorn, right?" I inspected the jar.

"Yeah. Peppercorn. Oh, I'm so glad you like it. Okay, try the other one."

Clive and I each took a slice of the other dill. As soon as I crunched down, I knew I'd made a horrible mistake. My eyes started to water, and I was very aware of the air moving in and out of my nose. Clive's face reflected my horror. "It's so good, Shelby. Try one." I held out the cutting board. Clive turned away so she couldn't see his expression.

"Thanks." She took a bite, then looked at me like I'd kicked her puppy. She swallowed loudly. "My God. This is what sin tastes like. Why would you let me eat that?" She took deep breaths through her mouth.

Clive started to laugh which made him cough. "To be fair, you made us eat it first." He took a sip of beer. "That helps. It kills the vinegar just a little bit."

Shelby and I each took a long drink.

"So, the first one?" Shelby asked.

"Unless you want to kill someone," I said.

"Shut up." Shelby handed me a slice of baguette with creamy herbed cheese. "Try this."

"You're not making cheese now too?" I was skeptical.

"No. I'll stick with brining, thank you. I traded with the woman who makes cheese at that little farm outside Camino. She wanted produce; I wanted cheese."

"I told you she's bringing the barter system back, right?" Clive asked.

"Yeah, but I didn't know she would be so sincere about it."

"Sure. Mock now. You haven't tried the cheese yet." Shelby gave me a look so I took a bite. I tried to tamp down my Shelby-like excitement. "Well?" she asked.

"You might be on to something with this barter thing."

CHAPTER NINE

After a long debate, Nate and I decided to arrive at the coffee shop early. He had suggested that we arrive late to show that we were in control, but then we realized that we were definitely not in control. Jerome arrived on time. We waited while he ordered a pink iced tea, poured a pre-diabetic's worth of sugar in it, then finally joined us. Our table was outside. No one else was dumb enough to sit outside in the heat, so we had relative privacy.

"What do you want to talk about?" Jerome slurped his tea.

"We're sorry," I said.

"All right."

"As a show of good faith, we want to sell you the remaining X. It's yours," I said.

"How do I know it's any good?"

"Come on. I know you've asked around. It's awesome," Nate said.

"What if I don't want to buy it?"

I shrugged. "I'll flush it."

Jerome looked at me skeptically. "You'll flush it? What, you only got half a pill left?"

"No." I set a paper bag on the table.

Jerome opened the bag, dug around in it. "There's a grand worth of X in here."

"Yeah."

"And you expect me to believe you'll flush it?"

"It's a peace offering, not a measure of trust."

Jerome grinned. He liked that response. "How much you want for it?"

"Eight hundred." I was being downright charitable.

"Five hundred and I promise not to poach on your customers," Jerome said.

"Eight hundred. I'm knocking off two for the promise. It's not worth much." We were drug dealers. We had a modicum of honor, but most of our loyalty was tied up in opiates.

"And your promise is worth something? I'm not the one who moved in on someone else's territory. I'll give you six."

"Seven. I'm basically giving you free drugs."

"You know, last week a narc approached me in a bar in Davis." Jerome played with his straw and gave me a look that bordered on coy.

"Huh. You don't say. Was that the same night you followed me into a bar and threatened me?" I asked. Jerome wasn't the only one who could feign demure.

"Six fifty."

"Deal." I held out my hand. Jerome shook it. Nate gave me a look, but kept his mouth shut.

"Follow me out to my car." Jerome nodded to the silver Cadillac parked on the street.

Nate and I stood and let Jerome lead us to the street. He popped the trunk. We stayed back a respectful distance until he nodded me forward. Jerome handed me a wad of cash. I unfolded it and started counting.

"You don't trust me?"

"I thought we had already decided that we don't trust each other," I said. I finished counting. It was all there. I gave him the bag of ecstasy. "Pleasure doing business with you."

"You couldn't make that sound remotely convincing, could you?" He closed the trunk.

"Nope. See you later."

Jerome saluted us with his drink and climbed into his car.

"Let's not sell X anymore, okay?" Nate asked.

"I like your business sense."

❖

When I got home, I called Clive. He had asked to be kept in the loop and I was trying to indulge him. Most of the time, I simply told him I was keeping him in the loop. Saying it almost made it true. In reality, I wanted him to know as little as possible. It was my way of protecting him. I took a number of security measures to make sure we were insulated. I never wrote anything down that could be interpreted as drug related. I was careful when I spent cash so that it wouldn't look suspicious. I made sure our books were impeccable. I screened my regular customers very carefully. All of it was for protection. Clive had worked too hard to make his farm a reality. I wasn't going to let some ambitious cop take that from him. On the off chance that someone did manage to nail me, I wanted to make sure Clive was removed enough to feign ignorance.

"Hey, kiddo."

"Hey."

"Did you meet with Jerome?"

"Yeah, I just got home."

"How did it go?"

"Well enough. We sold the lot for almost nothing. I made it clear that the price was a show of good faith that he wouldn't come after our customers."

"And he agreed to that?" Clive sounded skeptical, which was probably wise.

"He said he did."

"You don't believe him?"

"Not entirely. But it would be in his best interest to back off. He's smart enough to see that. Right now, we aren't competition. I'm sure he would like to move into prescriptions because his customer base would like it, but he can't afford to have us dealing party drugs." I was relying a lot on that logic. It was sound, but it also assumed that Jerome was logical. That was the piece I didn't trust. It was possible, likely even, that he would judge that the risk was worth it. Hell, he was probably confident that he could push us out.

"That's true. I suppose we will just need to let this play out."

"That's the plan."

"Well, thanks for calling. I miss you." That's what I liked about Clive. He wasn't afraid of talking about his feelings. But he also didn't feel the need to dig into them.

"I miss you too."

"Bye, kid."

"Later."

When I hung up the phone, Nickels meowed at me. She was stretched out on the floor. Her pupils were dilated.

"Do you want to play?" I asked. She meowed again. I sat on the floor with her and tossed one of her mouse toys in the air. She tracked its movement, but made no effort to grab it. Instead, she grabbed my hand and dug her claws in. I froze. Once she had flesh, it was best not to argue. My palm got a wet sandpaper bath. "Thank you. That's exactly what I wanted."

When she was done, I tossed the mouse again. She smacked it with her paw and sent it skittering down the hallway. She ditched me to give chase. Her nails clicked and scraped across the hardwood as she disappeared from sight.

"Okay, cool. Later, Nickels." Abandoned by the cat. There had to be a metaphor there.

The temperature had dropped with the sun, which was rare but welcome. I took my book to the back porch. It didn't take long for me to realize that the neighborhood sounds were too distracting so I put the book down and listened. Nondescript noise had always been soothing to me. It was the same with the haze of light that always hung over the city. I loved Clive's farm, but nights there weren't peaceful for me. It was unnaturally dark. The silence seemed barren. But then, I'd always been a city type.

"You mind some company?" Robin was standing in the darkened doorway behind me.

"Not at all. Just listening."

"Want a beer?"

"Love one. You mind if I turn off the lights?"

"Perfect." She disappeared inside.

I picked up my discarded book and brought it inside. Nickels sat up in her bed, blinked at me, and put her head back down. I pushed the button for the outdoor lights. That light switch was the reason I knew this duplex had been the one for me. It predated the usual flip switch. Instead, it had two round buttons. I'd never seen anything like it. Clive had loved it too. A week after I moved in, I'd banned him from touching the switch because he played with it too much.

Robin came back out as I was sinking into my chair. She handed me a bottle and stared at the backyard. A combination of moonlight and light pollution made everything glow. When I'd moved in, the yard had a spread of patchy grass. In the summer, it was dirt. Grass was useless. Robin and Andy had moved in a few months later. Almost immediately, Robin had directed a twelve-year-old Andy to destroy the lawn. Robin and I built massive planter boxes out of scrap wood from the farm. Andy stole my tool belt and was not helpful. We spent all Robin's days off planting seedlings and constructing barriers against the urban wildlife. Raccoons were shifty little scavengers. It had been a stupidly large undertaking that resulted in bonding the three of us. Robin and I found that we made a good team. Our communication was seamless. And Andy was adorable back then, before her snark and vocabulary kicked in.

After the first year, we realized that edibles were pointless. Clive kept us pretty well in produce. Now, we had a spread of flowers that kept the yard in color and smelling of honeyed sweetness. One of the smaller boxes had herbs that I never used and Robin constantly berated me to remember.

Robin leaned over and tapped the neck of her bottle against mine. We drank and watched the flowers ripple in the easy summer breeze.

"Where's the little tiger?" I asked.

"Out somewhere. I've been assured she will be home for curfew." Robin pulled out her phone and checked for text messages.

"She still has an hour."

Robin waved her hand like it wasn't a big deal, but I knew it was. "Big plans this week?"

I shook my head. "Just living the dream. You?"

"Same." She chuckled.

I took a sip of my beer. I was happy. I had a summer night, a cold beer, my friend. It didn't take much. "We should barbecue one night."

"Yes, let's. Tomorrow's high is ninety."

"Perfect. I won't have to barbecue in the dark." That had been a disaster last time.

Robin laughed. "I thought you liked the challenge."

"You realize your kid is going to want to take over and play with fire too?"

"Daytime is much better for barbecuing."

I nodded. "I'll hit the store after my haircut. We can start the grill around seven?"

"Perfect." Robin sipped her beer. "Haircut?"

"You know me. Drives me crazy when I can feel hair on my neck." I rubbed the back of my neck. Stubble. Gross.

"You, uh, still going to that barbershop?"

"Yes. Why are you interested in my haircut?"

"Well, Andy has been bugging me," she said. I waited for her to finish. "She wants to go way shorter, but I don't think the salon is the right place anymore. They keep recommending ways to keep her style feminine. It's frustrating for me and demeaning for her."

I smiled. "You want me to take Andy to get her hair cut off?"

"You don't have to."

"I'd love to." This was exciting. "Wait. Don't you want to take her?"

"Yes. But I was there for the initial cut when we donated her ponytail. I think she needs some space for this one."

"You sure? You can totally tag along."

Robin took a deep breath. "No, it's okay. It's a good outing for the two of you."

"I'll take a ton of photos."

"I'll wait to fawn over them until Andy is out of the room."

"You're the best mom ever."

"I know."

I pulled out my phone and went on my barbershop's website. We were in luck. My barber had an appointment right after mine. I logged in and reserved the appointment. "Done. Scheduled with Caleb for one and one thirty." I pulled up my email, clicked the confirmation, and forwarded it to Robin.

"Oh, she'll be so excited. You're amazing, Cash." She leaned over and squeezed my arm. "Really. I don't know what we would do without you."

"Probably drink less beer." I couldn't handle sincerity very well.

"And go to fewer art shows and read less. And my kid would be floundering." She was wrong, but I didn't know how to tell her that.

"Hey, I know what floundering is, and I'm doing just fine, thank you," Andy said.

Robin and I turned and found Andy grinning at us from the darkened doorway. She pushed through the door and sat on the arm of Robin's chair.

"You're back. Did you have a good time, honey?" Robin put her arm around Andy's waist and Andy let her. Big night.

"Yeah, it was cool." Andy didn't elaborate.

"Did you thank Sophie's mom for giving you a ride?"

Andy sighed. "Yes, Mom."

"Guess what we're doing tomorrow," I said.

"Ice skating?"

"Barbecuing," I said. Robin laughed.

"Cool. Can I start the barbecue? Are we doing burgers? I can make them."

"Ask her what else you're doing," Robin said.

"What else are we doing?" Andy asked.

"Going to my barbershop."

Andy's jaw dropped. "No way. Really?" Robin and I nodded. "And you're cool, Mom?"

"I'm the coolest."

"Thanks!" Andy hugged Robin. Then she leaned over and high fived me. She had told me high fives weren't cool anymore so I knew she was indulging me. It was pretty epic.

CHAPTER TEN

The door to the barbershop was propped open as usual. Andy hesitated so I went ahead of her. She seemed nervous. We sat in the leather stadium seats along the wall. Another strip of stadium seats faced us, and a pair of small club chairs bookended the waiting area.

Andy looked around, but tried to make it look like she wasn't. She tapped her hand against her thigh to the beat of the blues playing.

"Hey, Cash," Caleb called. "I'll be with you in a minute. You want a beer or something?"

"I'm good, thanks," I said. He nodded and went back to sweeping.

"That's our barber?" Andy asked.

"Yeah." I managed not to smile at her. Her seriousness was enviable. "You want to go first or second?"

"I think I want to go second."

"Cool. You want to come up and watch?"

She seemed surprised. "Oh, is that okay? I don't want to get in the way."

"It's fine."

"Then, yeah. That would be dope."

Caleb leaned over the opposite row of stadium seats. "Cash, you ready?"

"Yeah." I skirted one of the club chairs and went to Caleb's station. Andy followed. "Caleb, this is Andy. She's your next appointment."

"Hi, Andy. I'm Caleb." He shook her hand. "First time in a barbershop?"

"That obvious?"

"Just judging by the haircut." Caleb smiled in a way that made it seem like they were buddies.

"Yeah, I guess that's a giveaway. Cash said I could watch."

"Sure. Take a seat, Cash. I'll be right back." Caleb disappeared down the hallway to the storeroom.

I sat down and watched Andy. She was still looking around, but she wasn't fidgeting as much. "I like this place," she said.

"Yeah, it's pretty cool."

"Here you go, Andy." Caleb set a tall stool next to his station, just out of the way of foot traffic.

"Oh, dope. Thanks." Andy climbed on the stool and swung her feet a little.

He draped a smock over me. He tucked a slip of cloth around my neck. I put my head down. He tugged my shirt away from my neckline and clasped the smock. "So what are we doing today? The usual?"

"Let's go two on the sides. It's been hot."

"Sure thing." Caleb spun me toward the mirror. "What about the top?" He ran his fingers through my hair a few times, then pushed it vertical. "Five inches? About here?" He pulled the front of my hair up and stopped an inch shy of the end.

"Perfect."

Caleb spun me back around. He carefully combed the top up and out of the way. Before turning on his clippers, he turned to Andy. "Cash asked for a two, which is a quarter inch. The numbers go up in eighths until you get to an eight, which is an inch. The numbers refer to clipper guards, but most barbers use a comb and clippers."

Andy nodded like he was a hero.

When he started on the sides with clippers, he angled the chair so Andy could see what he was doing. Haircuts were one of my favorite things. I loved the dull hum of the clippers and the crisp zip along the comb. Caleb worked his way around from one side to the other. My favorite part was when he cleaned up around my ears and neck. The clippers buzzed and brushed each line into order. I'd had plenty of haircuts where the stylist or barber seemed to forget that the hair they were cutting was attached to a human, but Caleb was always careful. If this was meditation, I would probably do it more often. Hell, this was my meditation.

When the back and sides were finished, he spritzed with a water bottle and started combing. There was a quiet snick of shears as he cut. Clumps of hair brushed my neck and fell into my lap. He combed again, then blow-dried. He cut anything out of place, and dry wisps tickled my nose. He brushed my ears and forehead with a thick, soft brush to remove the little pieces of hair.

Finally, Caleb pumped hot lather onto his fingertips and painted around my ears and neckline. The lather rapidly cooled. He used a finger to smooth the lather by my ear and efficiently swiped his straight razor down. Around my ear, he used quick, steady movements with the razor. I loved how clean I felt after each cut. The press of the razor, the rough drag, seemed to slough off something that had been weighing me down.

Caleb wiped away the excess lather and dusted everything with talcum powder. He combed back my hair, parted it again, and smoothed it into place. There was another quick cut with the scissors before he was satisfied. He grabbed the tub of pomade at his workstation and worked it through my hair. When he was done with the pompadour, he handed me a mirror.

"Perfect." I grinned and felt along my neckline.

"Cool." Caleb pinched the bottom corners of the smock, brought them up to the top, pinched there as well, and drew it away.

I stood and rubbed the back of my head. It felt clean.

"My turn?" Andy asked. She seemed excited again.

"In just a sec. Let me clean up." Caleb flashed Andy a smile and grabbed the broom. She watched him sweep, seemingly mesmerized by everything he was doing. "All right. Have a seat." He rapped on the chair. Andy jumped off her stool and settled into the barber's seat. I took the stool. Caleb repeated his dance with a new smock. "So what are we doing?" He ran his fingers through her hair, pulled it out at the sides, stood it on end.

"I was thinking like an undercut? I think that's what it's called. I have pictures?"

"Great. Let's see them."

Andy wrestled her phone out from under the smock and unlocked it. "Something like this, but a little longer on the sides."

"May I?" Caleb held out his hand. Andy gave him the phone and he swiped back and forth between the screenshots. "Very cool. So the sides here are about half an inch, a four. Do you want to start with three-quarters of an inch? We can go shorter from there if you want." He handed the phone back.

"Yeah, you don't mind if I want to go shorter?" Andy tucked her phone away.

"Not at all." He turned her toward the mirror. "How long on top?" He threaded his fingers in the front and pulled up. "Six inches will lay about this far back once we've styled." He brought the hair back and tapped her head.

"That looks good." Andy grinned.

"Do you want a hard line between the top and sides or do you want it to fade?"

"I don't know. What's the difference?"

"The hard line means your hair will go from one inch to six inches." Caleb combed to show her. "There will be an obvious part. With a fade, it will be more gradual. One inch to two." He put his hand next to her head and moved it up with each count. "Cash's is more of a fade, but she has a different cut."

"I'm not sure. What will look better?" she asked both of us.

"It's really a matter of preference. The photos you showed me were disconnected, a hard line," Caleb said.

"Okay, let's do that, then."

"What about the sides? We can taper them." He drew a diagonal in front of her ear with his fingertip. "Or leave them longer, or cut them blunt." He drew a sharp, short horizontal.

"Blunt."

Caleb smiled. "Well, that was easy."

Andy shook her head. "At my mom's salon, they always say that longer sides will maintain my femininity."

"I'm thinking you're not too worried about maintaining femininity." Caleb swept her hair back and held it in place so it almost looked like her head was shaved. "I don't know, Cash. If I do this, she might be competition for you." Andy started laughing with relief. Robin had been right. The barbershop was the place for her.

"Damn right," Andy said.

"Cool." Caleb spun her back. He parted all the way around her crown and pinned up the top. He used shears to take the length down, then switched to clippers and a comb. Honey brown curls began to litter the floor. Andy held admirably still as he combed and clipped her sides and back. I took a few photos before she caught me.

"Are you taking pictures?"

"No," I said.

"Liar."

"It's for your mom. This is a big deal."

"Cash." She drew my name out.

"Suck it up, kid," I said. Caleb laughed. Andy sighed.

Caleb took the clip out of the top and tossed it aside. He sprayed Andy's hair and started combing back. I'd never watched him cut because I'd always been on the receiving end, but he held the shears weird. The free end swung back and forth with seeming abandon. It was unsettling. He took a lot off the top. Andy seemed delighted as each chunk dropped. He sprayed and cut and sprayed and cut forever. It finally started to take shape.

Andy flinched when he blow-dried, but rapidly realized the blow-dryer was not going to attack her. There was more cutting and then he stopped and handed her a mirror.

"I still need to finish and style, but tell me how you like the sides."

Andy lifted the mirror and smiled. I took a photo. "It's badass," she said.

"Feel the back. Does it seem short enough?"

She ran her fingers through the back, traced up to her ears. "It's totally short enough."

"Good." Caleb grinned at her and took the mirror. He got some hot lather and dabbed it along her neckline. He dragged the razor down her cheek, traced the edges of her ears. At her neckline, he loosened the smock and lightly tugged her T-shirt away from her neck. He smoothed the lather over her neck and drew a careful line with the razor.

"Are we done?" Andy asked.

"Almost." Caleb wiped away the remaining lather and powdered everything he had just shaved. "Do you want me to style it?"

"Yeah, that would be dope."

"Do you want to watch so you know how?" Caleb asked. He was apparently feeling generous. I'd never seen him offer to teach someone.

"Please." Andy nodded emphatically.

Caleb spun her to face the mirror again. He sprayed her hair and towel dried it. He spritzed on a product and worked it through, then combed the hair back until it lay just right. When he blow-dried, he focused on a bit of volume in the front. He brushed and followed each stroke with the dryer. When the top was mostly dry, he set aside the dryer.

"Drying allows you to sculpt the shape you want and the heat locks it in." He picked up a tub of paste. "This paste is matte, but you can get it with shine if you like that look. You don't need much." He showed Andy the amount of paste in his palm. "Work it through front to back, but make sure you follow through." He finger combed the product in, smoothed the sides, pulled the front to attention, combed everything again. "Make sure you put a little product on the back and sides too. It'll help it stay in place since yours is a little longer on the sides. Plus, it looks weird when the top has product, but it's not anywhere else." He worked the excess product off his palms and into her head. Andy leaned toward the mirror and turned her head back and forth. Caleb pulled away her smock and handed her a mirror.

"This is the best haircut ever. Like, ever. I checked."

Caleb laughed. "Here, look at the back." He spun her so her back was to the wall mirror.

Andy tilted her head so she could see the neckline. She ran her hand down the back and felt her bare neck. "This is awesome." She gave the mirror back and stood.

I took a few final photos. Andy ran her fingers through her hair, directed the length to one side, shifted it back.

"Does it look like you were hoping?" Caleb asked.

"Yeah, exactly. Thank you. Seriously."

"You're welcome. Do you need hair product? Or do you already have some?"

Andy looked at me. "I don't know."

"I've got some she can play with," I told Caleb. "When you figure out what kind of paste you like, we'll get you some of your own. Sound good?" I asked Andy.

"Yeah, that would be cool."

"Good idea." Caleb shook Andy's hand again, then mine. I handed him money for my haircut and severely over tipped him. Andy followed my lead with the cash Robin had given her.

I led the way out and back to my car. Andy studied herself in every reflective surface we passed.

"So you like barbershops."

"I love barbershops. And Caleb is so cool. He did a really good cut, right?"

"Totally. It looks amazing."

"Do you think I'll be able to style it on my own?" Andy asked.

"Yeah, you will get the hang of it really fast. And I can help if you need it."

"Thanks, Cash. For taking me and everything."

"Anytime." We got in the car. "You still cool if we go to the grocery store?"

"I guess." She made it sound like she was doing me a huge favor.

We had worked through half the grocery list when I realized Andy was obsessively rubbing at her collar.

"Itchy?"

"It's like torture." She juggled the three bags of chips she was holding so she could scratch more vigorously.

"Stop that. It's all the little pieces of hair stuck in your shirt collar. When you go short, it's part of the bargain."

"Well, make it stop."

"We will be home in fifteen minutes. You can shower then." I added buns to the produce and cheese in my basket.

Andy sighed. "What else do we need?"

"Ground turkey. And soda, if you want it."

"Oh, can I get the good kind?"

"Sure thing. We're basically celebrating your haircut."

"I thought you decided to barbecue before you decided to take me to get my haircut," she said.

"Yes, technically. But it really lends some legitimacy to the whole affair." Kids didn't understand anything.

"You're so smart."

"I know." I tossed in a couple pounds of ground turkey. Andy led us to the cold drinks where I let her pick out three packs of Jones. I was way too indulgent.

"Hey, Cash?" Andy asked as we left the store.

"Yeah?"

"Thanks again."

"You're welcome." I resisted the urge to ruffle her hair. That wouldn't go over well. "Besides, now I have someone to go to the barbershop with."

"Selfish."

CHAPTER ELEVEN

I was stretched on the couch. Nickels was curled up next to me. I had a book propped on my other side. It was too hot to go outside. It was too hot to have a cat sleeping on me, but Nickels wasn't great at listening. My phone buzzed and I had no desire to look at it. Robin wouldn't be home for a while. I didn't need to start the charcoal for another hour. I just wanted to snuggle with my cat and read my book. But then I decided to be a big kid. So I looked at the phone. It was Laurel.

What u up to?

In response, I sent a photo of Nickels and my book.

Casual midday poetry read?

I smiled. That photo had been way more Instagram than I realized. *It's Audre Lorde. She's best in the light of day.*

What the hell does that mean?

I laughed, which Nickels did not appreciate. *No fucking clue. Thought it sounded cool. What r u doing? Want to come over for a BBQ?*

Yes.

That was it. Simple. I liked it.

Come over. I'm starting the grill in an hour. That was super casual. I was owning this dating thing.

Fifteen minutes later, I'd managed to disentangle myself from the cat. I debated putting a button up over the tank top I'd put on after my shower, but Laurel wasn't the only one who could rock a tank. I finished styling my hair in record time. I was rinsing hair product off my hands when there was a knock at the front door followed by a knock at the back door. I wasn't usually so popular. I answered the front door first because I figured it was Laurel. It was. I got a kiss and a six-pack with two limes tucked into it.

"So, hi."

"Hey. Come in," I said. The knocking at the back door picked up. "Sorry. That's probably Andy."

"Go ahead. I'll put this in the fridge."

"Perfect. Thanks." I went to the back door. It was Andy. Fresh from what had to be an hour-long shower and on the verge of tears.

"I don't know how to blow-dry."

"Whoa, it's okay." I squeezed her shoulder. "I have years of experience with blow-drying. Would you like to see my résumé?"

She nodded and took a deep breath, which seemed to calm her. "I won't settle for less than ten years' experience. My hair is the source of all my power."

"All right, Samson. Let's go."

"Hey, Andy." Laurel stepped out of the kitchen. "Whoa, killer haircut."

"Thanks." Andy grinned and pushed back her wet locks. "Cash took me to her barber."

"It looks fantastic."

"I feel like Romeo from that stupid version Cash likes, but I'm going to learn to style it."

"Not if you insult Baz Luhrmann. His version of *Romeo and Juliet* is clearly the best," I said. Andy rolled her eyes. "Sorry, Laurel. We have a hair styling session. Would you care to join us in the bathroom?"

"Not an odd request at all. I'd love to."

We traipsed into my bathroom. Laurel sat on the edge of the tub. Andy stood in front of the mirror while I plugged in the blow-dryer. I leaned around Andy to get a brush and some product out of the medicine cabinet.

"First up is a sea salt spray. It adds texture without adding weight. Then we do a heat protectant because you'll be blow-drying a lot." I gave her both bottles. "Just a little of each."

"Okay." Andy sprayed both products lightly. I nodded and she ran her hands through her hair to distribute the product.

"Good. Now, remember how Caleb brushed while he blow-dried? You need to keep the blow-dryer right next to the brush. Pay attention to how I add volume to the front." I repeated the process Caleb had shown her. In between strokes, I glanced over at Laurel. She was grinning at us, seemingly enchanted at the sight of me helping my little baby dyke neighbor style her hair. But there was something more. As if she thought the whole thing was hilarious. It was that snark coming through. Laurel realized I was watching her and she narrowed her eyes. It was both an invitation and a warning. I really wanted to give in to the invitation. And I didn't care about the warning.

When Andy's hair was mostly dry, I turned off the dryer and set it aside.

"More product now?" Andy asked.

"Yeah, this is similar to the paste Caleb used. Do you want to put it in?"

"Sure." She unscrewed the top and scooped out a glob of paste. "This much?"

"That's good. Rub it in your palms, then spread up to your fingertips a little at a time."

Andy spent more time than necessary carefully rubbing the product into her hands. She started with a little paste in the front and finger combed it back. When she ran out of product, she gathered more from her palms. There was a cowlick on the back of her head, but she quickly figured out which way it was pushing her hair and went with the flow.

"You've really got the hang of that," Laurel said.

"I think I do." Andy sounded excited. "What do you think? Am I done?"

Laurel and I nodded. "Totally. Do you want hairspray?" I asked.

"I don't know. Do I?"

"Your call. I don't like it because it makes my hair feel too stiff," I said.

"Okay. I'll skip it." Andy washed her hands.

I packed away the dryer and pulled out more hair product. "Try these." I handed her three tubs and one tube, plus the two sprays she had already used. "Let me know what you like and what you don't like."

"Thanks." Andy cupped the products in her shirt and led the way out of the bathroom. "Can I break into that soda now?"

"Fine with me."

"Dope." Andy left through the back door. She even remembered to close it.

"Thanks for being so patient," I said to Laurel.

"No problem. I like watching you with her. It's cute."

"Super. I totally want you to think I'm cute."

"Oh, sorry. I meant sweet."

"Awesome."

"Tender? Delightful?"

"So you want a beer?" I asked.

"Nice sidestep. Yes, please."

I sliced up the lime and grabbed two beers. "Porch?"

"Sure."

Outside, I opened the bottles with the opener mounted on the railing. Laurel took her bottle and sat in one of the big chairs. Half a second later, Andy joined us with her fancy ass soda and sat in the chair next to Laurel. I leaned against the railing.

"When are we starting up the grill?" Andy asked.

"When your mom gets home," I said.

"But we could start it earlier if we wanted."

"We could."

"So when are we starting up the grill?"

"When your mom gets home."

Andy rolled her eyes. "Cash."

"Anderson."

"Oh, an impasse. What will happen now?" Laurel said.

Andy laughed. "Cash will win."

"Damn right. Now, go put on some music."

"Fine." Andy pushed herself up and went into my side of the house.

Immediately, I took the chair she had vacated.

"Smooth," Laurel said.

"I've got to make sure she knows who is in charge."

"Yeah, you really put that foot down."

"Thanks, I know."

Music streamed from the speakers, but it was too low to hear. I pointed up so Andy could see me through the window. The volume went way too high. I pointed down. It equalized and I gave her a thumbs-up.

"Blondie?" Laurel asked. "She doesn't know The Cranberries, but she knows Blondie?"

"I'm teaching chronologically. We haven't reached the nineties yet."

Andy opened the door. "Hey, you took my seat."

"Sucker."

"Jerkwad." Andy flopped into one of her mom's Adirondacks, which was great because they were angled so she could check herself out in the window.

Laurel and I watched her play with her hair and tried not to laugh. She threw bottle caps at us. By the time Robin got home, we had worn ourselves out from laughing and a brief, impromptu game of tag.

"I leave for a few hours and the place goes to hell." Robin closed the door behind her.

"It was Cash's fault," Andy said. "She stole my chair."

"Anderson." Robin saw Andy's hair and started smiling. Maybe tearing up a little. "You look so good. Spin around, let me see." Andy spun slowly. Robin ran her hand over the back. "I love it. It's perfect on you."

"You think so?" Andy asked.

"Definitely. Did you like the barbershop?"

"Yeah, it was so cool. Caleb—he's our barber—showed me how to style it and he asked all these questions and it was totally dope." Andy ran her hands through her hair, pushed it to the right, then back to the left. She was already mastering the casual hair tousle. "And he used a straight razor."

"No way." Robin rubbed the soft, freshly shaved skin on the back of Andy's neck. "I'm so glad you had a good time. I'm also glad you like the cut. It really suits you."

"Thanks, Mom." Andy ducked her head.

"And you must be Laurel." Robin reached over me to shake Laurel's hand. "I'm Robin Ward. My boys speak very highly of you."

Laurel laughed when Robin said boys. "It's great to meet you as well."

"Are we starting up that grill?" Robin asked me.

"We can do that," I said.

"Good. You and Andy need a distraction so I can talk to Laurel."

Andy and I did a mutual eye roll. I took the cover off the grill and started assembling supplies.

"Hey, Mom, Cash let me get Jones. You want one?" Andy asked.

"I think I'll probably do a beer, but thanks."

"There's more in my fridge, Andy. You want to grab one for your mom?" I asked.

"Okay."

"Make that two." Laurel held up her empty bottle.

"Good call. Three, please."

"Demanding." Andy took our empties and disappeared into the house.

"So how did she do at the appointment?" Robin asked.

"She did great. Asked good questions, listened to what he was telling her." I pulled up the photos on my phone and handed it to Robin. She made an excited noise.

Andy returned and handed out beer. Robin barely looked up. She was engrossed. "Oh, he's cutting so much…What a funny way to hold scissors…Andy looks so calm…Look at how much he's paying attention to detail."

We ignored her.

I motioned Andy over so she could start the chimney. She expertly filled the base with newspaper and scooped charcoal out of the tub until the top was rounded. I gave her the barbecue lighter and watched as she lit strategic points of the paper.

"Nicely done."

"Thanks."

We tucked away the flammable supplies and backed away from the smoke.

"Should we prep the burgers?" Andy asked.

"Sure." I glanced at Robin and Laurel. "You guys mind if we go prep the food?"

They waved us away. I grabbed my beer and Andy followed me into the kitchen. She pulled out a large bowl and dumped the turkey meat into it. I assembled spices on the counter next to her. She washed her hands.

"Basil, garlic, oregano, pepper, salt, what else you want?" I asked.

"What did we do last time? It was kind of brown and orangey."

"Cumin?"

"Yeah, let's do that."

"Anything else?"

Andy looked at the spices and thought hard. "Truffle oil."

"Kid, you're a genius." I grabbed the bottle.

"I know." Andy started dumping spices into the meat. She managed to not go overboard, which was good. We'd been working on that.

I started slicing veggies and dumping them in a bowl.

"Hey, do you mind grabbing a tray for me? I forgot." Andy was holding a half-formed burger and had no place to set it.

"Sure." I rinsed my hands. She waited while I pulled out a tray and lined it.

"Thanks."

"How you guys doing in here?" Laurel came in the back door.

"We're the awesomest," Andy said.

"Did Robin quiz you too hard?" I asked.

"No, she got a call. You need some help?"

"Sure," I said. "I'm cutting veggies to grill. You want to slice produce for the burgers?"

"I'm basically a master at produce slicing." Laurel stood a little too close to me so she could see what I was doing. "You know, that bowl is never going to survive grilling."

"Gee, thanks." I got out another cutting board for Laurel and gave her a knife. "Produce is there, pickles are in the fridge."

Laurel looked at the plastic bags of produce. "You own a farm and buy produce at the grocery store?" She was judging hard. Andy laughed.

I sighed. "Yeah, I know. I would have brought some down, but I didn't know we were going to barbecue. Plus, there isn't a farmer's market today."

"Excuses, excuses."

"But get this, Braddock Farm is going to start making pickles."

Laurel started in on the tomatoes. "Pickles?"

"I'm a little bit obsessed. I've been begging Clive for years, but he's been ignoring me. But Shelby finally convinced him."

"And Shelby is?" Laurel asked.

"Oh, she's this crazy girl he hired a few years ago to work in the farm stand. She ended up running the place. She's got some agreement with the local high school during the school year. The 4-H kids come volunteer. They help around the farm, work the farm stand. In summer, she hires the best kids from the school year."

"She sounds really put together," Laurel said. Andy started laughing again. "How old is she?" Laurel turned to Andy. "What is so funny?"

"Shelby is so not put together. She's all whimsical and floaty," Andy said.

"Whimsical and floaty?" Laurel asked.

I was going to deny it, but it was a good description. "Yeah, she's great at working out community programs and cultivating pickles, but she sometimes forgets things."

"Like pants," Andy said.

I looked at Andy. "She's never forgotten her pants."

Andy giggled. "Okay, but she totally would."

I thought about that. "Yeah, okay." Laurel stopped cutting to look at me. She raised an eyebrow. "She's a lovely girl, though. Really. And Clive says she's very helpful."

"I so want to meet this chick." Laurel went back to slicing.

"Okay, next week?"

"I get to go to the farm?"

"Sure. Why not?"

"I'm in," she said.

"Burgers are done." Andy nudged the laden tray.

"Should we see if the charcoal is ready?" I asked.

"Yeah." Andy grabbed the tray of burgers. She was excited. Barbecuing was her only chance to play with fire and not get in trouble.

"I'll be right back," I told Laurel.

"No worries. I'm almost done."

Andy led the way outside. The chimney had stopped smoking and the charcoal was glowing. Looked ready to me.

"What do you think?" I asked her.

"Looks good. Can I turn it?"

We both turned to look for Robin. She wasn't there. "Sure. But be careful," I said.

Andy grasped the wooden handle and slowly lifted. She gave it a little shake to knock off any newspaper ash or loose embers. Then, she flipped it and poured out the charcoal. Like a pro. Well, almost a pro. One small piece of charcoal jumped the barbecue and landed on the deck.

"Shit." Andy started to set down the chimney, realized it was hot and couldn't be set on the deck, and looked at me in panic.

"I got it." I kicked the charcoal into the grass and jumped down the steps. I crushed the embers into smaller pieces.

"Here." Andy handed me the watering can from the deck.

I poured water on the smoldering pieces. "We win."

"Totally. Let's not tell Mom."

"Deal." I gave the watering can back.

"So where do I put this?" Andy held out the chimney.

"It's cool now. Anything burning in it?"

Andy looked inside and tilted it back and forth. "Nope."

"You can put it on the deck."

After that excitement, evenly distributing the charcoal and putting the grill in place was easy. We didn't even light anything on fire. I left Andy with her spatula and her perfectly formed burgers.

"That was quick," Laurel said when I came in.

"She's done it before. I just supervise now."

"Brave."

"Well, she dumped the entire chimney on the deck once. After that, not much impresses me."

Laurel laughed. "Nice."

"Yeah. It didn't even catch fire. I replaced a couple of the boards because they were singed, but other than that, it was fine."

"Wait. You're serious?"

"Totally. Then again, she was twelve." I resumed my veggie prep. "Twelve-year-olds shouldn't play with barbecues." I imitated Robin's voice.

"Christ, you're not very smart, are you?"

"Not really, no." I dumped the last of the onions on top of the halved mushrooms in my bowl. "Looks like you're done."

"I didn't do pickles yet." Laurel went to the fridge. "I hear they're very important."

"The most important." I pulled out foil for me and plastic wrap for her.

"What exactly is your plan there?" Laurel nodded at the foil.

"Watch and learn." I poured olive oil and ground salt and pepper into the bowl. I tossed it a few times until everything down to the zucchini was coated. Then I pulled off sheets of foil and formed two big envelopes.

"Nice."

"This ain't my first rodeo." I divided the contents of the bowl between the foil envelopes.

"Really? Rodeo?"

"Yep. That's what I said."

Laurel nodded in a judge-y way. But she was smiling. When she finished the pickles, we wrapped the cutting board in plastic and put it in the fridge. I leaned against the counter.

"Do you need to help Andy?" Laurel asked.

"Nope, she's got this."

"So we don't need to go back out there?" She took a step closer to me.

"No."

"You know, we're in here being, for all intents and purposes, domestic as hell. But there's something about it that feels…"

"Queer?"

Laurel laughed. "Sure. Queer."

"We're not exactly wholesome, are we?"

"Well, you're not," she said.

"Says the chick who punched a drug dealer."

She stepped closer until we were almost touching, but not quite. "Not one of my finer moments."

"I don't know. It worked for me." I was suddenly very aware of the warmth radiating from her. It was a pleasant heat, a respite from the air conditioning that seemed to cling to my bare arms.

"Yeah? Violence does it for you?"

"Apparently. I'm learning all kinds of fun things about myself."

"Like what?" Laurel hooked her finger in the front of my tank top and looked down. "Fair game."

"It appears that I'm into chicks who fight my battles for me."

"Not very chivalrous of you."

"I never said I was chivalrous." I pulled her close and kissed her. She held back for a moment, as if she was going to keep it chaste like before. And then she let go. Her weight pressed into me. I tugged at her bottom lip with my teeth. She opened her mouth and let me in. I cupped the back of her head, pressed closer. I'd only meant to kiss her, but suddenly I wanted her under me. She slid a hand under my tank and dragged rough fingertips across my stomach. Something shifted and she was in control. Her lips moved away from mine, which was tragic. But then she was kissing my jaw, my neck. I gripped her hair and brought her back to my lips. We kissed, a simple press of her mouth against mine, but it was perfect. Her hands dug into my sides, pulling me harder. I slid my thigh between hers. Her breath hitched. That small catch seemed sexier somehow than the passionless joy of fucking someone else. I realized right then how deep I was, how fucked I was. She opened her mouth again and licked the edge of my lip.

"So I take it the buns aren't ready for the grill?"

Laurel jerked away from me. We turned to find Andy leaning against the doorway, her hands over her eyes, and a massive grin on her face.

"Perv," I said.

"I am not. I just want my burger buns and I'll be on my way." Andy stuck one of her hands out and stumbled blind into the kitchen. "I think I left them on the counter."

"Anderson, stop screwing around."

Andy coughed. "I hate to state the obvious here, but I think that statement might be a bit hypocritical." She found the edge of the counter and slowly felt her way forward.

"You just had to make her download a dictionary, didn't you?" Laurel said to me.

"I never said I was perfect."

Laurel scoffed. She grabbed the package of buns, took Andy's hand, and set the package in it.

"Thanks." Andy spun and booked it out of the kitchen.

"That was interesting," Laurel said.

"It sure was."

"We should probably go outside."

"I suppose you're right." I pushed up off the counter.

"One thing." Laurel leaned in and kissed me again. I tried to pull her against me, but she took a step back. I groaned. She trailed a hand down my chest and walked away.

"Tease."

CHAPTER TWELVE

I was going to have to call Henry. My supplies were tragically low. Maybe he would meet me at the farm again. Or maybe it was a bad idea to pick up drugs when I was giving Laurel her first tour of the farm. Yeah, that probably violated some rule book.

I sorted through what I had left and decided to only hit the big deliveries. My three in Land Park would take the rest of my OxyContin and Xanax. I wanted to make Brant wait another day or two, but I needed to be prepared after holding out on him. Last week I'd lied and said I was low so I only gave him a half order. But it was a timeout, nothing else. So I texted to see what he would need.

How much produce do you need this week?

I didn't need to monitor Peggy so I texted her the same message. She could probably hold out for a week, but she liked to have a little stockpile. She wrote back right away.

The usual order, please. How is Thursday? Peggy's texts were always flawless and polite. She was of the generation that had mastered texting, but refused the shorthand.

Perfect. I'll see you then.

Nickels watched me sort bags of pills with an air of disinterest that didn't hide her tiny kitty disappointment.

"I'll be back before you know it," I said. She meowed. "You'll fall asleep anyway. You won't miss me." She walked back into the living room and climbed in her bed. It was her equivalent of telling me to go fuck myself. "I love you too."

I had just started my car when Brant wrote back.

I'm good this week.

That was odd. *Really? You still have some?*

Yeah. I'm good.

Interesting. Brant never struck me as the self-regulating type. Not great for my bank account, but good for him.

I hit the first housewife in Land Park. I didn't even know her name. I called her Mrs. Peacock in my head because she reminded me of *Clue*. She wasn't a regular customer in the sense of time— I'd gone half a year without hearing from her and I'd delivered to her three times in a month—but she was like clockwork in that she called me whenever her husband went overseas on business. At first, I thought she missed him. Then, I thought she was drowning her sorrows. It wasn't until I ran into a nineteen-year-old rent boy coming out of her house that I figured it out. She wasn't buying drugs for herself. She was paying for services with them. Lovely woman, though. Always offered me fresh baked cookies. Today, it was a package of biscotti.

My next stop was three streets over. I was parking when my phone rang. It was Nate.

"Hey."

"Okay, so in a week you'll make fun of me, and in a month this will be your favorite joke, but right now I'm being totally serious," Nate said.

"I'm intrigued."

"I think I'm being followed."

"What?" That didn't sound remotely funny.

"I'm probably just paranoid and I'm fine with that. But I swear I'm being tailed by a dark blue, late nineties Civic. I haven't gotten a decent look at the driver yet, but they are tall. The windows are tinted so that's all I can see from a distance." He sounded clinical, which meant he was panicking.

"Start at the beginning."

"Last night, I hit some of my usual rounds. I started at that bar in downtown Davis. Not the one that cop was at. The place without a name."

"The one with the bright blue walls?" It was always Nate's kickoff point. The bartenders didn't mind because he tipped them well. Okay, he bribed them a little.

"Yeah. Then I did a few house calls and a frat party. I noticed the car at my first house call because the license plate starts with eighty-four and that was my lacrosse number in high school." Nate played lacrosse in high school? "Anyway, I saw it outside the frat party later and thought it was weird."

"But it could be a coincidence. Was your first delivery in a college neighborhood?" I asked.

"Yeah. I know. You're thinking maybe I just saw the car and then the owner went to the frat party."

"Exactly. Nothing to worry about."

"That's what I thought too. But I was on campus all morning. When I left, I thought I saw it again when I was leaving the parking lot. It was like four cars behind me."

"See? So they're a student."

"Except I just did two deliveries in East Sac. I saw the Civic parked in the apartment complex next door at my first stop and on the street at my second stop."

"Fuck." Davis and East Sacramento were both college towns, but that was where the similarity ended. They were separated by twenty miles, a county line, and very different brands of militant liberalism. The chances that a Davis student would end up near Sac State were nonexistent.

"Damn right."

"Fucking motherfucker." I took a deep breath in addition to the profanity and that didn't help either. "Okay, did you see any more of the license plate? I can have Henry run it."

"I'm not a fucking amateur. I have the license plate and photos including two of the driver. Like I said, you can't see any detail, but it's better than nothing. I'll text you everything."

That seemed to help in ways the breathing and cursing hadn't. "You're fucking professional as shit."

"I know."

"Go home. Take a long route. Lock the door and chill."

"Done. But, Cash, there's one more thing."

"What?" This shit show wasn't enough?

"If I'm being followed, you probably are too."

It took Henry five hours to call me back. I knew it was because he was on shift, but logic wasn't exactly helping me freak out less. By the time my phone rang, I'd given up on my usual distractions and settled on pacing the kitchen.

"Good news or bad news?" Henry asked.

"Just tell me what you found out."

"It's not a cop."

"Thank God."

"The car is registered to Raymond St. Maris. Younger brother of alleged drug dealer Jerome St. Maris. Raymond has a record, but nothing compared to his big brother." All of my profanity failed me. "Cash, you still there?"

"Yes." This was bad.

"It looks like Raymond works with or for Jerome."

"What does he look like?"

"Similar to Jerome. Six one, two hundred and forty pounds, Caucasian, dark brown hair. Left arm tattooed."

"Does it say what the tattoos are? Is there a Catholic looking saint and some text?" I thought hard about the guy I'd seen working with Jerome. There were three guys I'd seen most often. The tallest had to be Raymond.

"Says here that he has the Virgin Mary and the word respect on his outer forearm."

"Yep. I've met him. He's not as smart as his brother and a lot meaner."

"That matches his record. Jerome's is a lot of minor drug offenses, but Raymond's got assault, battery, sexual assault, and a manslaughter charge that didn't stick. Cash, you and Nate need to be real careful." He was using his big brother voice. That was never good. It meant he would try to help and get in the way.

"I understand. We won't take any risks." I mostly just said it so he wouldn't play hero. "What else can you tell me? What does Jerome drive? I've seen the Cadillac, but does he have any other vehicles? What about his other lackeys? I want to make sure I'm not being followed too."

"Umm." Henry's voice trailed off. Christ, I was tired of micromanaging. "I'll look it up. You going to be up a while?"

"Yeah, sure." It was only midnight. I'd chosen my job so that I could stay up all hours of the night whenever it suited me.

"Cool." He hung up.

I flopped onto the couch. Nickels jumped up and curled up on my chest. "Hey, Nick, Nick, Nickels, don't answer the door if I'm not home, okay?" I rubbed behind her ears. She scooted closer until her little gray nose was an inch from my chin. "I love you too."

I tried reading, but quickly conceded defeat. How the hell was I going to get Jerome to back off? I'd had some minor issues before, but a visit from Nate and me and a well worded threat generally did wonders. Maybe Henry could dig up something we could exploit. An hour later, Henry texted. *New silver Cadillac CTS. Blue '98 Civic. Black Ford F-150. '84 Volvo station wagon.*

I thanked him and tried to review my entire day. I could have been followed so many times, it was barely worth considering. I thought about the drive from my place to the light where I liked to turn. I thought about the small side streets I passed and the nearly perfect grid of midtown blocks. Envisioning did nothing for me. The streets never changed, the cars and people constantly did. I could get up and look out the window and see a vehicle matching at least one of the descriptions Henry had given me. I stared at the white and gray tips of Nickel's ears. She was perfect. My crown molding looked fantastic. Paying Andy to paint had been a good idea. I was on the edge of sleep when my phone rang. Nate at two in the morning. That couldn't be good.

"Hello?"

"Cash?" Nate was almost whispering, his voice was so low. "You're up. Good, I'm at your back gate, but it's locked. Let me in."

"What are you doing at the back gate?" I asked, but I was already nudging the cat onto the couch and kicking into my shoes.

"I'll explain, just let me in quick. And, hey, don't flip, okay? I'm fine."

Well, that got me moving.

I fumbled the door open, vaulted down the steps, and crossed to the gate at a half-sprint. I swung the gate open. Nate was wearing a hoodie and basketball shorts, which was very unlike him. He was more of a sweater guy. I closed the gate after he slid into the backyard. He was moving too slow for my liking, but I didn't prompt him. I trusted him to be honest about what he needed.

When we got in the house, Nate pulled back the hood. His eye was swelling and there was blood crusted on his left nostril.

"What the fuck happened?" I led him to the kitchen and motioned for him to sit.

Nate shook his head. "I'll stand. My ribs are on fire." He stood by the chair I'd pointed to and gripped the back.

"Why?" I leaned back against the counter. I didn't know how to help him.

"I got jacked. Three guys broke into my apartment. They ransacked the place and took my stash and the money from my sales this week."

"Fucking Jerome."

"Yeah. One of them looked just like him, but younger and maybe a little shorter. And I've seen the other two with him. I'm so sorry, man."

"What? Why? It's not your fault."

"I should have done more. Maybe hid my shit better."

"No. We can replace the drugs." I was pretty pissed about that, but I wasn't pissed at Nate. "Wait. How much did they take?"

Nate grinned. "Joke's on them, I guess. I'm almost out of everything. I had twenty Adderall, ten Oxy, and fifteen Codeine. It wasn't much."

"See? No big deal. So what did they do to you?"

"Couple face hits. Kicked me in the ribs a few times. The big one sat on me while the other two trashed my place."

"So it was a warning?"

"Basically."

"How did you get here?" I assumed he had been careful what with calling from the back gate and all, but it was probably smart to ask.

"I took the long route down to Cosumnes, parked at that grocery store next to campus, walked through CRC, caught light rail, walked here. It was actually kind of badass. I'm like a spy."

"Super badass. So can I take a look at your ribs?"

"Sure." He tried to strip off his sweatshirt, but moving wasn't working for him.

"Let me." I gripped the edge of his sweatshirt and worked it up over his torso. He gritted his teeth when I made him lift his arm to free it from the cotton. "Shit." Deep purple bruises spread from his hip up toward his armpit.

"You think they are broken?"

"No idea. We will have to ask Robin."

Nate nodded. "Don't wake her up. I can wait until morning."

"Are you sure?" That was chivalrous of him.

"Totally. It's going to hurt either way."

"Don't worry." I smiled. "I'm a drug dealer."

That made him laugh, then grimace. "Good. I'd love some drugs."

"Come with me. Let's clean you up."

Nate followed me to the bathroom. I gave him some Codeine from my private supply, which he dry swallowed. I got a washcloth wet and dabbed at the blood on his nose.

"It's not broken. You don't need to be careful," he said. I swiped a few more times before he took the washcloth and leaned to look in the mirror. "I got it."

"Sorry. I don't want to break you."

Nate smiled. "I've taken worse hits. Not all at once, but still."

"How can I help? Ice pack for your eye?"

Nate groaned. "An ice pack would be amazing."

"Done. One erotically charged ice pack coming up."

"Fuck you." He shook his head and smiled at me in the mirror.

I went back to the kitchen and poured ice into a plastic bag and wrapped it in a towel. At this rate, I was going to need to buy some actual ice packs. I wondered if that was tax deductible. It was a work expense, after all.

When I got back to the bathroom, Nate was scrubbing blood off his chin. "How does this shit get everywhere?"

"Maybe you should consider not getting punched in the face?"

"Brilliant idea. I'll try that tomorrow."

"Here." I gave him the ice pack. "I'm going to put sheets on the couch in the study. I'll have it made up in just a minute."

"I just need a pillow and my dignity and I'll be happy." Nate wrung out the bloody washcloth and hung it.

"Would you settle for a pillow, a blanket, and shame?"

"Sold." He put the ice pack against his face and sighed. "God, that's good."

I left him to the joys of frozen water. I pulled a blanket and pillow from the hall closet. Nate stumbled into the study as I was spreading the blanket. "Thanks for putting me up." He toed off his shoes.

"Anytime. Try to get some sleep. I'll have Robin check you in the morning."

"Sounds like a party." He slowly stretched out on the couch. "Until then, I'll just enjoy my drugs."

"'Night." I hit the light and pulled the door closed.

I went around and cleaned up the detritus of Nate's visit. I double-checked the locks on all the doors and windows. Nickels was already asleep on my bed when I finally crawled in. I typed quick, vague texts to Henry and Clive. They would be upset if I didn't give them a heads-up. I sent a separate text to Robin asking her to drop by in the morning.

Nickels scooted until her butt was against my hip. She flicked me with her tail, started purring, and fell back to sleep. I wasn't blessed with her skill set, so I succumbed to a far less peaceful sleep.

CHAPTER THIRTEEN

I woke to the smell of coffee brewing. This was why people got housewives. I wondered where I could buy one of those. I grabbed my cutoffs from the day before, underwear, and a clean T-shirt. I needed a shower if I was going to face this day. I realized about two minutes in that it was too hot for a warm shower so I turned the dials to cold, which did very little for my comfort, but certainly woke me up.

I found Nate at the kitchen table making awkward faces as Robin felt his ribs.

"Is he going to die?" I poured myself a cup of coffee. They both already had one.

"Eventually, yes. But not for at least a few years," Robin said.

"Good. His mother invested a lot into his education." I sat across from Nate. Robin moved to his other side and prodded some more.

"Hey, remember when you gave me those drugs? That was awesome." Nate had apparently lost the art of subtlety.

"What kind of drugs?" Robin asked.

"Codeine."

"How long ago?"

I looked at the clock and counted. "Seven hours."

"He can have some more," Robin said.

"Yes! I love drugs."

"And I hired him because he doesn't like drugs," I told Robin.

"I think the fractured ribs might have something to do with it." Robin pressed a stethoscope to various points of Nate's chest and told him to breathe.

I left them to it. When I got back with Nate's drugs, Robin was helping him stretch out on the couch. She arranged two new ice packs against his side. I gave him the pills and he struggled to sit up enough to swallow them.

"Easy. Move slow." Robin supported his back, then guided him back down. "Make sure to take deep breaths regularly. And ice it when it gets sore."

"How long is he going to be out for the count?" I asked.

"It will take a few weeks to fully heal. Six, maybe. But he will be mobile in the next few days." Robin checked the placement of the ice. "That feel okay?"

"Like a million bucks. Thanks for taking a look at me," Nate said.

"Any time. Of course, I'd rather you not let people kick you in the ribs."

"Agreed."

"See, man? I told you having a nurse around was awesome," I said.

"If we could stick to opinions about cough syrup and runny noses in the future, that would be great," Robin said.

"Yes, ma'am. If I see anyone with cold or flu symptoms, I'll rub them all over my face." I had to dodge Robin's backhand.

I stepped outside to call Henry. He'd been blowing up my phone for thirty minutes. But Robin had gone to drop Andy off at a friend's, Nate was finally asleep, and the dregs of my coffee were still almost warm, so I finally had the privacy and inclination to call him back.

"Finally. Jesus. What is going on?" Henry asked.

"Jerome's friends paid Nate a visit last night. Beat him up, took his stash and the money he'd made this week."

"Fuck me."

"Yeah, he's asleep on my couch. Robin just looked at him. He'll be fine."

"Oh, okay. Well, that's good. How much does he owe?" Henry asked.

"What?" I replayed his sentence. There was no way he was asking what I thought he was asking.

"Between the drugs and the money. How much does Nate owe us?" Of course he went there. Why was I surprised?

"Nothing. Are you a callous bastard or just stupid?"

"You're not going to make him pay?"

"No."

"But—"

"No."

Henry sighed. "Fine. Whatever. You want to be a pushover, that's your business. But this is why people fuck with you."

"Henry, I don't have time for this." I never had time to deal with his bullshit, yet I always seemed to. But this time I wasn't going to coddle him like I usually did. "I'll deal with my business. You know what I need you to do? Get me everything on the St. Maris brothers. I need specifics. Addresses, vehicles, illegitimate children, legitimate children, parents' names. Hell, I want their medical records. If they jaywalked in the fourth grade, I want to know about it. Same for Jerome's other two lackeys. And any other known associates. Get me everything."

"Yeah, okay." He sounded pouty. "Am I looking for something specific?"

"I need leverage. Something I can use to get them to back the fuck off. But bring me everything and I'll figure it out from there."

"Got it. You want to meet at the farm later?"

"I don't think I should leave Nate alone."

Henry sighed. Loudly. "Okay, I'll bring it to you. Three o'clock?"

"See you then." I hung up. He never waited for me. This was my small rebellion. Yeah, I was a badass.

❖

Henry was punctual as always. I heard the roar of his overpriced engine at seven till, but it was three on the dot when the door slammed. I opened the door as he was climbing the steps. He was carrying a large stack of files.

"Looks like you found some stuff," I said.

"Not really. But I brought everything, just like you instructed." Henry strode past me. He set the files on the table and went straight to the coffee machine. "We're going to need this."

"You know how the burr grinder works?" I asked.

"I'm not an idiot," he said. What a fussy pants. I started separating the files. "Hey, Cash?" I turned. "How the hell does this thing work?"

I rolled my eyes. Henry turned the dial and peered at the bean hopper. I pushed his hand away, reset the grinder, and pushed the button. Henry shrugged and started filling the pot with water.

The files were all labeled with names. There were eight in total. Jerome's and Raymond's files were sizable, but one labeled Jerome St. Maris Sr. put them both to shame.

When the coffee was finally brewing, Henry sat across from me. "St. Maris Sr. is the father. He has all the qualities of his sons without the charm and ability to run a business."

"How so?"

"Domestic violence record forty years long."

"Lovely."

"Jerome and Raymond also have hefty records." Henry placed all the St. Marises in a pile. "Not much personal information to exploit in there, but a pretty decent picture of how Jerome makes his money."

"I'll probably start there. If I have questions or want something followed up, how quickly can you check?"

Henry hauled out his laptop. It was clearly sheriff department issue. An inch thick, black case on a black computer, and he was holding it like it weighed too much. "I've got remote access. It's slower when I'm not at the station, but it works eventually."

"Badass."

"We also have Julio Aragón and Jeremy Norris." Henry handed me two of the midsize files. "Both appear to be regularly employed by Jerome. We should show their photos to Nate. I'm guessing they were the guys who jacked him with Raymond."

"When he wakes up, I'll ask him. Does that cover everyone? What else you got?"

"Robbie Tran and Christian Dilsey. They don't show up as regularly in my searches, but they are known associates. Robbie Tran had some sort of break with Jerome two years ago. Christian Dilsey still works with Raymond every so often, but it doesn't look like he works for Jerome." Henry created a third pile. Those files were even smaller than Aragón and Norris. Henry probably only included the information that tied Tran and Dilsey to the St. Maris family. Which wasn't great. There was no telling what piece of information was going to be interesting.

"And the last one." Henry waved it at me. It was about the same size as Jerome's. "Eleanor St. Maris. Deceased. Jerome Jr. and Raymond's mother and Jerome St. Maris Sr.'s punching bag. Died of an aneurism four years ago. She had racked up an impressive number of concussions and an array of other injuries. All indicative of years of abuse. The aneurism could have been caused by the previous injuries, but the case was never official."

"So we have lot of fun, light reading?"

"Yeah. I only skimmed as I was researching. Like I said, I can run more searches if we see anything interesting. Tell me any names, vehicles, or property that comes up in the files, and we can decide if it is worth digging deeper."

This wasn't going to be fun. Henry had been right about the coffee. I got up and poured a mug for each of us. Henry took the files for Aragón and Norris and I took the St. Maris brothers. Jerome was up first. He had a number of minor drug offenses in his teens and early twenties. Those tapered off pretty quickly. There were a handful of assaults. None of his crimes were particularly impressive or illuminating, which wasn't surprising because I was certain he had gotten better at not getting caught. His name turned up in a handful of other investigations, but it never seemed to lead to a conviction. Witnesses tended to recant their statements. In one case, the evidence was logged incorrectly. In another, a rival drug dealer was tried and convicted instead of Jerome, despite the early evidence pointing strongly at him. Nothing seemed to stick to this guy. It didn't really matter much to me if he got nailed for dealing. I mostly wanted something that could be used against him.

Raymond's file was more of the same except he had more violent assaults and fewer drug convictions. His assaults diminished, but didn't entirely disappear. Bar fights, or beatings made to look like bar fights, were common. He had a few domestic violence charges against three different women. Each relationship lasted about six to nine months after the initial assault. Unlike Jerome, Raymond had spent time in county. It looked like the final girl's father was in law enforcement in Nevada. His influence was impressive considering the state line between them. Still, nothing stood out. His tattoos were interesting. There was a piece on his back with his grandfather's name. Then again, it was obvious that familial ties were important what with the brotherly drug dealing business and all.

"How are you holding up?" I asked Henry.

"I got nothing. You want to go wake Nate up and ask if he knows these guys?"

I hesitated because Nate and Henry had only met in passing. I'd been careful to make sure they never developed a relationship. Part of it was for my protection, most of it was for Nate's. I didn't want to give Henry access to bully him. But that was kind of out the window.

"Sure. I'll go get him," I said.

Henry nodded. He seemed oblivious to my turmoil.

I stuck my head in the study. "You awake?"

"Yeah, just resting." Nate rolled carefully to his side and pushed himself up.

"How do you feel?"

"Less shitty than I did. My face isn't throbbing like last night." He slowly twisted his torso and stretched. "But I think I'm ready for more ice."

"Come take a look at some photos first. Henry thinks he knows who jumped you."

"I was wondering if that was Henry's voice. You cool with this?" Nate kept his voice low enough that Henry couldn't hear.

"Yeah, it's inevitable, right?"

"Probably."

"Just, you know, don't give him any leverage."

"I won't."

Nate followed me down the hall to the kitchen. His gait was slow, but he definitely had some mobility back.

"Henry, Nate."

Henry stood. "Hey, Nate." He extended his hand. "Nice to officially meet you."

Nate shook his hand. "You too. Cash said you have some photos."

Henry grabbed the two files in question. "Yeah, here. This is Julio Aragón." He flipped open the file and handed it to Nate. "And Jeremy Norris." He opened the second file.

Nate studied Aragón. "He was definitely there." He handed back the file. "But this guy wasn't." He tapped Norris's photo.

"Okay, good. Look at these." Henry repeated the process. "Robbie Tran and Christian Dilsey."

"Dilsey. That's the other guy."

"Show him Raymond," I said. "I want to confirm that it was him."

Henry handed over the file. Nate studied it and nodded. "Yep. That's him. And I think that's the guy who was following me too. He drive a blue Civic?"

"Yep," Henry said.

"So you want to help us read files?" I asked.

"Sure. What else do I have to do?" He tried to sit at the table and grimaced. "But I think I'll sit in the comfy chair."

I managed not to laugh at him, which I thought was impressive. "Here, I've already read Jerome and Raymond. See if you can find something I missed." Nate took the files. "I'll prep another ice pack."

"You're too good to me."

"You're easy to please."

Nate made a face, then nodded in acknowledgment. "Yeah, not arguing." He went into the living room and collapsed in the chair next to the couch. I brought him an ice pack. He tucked it against his side. "Living the dream right now."

CHAPTER FOURTEEN

I decided to dive into Eleanor's file. Maybe it would offer insight into her sons. I started at the beginning, which was depressing. The early police reports listed her as the perpetrator. All of the reports stated that Eleanor was hysterical when the police arrived on scene. She had no visible injuries, but her husband's arms were scratched. Grainy photos showed obvious nail marks gouged into his arms.

"What's the deal with this?" I showed the photos to Henry. "The reports say Eleanor was abusing Jerome Sr. They say he was calm, but she was ranting. Did the abuse shift later on? Was she abusing him?"

"How long ago?" Henry took the photos and looked them over.

"These are the early reports. Thirty, forty years ago."

He grimaced. "Yeah, back then that's how most domestic violence was recorded. The police show up on scene, the victim—usually the woman—is crying, shouting, the abuser appears collected. The police assume the crazy person is the abuser. It's because the abuser has spent all their adrenaline, they already dealt with their aggression. The victim, however, is still reeling from being assaulted so they appear to be overreacting."

That was insane. It didn't make sense. "Overreacting to being beaten?"

"Well, the police show up after. They don't see the beating, so in the aftermath, yes, it looks like an overreaction to a cool, soft-spoken man."

"But wouldn't the victim have injuries?"

"Most good abusers—not good." Henry shook his head. "Most proficient abusers do things that can't be seen. Blows to the top of the head where bruising is hidden, hitting or grabbing arms or wrists, that sort of thing."

"That's sick." I'd gotten distracted from my task in the worst possible way. This was the home that Jerome and Raymond had grown up in. I didn't want to feel sadness for them, but it was there nonetheless.

"Umm, we are talking about people who habitually hit other people. Of course it's sick. Look at her hospital records. I bet Eleanor was very clumsy. She tripped a lot, bumped into walls, had minor car accidents." Henry leaned over and flipped a few pages. "See? She was in the emergency room about once a month."

I read the highlights of the hospital reports. Henry was correct. All the paperwork suggested that Eleanor was very accident-prone. I continued reading. It was tragic, but compelling. In the nineties, the police reports started to shift. More and more listed Jerome Sr. as the abuser. I snagged his file and turned to the middle. It matched up. He was arrested more frequently until the late nineties when they started arresting him exclusively.

"What happened in the nineties?" I asked. There was probably a more articulate question, but I was beyond asking specific questions.

Henry came around the table and read over my shoulder. He turned a few pages. Matched up the dates like I had. "Police departments started training the officers in recognizing certain behaviors indicative of abuse. All the stuff I just explained about how the abuser and victim behave initially. That wasn't included in trainings until the nineties. Now, it's standard. In California, we are required to arrest one party on domestic violence calls. They are big on giving us tools to identify the appropriate party."

"So this is a new idea? Make extra sure you don't arrest the victim?" I scoffed. My estimation of police officers was rapidly dropping. And it was already pretty low because, well, I was a drug dealer.

"Hey, man. I didn't build society, I just live in it." He sat back on his side of the table.

"Yeah, whatever."

"Up the hill, we have really cool trainings. The Women's Center comes in and terrifies all the rookies. It's great."

"Or they come in and teach you guys better ways to beat your significant others."

"Fuck you. I'm not a bad cop."

I stared at Henry. He was upset. The dirty cop who stole drugs from the evidence locker, gave them to a drug dealer, and took a cut of the profit was telling me he wasn't bad. We were sitting at a table covered in files that he had obtained illegally, and I was the asshole for suggesting that cops weren't perfect?

Then again, pissing off the dirty cop was probably bad.

"Sorry. Bad joke," I said.

"You're damn right. Don't be a dick. I don't have to be here helping you."

"Yeah, I know. Thanks. I really do appreciate it. And so does Nate." I looked into the living room. Nate was asleep, the files open and spread across his thighs. Real hardcore team I had.

"Yeah, okay. I'm sorry too. I know you weren't talking about me. And there are some guys on the force who do that kind of shit. It pisses me off. I don't like to be lumped in with them."

"Of course. I really wasn't talking about you." I closed Eleanor's file and turned to the elder Jerome. Henry seemed to realize that I was letting it go and returned to his files.

I skimmed the abuse reports because I didn't think I would learn much from them. His hospital records were fewer than Eleanor's, which wasn't surprising. Four years ago, the domestic violence calls stopped. Eleanor was dead so Jerome Sr. didn't have anyone to push around. He had two bar brawls. There was a DUI. It was his second. The first was in 2001. I knew the answer to that one. My grandfather, Clive's dad, had been an alcoholic. When Clive was a kid, the police used to follow my grandfather home from the bar to make sure he got home safe. No regard for anyone else on the road. I was guessing Jerome Sr. had enjoyed the same treatment.

I found my first interesting piece of information a year after the DUI. It was a hospital record. Jerome Sr. had a stroke. The hospital report didn't have much information, but the accompanying probation report did. He was confined to a nursing home. He wasn't yet seventy so that was unusual. The stroke must have done some damage.

"Probation officers file regular reports, right?"

"Yeah," Henry said.

"I thought so. Jerome Sr. is still on probation, but the reports aren't included here."

"That's odd. Let me see." I handed him the file. He skimmed it. "Oh, he had a stroke? Just a minute."

He handed back the file and opened the laptop. It took ten minutes to boot and connect to the El Dorado County Sheriff's server. It was a lifetime. I filled our coffee cups. I retrieved the files from a sleeping Nate. I checked the time. We had been reading for two hours.

"Got it." Henry leaned back and turned the laptop so I could see. "He can't walk. His motor functions are almost non-existent so he can barely feed himself. Speech is restricted."

"So they don't report on him anymore?"

"There's no point. The reports after his stroke detail the medical trauma, and the first report after he was put in the nursing home gives information about his inability to function, basically."

I sat back down. "Don't they still have to do reports though?"

"Yeah, but the reports are bare bones. They just say that he can't go anywhere and doesn't have the inclination to even if he was physically able."

"So we got nothing," I said.

"What exactly were you hoping was there?" Henry was skeptical.

I thought about that. I didn't really have an answer. "I don't know. It would be nice if the reports said, 'oh, and by the way, Jerome Jr. has a weak spot for puppy dogs,' or 'Jerome Jr. has a prize motorcycle and his father hid it and here is a treasure map to find it.'"

Henry laughed. "Yes, I can see why you would think that might be in old police reports about a guy who terrorized his wife and children."

"He didn't though, did he?" Nate asked. Henry and I looked at the doorway and found Nate leaning against the wall. "Granted, I only looked at Raymond's file and half of Jerome's before I fell asleep, but I didn't see anything about childhood abuse."

"He has a point," I said. There hadn't been even a rumor of child abuse in any of the St. Maris files.

"He does, but I'm not sure what it is," Henry said. "What does that tell us?" he asked Nate.

"It means big Jerome didn't beat on little Jerome or little Raymond."

"Yes, we've established that," I said. Nate was making me feel particularly dense.

"Maybe the boys weren't scared of their father. I mean, they could have just learned to be misogynistic pricks from Dad instead of learning to be cowering victims like Mom. It's pretty classic, in a way. Boys who grow up in violent households tend to grow into men who beat their wives, right?"

"Yeah," I said. Henry nodded.

"The only thing we don't know is how Jerome and Raymond feel about their father. This nursing home Jerome Sr. is in. Is it expensive? Who is paying for it? I bet half a rib that it's Junior." That speech seemed to take all of Nate's energy. He pulled out a chair and collapsed into it. "Okay, no more Codeine for me."

"This is why you shouldn't do drugs, little boy," I said.

Nate rolled his eyes.

"He's right. Nursing homes cost a ton of money. Especially if they are high quality," Henry said.

"So we need to find out if Jerome and Raymond are paying for it." This was fantastic. We had a plan finally. I loved having a plan. Nate gave a silent nod and closed his eyes.

"Okay, I'll call and play the sheriff's card. See if they will tell me." Henry pulled out his cell phone. I looked at the probation report and pointed out the phone number. He punched it in.

Nate retrieved his melting ice pack and dumped the remainder in the sink. Henry sighed at the noise and went into my study. I could hear the rumble of his voice as he paced.

"So what do you think? What if they do like the old man?" Nate looked down at his T-shirt and realized there was a large wet spot from the ice pack. "Damn it." He stripped off the shirt.

"Then we have something to exploit, I guess. Of course, even if they are paying for it, it doesn't mean they like him. It could just be obligation."

"Or Jerome Sr. has money and they are funneling his money into his care." Nate balled up the towel and his shirt and tossed them into the small laundry room off the kitchen.

"Good point. You want a fresh shirt?"

"Yes, please. Any chance you have something that will fit me?"

"Not really, but you'll look cute in a belly shirt." I laughed as I pictured it. Nate didn't laugh. I went into my room and found an oversized shirt. It would do.

Nate pulled on the shirt that I tossed him. It wasn't a belly shirt, but it was snug. "Oh, good. Now, I can count my nipples. You know how sometimes you're like, oh no, did my nipples fall off? But fear not, I can look down and count them." Nate pointed at his nipples. "Yep, both are still there."

"Glad I could help."

Henry came back into the kitchen. "They wouldn't discuss billing."

"Shit," I said.

"But they were very confused about why the sheriff's department was inquiring about those nice St. Maris brothers." He set his phone on the table.

"Nice St. Maris brothers?" Nate asked.

"Yeah. It sounds like they regularly visit their father. Jerome was just in for his weekly lunch, and he brought a new set of audiobooks for his dad."

"Huh?"

"Audiobooks?"

"Yeah, I guess Jerome Sr. can't hold books very well and his eyesight is shot, but he loves to read. When the boys—this lady sounded about eighty and she kept calling them the boys—so when the boys are busy they bring him audiobooks. When they aren't busy, they read to him."

"You've got to be fucking kidding me," I said.

"Isn't that insane?" Henry didn't look like he believed it and he was the one who had called.

"This is perfect." Nate looked like we had hit the jackpot. "We have our leverage."

"Yeah, but we can't exactly access the guy." I hated to be a downer, but I didn't think we would be able to walk in to a nursing home and threaten the old man.

"No, but we can go tour the place." Nate had a look that I'd only seen once before. The last time, we had ended up crossing the Canadian border with a trunk full of drugs and a very angry, very crazy stripper following us. We managed to lose her in South Dakota, but it was a road trip I didn't want to repeat. South Dakota was really boring.

"Are you totally freaked out by him right now?" Henry asked me.

All I could do was nod.

CHAPTER FIFTEEN

Nate and I were watching *Ren & Stimpy* when my phone rang. I assumed it was Henry so I swiped without looking. Nate paused the show.

"Hey."

"Hey." Definitely not Henry.

"Laurel. How's it going?"

Nate raised his eyebrows and grinned at me. I turned away.

"All right. What are you up to?" she asked.

"Watching *Ren & Stimpy* because I'm a big kid."

"Wow, you are a big kid. Are you allowed to watch that without supervision?" Her tone was pure condescension.

"Well, Nate's here. So I'm actually babysitting him."

"You're watching nineties' cartoons with the guy who deals drugs for you? Is that normal?"

"He got the shit kicked out of him last night. We figured he deserved an evening of cartoons." I was aiming for casual and failed.

"What?" She didn't sound playful anymore.

"Yeah. You know that guy you hit in the face?"

"Yeah?"

"We accidentally moved in on his territory and he got mad. We paid him off, but apparently, the fee was higher than we realized," I said. Nate was frantically motioning for me to shut up, but I waved him away.

"So he beat up Nate?"

"Pretty much."

"That's fucked," she said.

"Agreed."

"I guess there's only one thing to do."

"What's that?" I asked.

"I'm bringing over pizza and beer. Can Nate have beer?"

"No, but we can. I think some of Andy's sodas are still in the fridge for the little baby." Nate threw a pillow at me and then looked sad that he didn't have a pillow.

"I'll see you in thirty."

"You're awesome."

"No, I'm dope. Ask Andy."

When Laurel showed up, she rang the doorbell about five times. Nickels sprinted for my room. After half a day of Henry, the assault of a doorbell was too much for her. I kept forgetting to disconnect the damn thing. I answered the door and realized why Laurel was leaning on the bell. Her hands were full.

"Hot chick with beer and pizza? This is better than Christmas."

"Shut up. Take the beer. I'm going to drop it."

I obliged and held the door. "Laurel, Nate. Nate, Laurel."

Nate tried to get up, but by the time he had managed sitting, Laurel had crossed to the couch, set the pizza on the coffee table, and extended a hand.

"Nice to meet you," she said.

"You too." Nate shook her hand. "I usually make a much better impression." He tried to shrug, failed, and settled on a grin.

"Don't worry. Cash's T-shirt looks good on you."

Nate looked down at the snug shirt. "I think it really shows off my muscles."

"You have muscles?" I did my best to look shocked.

"She's kind of an asshole. You ever noticed that?" Nate asked Laurel. She nodded. "You, on the other hand, brought pizza, which makes you my favorite."

"I brought beer too, but Cash says you can't have any."

"See? Asshole."

I was going to dispute it, but I didn't have much of an argument. So I got plates instead. I handed them out while Laurel opened the pizza boxes. She offered each one to Nate first so he didn't have to lean forward.

"I thought you said she was a dick, Cash. She's being nice to me." Nate settled back into his comfy chair. He took the soda bottle I held out to him.

"I'm totally a dick, but only to Cash. I'm sure it's 'cause I have Daddy issues or intimacy issues or something." Laurel pulled two beers out of the six-pack she had brought and opened them.

"I like that you own it." Nate saluted her with his soda.

"When I own it, I'm an asshole, but when she owns it, it's charming?" I asked.

"Pretty much," Nate said.

"So I dig your friend Nate," Laurel told me. Nate started laughing.

"Shut up." I pointed at Nate with my slice of pizza. "Or I'll break the ribs on your other side."

"Dare you." He stuck his chin up defiantly.

"Yeah, so what's up with that?" Laurel asked.

"The broken ribs?" Nate asked. She nodded. "It's cool. We're handling it."

"I hesitate to ask," she said.

"We're going to threaten the guy's wheelchair bound father."

"Charming. Is this a normal occurrence?" Laurel asked.

I threw a pillow at Nate. "Keep your mouth shut."

"Well, we are drug dealers." He acted like that was an explanation.

"Wait. You're actually going to threaten some old guy in a wheelchair?" Laurel looked back and forth between Nate and me.

This was so not helping me get the girl. "It sounds worse than it is. And, no, it's not normal."

Nate grimaced as he realized what he had said. "She's right. It's not that bad. I can explain." He set down his pizza and mustered all his strength to get out of the chair.

I really hoped he wasn't doing what I thought he was doing. But then he came back in the room with a stack of files. Of course he was doing exactly what I didn't want him to do.

"What's this?" Laurel took the files he handed her.

"Police files. The top one is the guy you punched. Asshole, but not in the fun way like Cash. Next one is his brother, who gave me these lovely presents." Nate pointed at the bruising on his face. "But that thick one at the bottom is their father, the guy we are going to threaten. His whole file is just him beating on his wife for like half a century."

Laurel shook her head and set her pizza down. She flipped through the files on Jerome and Raymond. "These guys are like sweet little puppy dogs, aren't they?"

"Wait till you get to Dad. He's a real piece of work," Nate said.

This was exactly what I didn't want to involve Laurel in. To be fair, I didn't want her involved in anything related to my dealing, but I really didn't want her looking at police and hospital records that I'd gotten from a dirty cop.

"Okay, you did your show-and-tell. Can we put away the police files now?" I asked Nate.

"Fine." Nate caught the look I was giving him. He collected the files. "I'm just saying. These are not nice people. It's not like we are threatening sweet old grandmothers."

"Noted. They're bad, you're not."

"See, Cash? She gets it." Nate was a little nervous now. Too late for that. The line had been crossed.

"So how the hell did you get those files?" Laurel asked. And that was why I hadn't wanted to show her.

"Oh, a friend of mine is a sheriff. He does the occasional favor for me." I felt terrible lying, but I couldn't exactly tell her the truth either.

"That's some favor."

I scoffed convincingly. "Yeah, I'm going to owe him big."

"So what about you? We're drug dealers. What does Laurel do?" Nate asked.

"Don't ask that. It's embarrassing." Laurel drank her beer and hung her head.

"You realize you have to tell us now," I said.

"Yeah, but it's so boring." We waited. "Okay, fine. I work at my dad's law firm."

"Whoa. Establishment." Nate said what I was thinking. "Are you a lawyer?"

"God, no. I just work in the office. It's like nine to five shit, but then I don't show up and my father lectures me on being over thirty and irresponsible. He tells me I'll never be able to take over the firm if I don't go to law school. I tell him I don't want the firm. It's a thing we do." She took another slice of pizza and pretended that she had explained everything.

"Your dad should get together with my mother and write lectures on teaching responsibility to unruly children," Nate said.

"I think he would really enjoy that." Laurel leaned forward with her beer bottle and Nate tapped his soda against it.

"Thank you for making time in your schedule to meet with us." Henry was in full charm mode the moment we entered the nursing home. Our tour guide was a Mrs. Whittling. She was a lovely fifty something woman who looked like she belonged in the office of a sorority, not a nursing home. Perfect blond hair, tastefully cut to her collar. Perfect white suit, tailored to her perfectly trim frame. Perfectly cerulean eyes behind fashionable, but not trendy glasses. And she was already half in love with all of Henry's perfection, right down to his raw denim jeans and Italian loafers. They made quite a pair.

"Not at all. I'm happy to show you around. I think you will find our facilities have every amenity your mother could hope for. And, of course, our staff is highly trained to meet her needs. Why don't you tell me a bit more about her?"

And we were off. Henry wove the story of our mother who had recently suffered a stroke and was ready to move out of her hospital room. Yes, selling the family home was proving quite difficult. So many memories. Oh, and Mother was just beside herself, but we all knew that this was the right thing to do.

I trailed behind them, looking at every patient we passed. At some point Henry looped Mrs. Whittling's arm through his. She was utterly delighted. There were two sides to the nursing home. One was assisted living for the more mobile patients. The dining room there had waiters who worked with the regular attendants. It looked more like a day spa than a nursing home.

Henry directed us to the other side. Poor Mother had hopes of regaining her fine motor skills, but we needed to face the reality that she might not. As we passed through a series of doors using Mrs. Whittling's key card, I realized how much a facility like this was a prison. For the safety of the Alzheimer's patients, she explained.

We emerged into a common room filled with elderly people in wheelchairs. There was a quiet difference on this side. The conversation seemed more wild, outside of social standards. There was a feeling of wasting time. Waiting for an inevitable moment. Dreading that moment, but only out of obligation. Everyone was unfettered. When time was inconsequential, and mobility was based on the day's luck, and you realized how useless all of the constructions were, maybe irreverence was the only thing left.

It only took me a moment to find him. Mr. St. Maris looked exactly like his sons. Maybe it was a triumph of genetics, but—considering the violence they all surrounded themselves with—it seemed like more of a curse. He was dressed in designer sweatpants and two hundred dollar sneakers. His hair was trimmed into a close crew cut; it was both convenient and trendy. Jerome and Raymond's collective influence was obvious.

Henry saw him almost at the same time I did. He stopped walking and turned to Mrs. Whittling.

"Would it be all right if we spoke to some of the patients? I don't want to upset anyone. I just want to chat, see how they feel about the home."

"Of course." Mrs. Whittling patted his arm. "You'll find that some of them are non-verbal. And those with dementia and Alzheimer's may mistake you for someone else."

"That's perfectly understandable. You know, my sister volunteered in a nursing home in high school." He put his hand on my back and drew me into their circle.

"You did?" Mrs. Whittling was delighted. Okay, most of the things in life delighted her.

"Yeah, it started as a work study program and grew from there." I tried to match Henry's smile. "I just loved hearing their stories. So many of the patients I worked with had an almost childlike joy. It was infectious." And just like that, Mrs. Whittling loved me too.

"That is wonderful. It's so nice to hear from young people like the two of you. I truly hope you choose our facility for your mother. We could use your influence." She winked at us. Actually winked. We needed to get out of this place. "I'll let you two look around. I need to go speak to someone, but I'll be back in a moment."

"Thank you again, Mrs. Whittling." Henry was laying it on thick.

She smiled, perfectly, and left us.

It took all of my willpower not to go directly to Jerome Sr. Instead, I sat on a sofa with a woman older than God who was cradling a doll. She stared at me for a moment, then reached over and patted my hair into place.

"Look at this handsome boy. Haven't you grown?"

I didn't know what to say so I decided to go with it. "I sure have."

"It has just been years, hasn't it?"

"It has."

"Well, you certainly have grown." This was a winning conversation right here. "You know Harold used to wear his hair just like this." She petted my head again. "You never got to meet him, but I swear you look just like him. Doesn't he look just like his grandfather?" she asked her doll.

For some reason, I smiled at her. A genuine smile. She had no fucking clue what was going on around her and she did not give a fuck. She was just chillin' with her doll and patting strangers on the head. Well done, old lady.

I glanced over at Henry. He was perched on a coffee table next to Jerome Sr. talking to a lady with pink hair. His position was perfect to take an unobtrusive photo.

"I'll be back in a moment," I told my new friend. She smiled and nodded. I figured it wasn't a lie because she was going to forget me in two minutes.

I worked my way around the room until I was standing behind Jerome. Henry pulled out his phone and lifted it to his ear like he was taking a call. I leaned over Jerome's shoulder and smiled in the sweetest, most terrifying way possible. Henry nodded at no one.

"Henry." I reached out and tapped his shoulder as if he had been my goal all along. "I think we've seen enough."

He looked at his phone and quickly swiped through the photos he had taken. "Yep. I agree. We've got what we came for."

"Let's get out of here."

"We should say good-bye to Mrs. Whittling." Henry came around to where I was.

"Is that necessary? Can't we just go?" I kept my voice very low.

"Appearances matter." Henry put his hand on my back again. I leaned close like we were having a normal, private conversation. "I don't want to burn this bridge yet. We might need it. Plus, we don't want Whittling to realize that we are anything other than caring siblings helping out Mother. It would raise suspicion."

"You're right."

Henry smiled at a younger guy in scrubs. "Excuse me, we're looking for Mrs. Whittling. Is she around?"

"Yeah. If you want, I can grab her for you." The boy smiled at Henry.

Henry realized he was being cruised and smiled back. "That would be great, if you don't mind."

"Not at all." He disappeared down a corridor. Half a second later, he emerged with Whittling.

"Mrs. Whittling, thank you again for the tour. It was enlightening," Henry said.

I took a step back and let them lead us out. Despite my obvious gender presentation, Mrs. Whittling still seemed more comfortable with Henry taking the lead in our false sibling dynamic. It was fascinating, in a way, that she hadn't been thrown by my queerness at all, but she was still a little bit sexist.

When we got to her office, she handed Henry her card and a million pamphlets that outlined all of the paperwork we would need to institutionalize our dear mother. We each shook her hand and let ourselves out.

"So what's the plan?" Henry asked once we were in his car.

"Drop me at my place. I need to get my car. I'll stake out Jerome's house. You go get copies of the photo printed."

"Why are you staking out his place?"

"Because I want to break in and leave the photo for him to find. If he's there, that will be harder."

"You're disturbingly good at this," he said.

I decided to take that as a compliment.

CHAPTER SIXTEEN

I hadn't considered the possibility that Jerome might not be home. I'd been sitting outside his house for an hour and there were no signs of life inside. But that didn't mean he wasn't there. I wasn't dumb enough to break in to a house that was potentially occupied.

I was almost ready to ring the bell just to see if he would answer.

This neighborhood was disgustingly similar. The homes looked like they had been built in the late eighties, early nineties. Apparently, there had only been four models to choose from. In the intervening decades, people had added extra rooms and expanded garages, but the result was multitudes of cheap, identical houses screaming for their own identities and failing. I was a little bit surprised that Jerome had chosen such an unimaginative place to live. I couldn't imagine having a beige house with beige trim and a beige door.

My phone rang. It was Henry.

"Hello."

"How goes the stakeout?"

"It's shockingly boring. I have no idea if he is home. And if he isn't home, maybe I should just go in. Or if he is home and he leaves, I don't know if we should follow him just to make sure he isn't going out for milk and will be back in five minutes."

"Whoa, there. You need to chill. Is this your first stakeout?"

"Yes. Normal people don't do stakeouts. I don't like it."

"Okay, I'll be there in fifteen minutes. If he leaves, follow him and call me so I can take over. Sit tight."

I was pretty sure he was trying to reassure me, but it didn't help much. Thirteen minutes of drumming impatiently on my steering wheel, and Henry pulled up behind me. He got out of the car and came around to my passenger side. I rolled down the window.

"Any movement?" Henry asked.

"No."

"Here are the photos." He handed me an envelope from the drugstore down the street.

I opened the envelope. It was ten copies of the same photo. And the photo was perfect. I was leaning over Jerome Sr.'s shoulder and smiling rather wickedly. He looked like a clueless, drooling man. There was something nefarious about it. It was a facsimile of a sweet photo, but I'd managed to look predatory.

"This is disturbing," I said.

"Damn right." Henry grinned, pleased that everything was going according to plan, I guess. "You stay here. I'm going to drive around the corner and see if I can get a better look. He might be in the backyard. Hold on."

Henry returned to his electric blue muscle car and climbed in. He gunned his big ass engine and eased around the corner. So much for subtlety. Two minutes later, he pulled up behind me again. My phone rang.

"Nothing."

"So we wait?" I asked.

"Pretty much."

"Can you wait and I'll go buy a coffee?" I looked in my rearview mirror. Henry was shaking his head.

"You want a coffee?"

"No, I want an iced coffee. A big one. With crushed ice that I can chew on." Damn, that sounded amazing. I was going to die if I didn't have it right now.

"Hey, Cash?"

"Yeah?"

"When you drink a big ass iced coffee, how long is it before you have to pee?"

Damn it. "Like two minutes."

"I promise I'll buy you an iced coffee when we're done, okay?" He smiled at me in the mirror. "A huge one with crushed ice."

I didn't even mind how condescending he was being because I knew he was right. "Real big. Like the size cups they sell in the South."

"Do they have different cup sizes there?"

"In my imagination, when you go east of the California border, everything is bigger. Like, if you order a small iced tea, it's forty ounces and comes with a hat."

"And all of that is the South?"

Christ, it was like he had never studied geography. "Yes. Until you hit New York."

He started laughing. Hard. "Your brain is a very special place."

"Thanks. Clive says I was an imaginative child."

"Yeah, imaginative. That's you." Henry hung up the phone. He was still shaking his head at me.

I pushed my seat back and settled in for long wait. Between my attempts to see movement in the windows, I texted my regulars. I had drugs again. It was time to maintain those relationships. I got responses from eight customers right away. My housewives were feeling neglected. Two people wrote back and said they didn't need any. One would have been odd, but two? Something was off. Especially since one of them was Brant. He had a drug problem and money to burn.

I decided to text Nate. *My gay boy housewife just canceled his weekly order again.*

The one in fab 40s?

How many gay boy housewives do u think I have? I checked the street again. Still boring nothingness. Jerome's house, also nothing.

I don't kno, but I think I need one. Do they do laundry?

Of course. They're not heathens. Nate was proving distracting. Which was helpful with the whole boring stakeout thing, but not so helpful with figuring out what the deal was with Brant. *So that's weird right?*

Totally. Isn't he like a quarter of ur business?

Not quite, but close enough.

Maybe he got sober?

And didn't tell me? That was what bothered me. Brant was a social boy. If he was succeeding at cutting back or getting sober, he would have bragged to me.

So ask him. Dumbass, Nate said.

Well, that seemed logical. I texted Brant, *You sure? You haven't put in an order for two weeks.*

Brant wrote back right away. *Yeah, I'm cool. But thanks.*

I took a screenshot of the conversation with Brant and sent it to Nate. *Weird, right?*

Totally.

I still couldn't pinpoint what felt off about it, but maybe Nate would come up with something.

It turned out that all my whining was for nothing because I only had to wait another fifteen minutes. The front door opened. Christian Dilsey came out, and the door shut behind him. Jerome was home. Christian climbed into a Mazda parked a few houses down and took off. Ten minutes later, the garage door opened and Jerome's silver Cadillac pulled out. Henry waited to start his car until Jerome was at the end of the street.

Two minutes later, my phone rang.

"He's getting on the freeway. And it's definitely him behind the wheel," Henry said.

"So I'm going in?"

"Now or never."

"I'll call when I'm done." I hung up and tucked the phone in my pocket. I grabbed the envelope of photos. It was eight o'clock. Not dusk yet, which blew. But it was after everyone had gotten home from work. In a neighborhood like this, everyone was inside abusing their air conditioning. The people outside weren't crass enough to sit out front; they were all out back by the pool. I didn't see a single person as I crossed the street and marched up to Jerome's house.

I bypassed the front door. No chance it was unlocked so I didn't bother. The gate in the fence had a very convenient string looped over. I pulled it and the latch opened. I slid through and made sure the gate closed behind me.

The backyard was unremarkable. A cement patio, a couple of chairs. Next to the sliding glass door there was a single pot containing an impeccable gardenia. The flowers were a creamy white, the color of freshly churned butter.

I stared up at the house. There was a second floor about half the size of the first. The roof of the first floor ran around two-thirds of the house. I could easily climb onto it, but doing so would make me visible to the entire neighborhood, including anyone in their backyard. If I did that I'd have to wait for it to get dark, and I didn't want to sit in this sad, bare backyard any longer than necessary.

I walked to the side of the house. The windows were about a foot out of my reach. I went back to the other side. There was only one window and it was right at my level. It was locked. The other windows at the back of the house were high up. On a whim, I tried the sliding glass door. It opened. Jerome was an idiot. Or I was. Who would be dumb enough to break into a drug dealer's house?

I did a quick survey of the house. It was three levels, but not three stories. The bottom floor had a six-foot split between two levels. Not uncommon for the eighties. The lowest level had a living room and a game room, complete with two full size arcade games. I tucked the first photo into the corner of the Ms. Pac-Man screen. The middle level had a kitchen, family room, and dining room turned sleazy bar. Seriously, Jerome had installed a full bar. This guy's head was so far up his ass.

I walked behind the polished bar and tried to think like Jerome. I reached under the bar and found a shotgun hanging just out of sight. Classic, I guess. The pretty mirror and booze bottles behind me didn't offer much. I searched the cigar boxes stacked on one end of the bar and found cigars. The other end of the bar held a Victorian era cash register. I pushed a couple of buttons, but nothing happened. Not really surprising. It looked broken. And even Jerome wouldn't be dumb enough to keep his money in a cash register. I lifted up and shifted the various tins and jars stacked by the register. Then I tried to push the register to one side. It moved. Easily. I lifted it and found that it was hollow.

There was a wooden box underneath, not unlike the cigar boxes. Inside was the bag of drugs his boys had taken from Nate along with the ecstasy we had sold him. There was another bag of ecstasy and what looked like Oxy. A slim box underneath everything held a bajillion tabs of acid.

I pocketed the drugs they had taken from Nate and poured the Oxy into one of his fancy ass Scotch tumblers. I propped a copy of the photo against the glass and arranged the rest of the drugs around it. Jerome had quite a selection of booze. There was an unopened bottle of Johnnie Walker Blue on the top shelf of his display. I cracked the seal and poured a generous amount into the tumbler of Oxy. The pills swirled and settled nicely on the bottom of the glass.

The kitchen was unremarkable. Three kinds of beer in the fridge and an array of condiments. Olives. A green block of cheese that wasn't supposed to be green. On the outside of the fridge there was a reminder card for the dentist and a few photos. I added a new photo to the collection and moved on.

Upstairs, I found Jerome's bedroom, a guest room, and an office. I stuck a photo in the mirror in the master bathroom. Under the sink was a massive box of condoms. At least two of the three hundred condoms were still in the box. The box was almost expired. I rooted around in the drawers until I found a safety pin. I left the condoms on the counter with a photo safety pinned to the top. He would have to guess if I had used the pin on the condoms. Guessing games were fun. I was sure Jerome would thank me for all this fun.

In the closet, I found the mother lode. Jerome's shoes were on a rack, but there was a stack of shoeboxes on the floor next to them. The bottom shoebox was filled with neat stacks of cash. I did a quick and dirty count. Thirty grand. Because that was a good place to hide thirty thousand dollars. In a shoebox in your closet. It was super hidden. I pulled out the box, upended it on Jerome's perfectly made bed. I took out the amount that his friends had stolen from Nate and wrote a receipt on the back of another photo. I turned that one face down so he would be sure to read it.

The closet in the guest room held a large shelving unit. Guns were shelved according to size. Handguns on the top down to assault rifles and shotguns on the bottom. Boxes upon boxes of ammunition were stacked along the side of each shelf according to caliber. This shit was why people judged drug dealers. Well, that and the drug dealing. But who the fuck needed twenty guns just chillin' in a closet? One would generally do the job. Any more than that was excessive. Personally, one was excessive, but whatever.

I scooped up boxes of ammunition and carried them into Jerome's room. It took me quite a few trips to carry it all. Methodically, I opened each box, poured out the bullets, and filled the pockets of all his carefully hung jeans, shirts, jackets. When I ran out of pockets, I started filling his shoes. It took longer than I would have liked, but imagining Jerome trying to find all the bullets and sort them by caliber made me happy. I wondered if he would take the time to replace them in their stark, sad boxes. I hoped so. Life was about the little joys. I tucked a photo in one of the filled pockets.

The boxes, I brought back to the guest room and left littered on the floor. I tossed a photo down among the chaos.

Jerome's office was messy, lived in. His desk was a cheap, particleboard monstrosity. I was amazed that he had taken the time and money to install a full bar in his dining room, but couldn't bother with a decent desk. A mass of cords was piled next to his laptop. Unimpressive stacks of paper covered the rest of the surface. Old cable offers, bills from the nursing home, part of his car lease agreement, takeout menus, pizza coupons.

The detritus suggested that a lot of time was spent here. There were discarded sneakers on the floor and sweatshirts tossed onto the couch. Coffee rings were on every piece of paper on the desk. The carpet was worn between the door and desk, the desk and closet. Why would Jerome invest so much in the facade and completely ignore his private, comfortable space?

I opened the closet expecting either an answer or another cache. Instead I found winter clothes, a couple of old photo albums, and extra linens. I dug into the linens and coats and found nothing. This appeared to be actual storage.

I settled for placing one photo on the keyboard of his laptop. I closed the screen to hide it. The last photo, I laid on the floor in the entryway.

I checked my phone for good measure. No updates from Henry.
Still cruising?

I waited for a response. I didn't want to walk out and find
Jerome leaning against my car with Henry hog-tied in the trunk.

Yep. You finished?

I exited through the front door and left it unlocked. My work
here was done. The sun was finally dropping below the horizon. The
already quiet neighborhood was zombie movie silent. My walk to
the car was thankfully uneventful. I waited to write Henry back until
my engine was started. Not that I was paranoid or anything.

All clear. You can head home.

Cool. Solid work today.

He was right. We had done solid work. Maybe our work was a
little different than normal people, but we still worked hard. Today
deserved a drink. And a pretty lady. I decided to call Laurel when I
got home. I had promised her a visit to the farm, after all.

CHAPTER SEVENTEEN

I spent most of my day anticipating. Laurel had said she was available Thursday for our farm tour. It was only Tuesday. It had been only a matter of hours since I left Jerome super fun presents. I knew that sometime during the night he had returned home. I wondered if he had found all the photos. I had a feeling that he found most of them, but the remainder would pop up in the next week or two. I wondered what his reaction had been. Part of me was quite pleased with my work. Part of me was very concerned about his reaction.

It was a very conflicted anticipation. Waiting to see a girl. Hoping I didn't see a boy.

It didn't help that it was hot and getting hotter. We were a day into a projected two-week heat wave. Nickels had chosen her spot on the cool hardwood and had informed me that she wasn't moving, touching wasn't allowed, and she didn't want to play. The power company was already sending emails suggesting ways to stay cool and save energy. Most of the emails suggested that blackouts were imminent. I unplugged the TV and computer.

My phone vibrated. It could have been anything. I checked the screen. Andy.

Remember when I was little and we made slushies?

Yeah? I did a mental review of my kitchen. There was ice, which was an important ingredient of slushies, but I didn't have much else.

I've got watermelon. You got lime?

I went into the kitchen and sorted through the fruit bowl on the table. Fruit bowl was probably generous. I had an orange and a handful of limes. That would do.

I've got some.

She wrote back immediately. *I walked to the store cuz watermelon. But this watermelon is heavy and I don't want to walk eight more blocks.*

I laughed. Andy was a strange kid. The store was ten blocks away. It was 104 degrees. I was amazed she had made it as far as she had.

Cross streets?

19th and P.

On my way.

I grabbed my keys and wallet and headed out. It took me five minutes to get to her. She was sitting on the curb with a massive watermelon in her lap, playing on her cell phone. I pulled into the bike lane and rolled down my window.

"Hey, little girl. Want some candy?"

Andy looked up and started laughing. "Gosh, I don't know. Will you give me a ride? This city is scary and strange."

"Christ, why does your mother let you out alone?"

Andy stood and hefted her watermelon. "I think she has some misguided ideas about me developing independence."

"Not too bright, your mother. I'll have to talk with her about putting a tracker on you."

Andy climbed into the front seat. She tried to put on her seat belt and failed due to the watermelon. I took it from her and set it in the backseat.

"Thanks."

"Anytime. So were you planning on sharing your watermelon slushie with me or are you using me for my car?" I pulled back into traffic.

"I didn't really think that far ahead. I mean, I forgot to check if we have limes before I left the house, so that's a problem. I mostly just knew I needed a watermelon."

"You're going places, tiger. I can feel it."

"I know."

When we got back home, Andy followed me in and set her watermelon on the table. I pulled the blender from under the counter and plugged it in. We got to work cutting up the melon and juicing limes. I let Andy run the blender while I got the massive margarita glasses off the top shelf of the cabinet. I'd never been a margarita person. Really, I'd never been a mixed drink person. But the glasses dated back to when Andy was younger and drinking out of fun glasses made everything fun.

She did a less than expert job of pouring the drinks. Pink slush dotted the counter and dripped down her knuckles. She licked her hand and gave me a sticky glass. I ignored the mess and took my drink. We adjourned to the living room. Andy put on her playlist of the week and flopped into the comfy chair. I took the couch. We bitched about the heat and relived Andy's childhood.

"So what's up with the chick?" Andy asked.

"Living vicariously?"

"I'm young and single. Don't hate on me." She gave me an arrogant look.

I rolled my eyes. "It's going well, I think."

"You're not sure?"

"I don't know. She's not big on talking about herself."

"Because you're such a big talker."

"Noted. But she talks less than me, so that's saying something. She was over here a couple days ago and I just found out that she works in a lawyer's office. I mean, we've been seeing each other a couple of weeks and I just found out what she does?"

"Which is super important because you're really into money and material things?" Andy was far too observant.

"I get you. I'm just saying, that's normal conversation. She doesn't talk about herself. It's weird. I feel like she's holding something back."

"I think you're paranoid. And haven't had an adult relationship since I was in middle school. Except maybe with my mother, which is awkward."

It was sad that she was right. How sad was it that Andy had never seen me in a romantic relationship? Great example. "I think you're nosy and cheeky and should stop analyzing me."

Andy shrugged and hit me with an epic amount of not giving a fuck. "I think these drinks are fantastic."

"It's true. We are very talented."

"We should be chefs."

"Chefs who make drinks?" I asked.

"It's a thing."

I grinned at her. I loved this kid. Not that I was going to tell her that. "So what about you, heartbreaker?"

"No hearts broken this week. But next week is full of possibilities."

"And life plans?"

"Totally. This week, I'm telling adults that I want to be a doctor, but really I want to be a ninja. Or Harrison Ford."

"Han Solo Harrison Ford or Indiana Jones Harrison Ford?"

"Both." Andy sipped her drink. "I'm young and naïve."

"I like your ideals, kid. You're going places."

When Robin got home from work an hour later, she found us asleep in the living room. The power had gone out and come back on at least once. The receiver wasn't playing music anymore, just flashing the wrong time.

"So glad you two are accomplishing something with your summer."

I sat up and blinked at her. "It's too hot to accomplish things."

Andy continued sleeping.

"I can see that." Robin grinned and shook her head.

"But I convinced her to go to the Crocker with me." I moved my feet so Robin could sit down.

"That's good. Because she really doesn't get enough culture."

"I'm sorry. Are you complaining that your child is too exposed to culture?"

She sighed. "I suppose taking her to an art museum is a good thing." We grinned at each other. We were hilarious. "Anyway, I better wake up the beast. We have dinner with my mom and sister tonight."

I grimaced. "Have fun with that."

"Oh, it will be super fun. Linda hasn't seen Andy's new haircut. I'm sure it will be demeaning for everyone."

"You are a patient woman."

Robin stood. "Not really. If she oversteps, we will leave. I'm done pretending that her hateful rhetoric is anything except hateful." She shook Andy's shoulder. "Hey, bud. Wake up."

"It's too hot to wake up." Andy covered her eyes.

"We have dinner with Grandma tonight."

Andy dropped her hand and scooted so she was almost sitting. "Cool."

"And Aunt Linda."

Andy groaned, dropped back down, and covered her eyes. "Nope."

"How about this. If she says anything about your haircut, or clothing, or Jesus," Robin ticked off points on her fingers, "then we can leave."

"What about you being an independent lady?" Andy pried up another of Robin's fingers. "Or how my father is a deadbeat?" She pried up another.

"Isn't your mom independent and your dad kind of a deadbeat?" I asked.

"Yeah, but Aunt Linda says it like independence is bad. And she somehow makes it Mom's fault that Dad is a deadbeat."

"Now, Anderson. That's not fair." Robin was using her condescending mom voice. "Last time, she suggested that it was your fault that your dad is a deadbeat."

Andy and I started laughing. "See? It's your fault," I said.

"You're right. Somehow my gayness at two years old made my dad a flake."

"Solid logic," I said.

"Let's get going, troublemaker."

Andy groaned and pushed herself out of her chair. Robin led the way to the door. Andy made a show of not wanting to follow her.

I gathered our discarded margarita glasses and went to clean up the kitchen. When that was done, I debated resetting the clocks, but I knew the chances were high that the power would go again, so I didn't bother. I checked my phone and found a series of messages from Nate.

I think I figured out the gay boy housewife issue.

And I got you a present. We're going out tonight.

I'll be there at three a.m.

Well, that was interesting. Three a.m.? I decided to call Nate.

"Hey," Nate answered the phone.

"Explain."

"It's actually really obvious. Gay boy isn't cutting back. He is buying from someone else."

I sat at the table. Nate sounded like he was settling in for a long explanation. "Yeah, but how? Who? No one knows my customer base. You don't even know where half my customers live."

"Jerome, of course. His guys followed me. Chances are decent they followed you. It's not rocket surgery."

"Rocket surgery?"

"Brain science?" Nate giggled. He was so pleased with himself.

"So we're going to follow Jerome? At three a.m.?"

"No. I don't have time for that shit. Jerome has a whole group of guys who do whatever he tells them. You don't have that."

"I don't? You won't do whatever I tell you? Why aren't you loyal like Jerome's guys?" I tried to sound shocked.

Nate laughed again. "You hired someone smart and loyal. He hired dumb and loyal. I'm worth more."

"You may have a point."

"Don't worry. The smartness paid off. I have a plan." He made it sound epic. I waited for the epic smartness. "I just bought six GPS trackers. You owe me for overnight shipping. They make them for crazy parents to track their kids and shit. It's got a magnet and you just stick it under their cars. We can watch the progress on a smartphone."

"I'm so glad I hired someone smart."

"We know Jerome parks in a garage, but everyone else lives in apartments or shares a house with fifteen other people. They probably park on the street. Tonight, or tomorrow morning, really, we are going to put trackers on everyone's car. Jerome will be more difficult, but we can get him at the grocery store or something."

"You're amazing. Have I told you that? I owe you big."

"Hey, these assholes kicked the shit out of me. I'm invested."

"So what do I need to do? Drink coffee and wear dark colors?"

"That and look up vehicles and addresses. You still have Henry's files, right?"

"Yep. So home addresses and cars? Anything else?"

"Anything that sounds relevant. If the file says they stay with a girlfriend or boyfriend or Mom and Dad, whatever."

"Done. I'll see you at three."

"Cool."

"Oh, and, Nate? You're a badass."

"I know."

Nate did me the favor of knocking instead of ringing the doorbell. I was thankful because Nickels would have never forgiven such an offense. I let him in.

"Hey." Nate handed me a cardboard box. It had six identical black boxes, each the size of a pack of cards. He was typing on his cell phone and juggling a second box of what looked like accoutrements for the first box. "These things are a bitch to set up."

I took the second box and got out of his way. He went to the kitchen table and sat down, while continuing to angry type. I sat across from him and started unpacking the second box. Chargers, cardboard envelopes with the SIM card punched out, instructions for the GPS trackers.

"What is the issue?"

"I can't get the fucking thing to register," he said to me. "No, I gave you the subscription number, now you text me, you fuckwad," he said to the phone.

I decided questions were not a good idea. So I read the instructions. As far as I could tell, they were translated poorly. There were also instructions in Korean and French, which was not helpful because I couldn't read Korean or French. I assumed that was why Nate was struggling. Unless he had forgotten to mention that he was trilingual, he didn't read Korean or French either.

"These instructions don't make sense," I said.

"No shit." He set down the phone and deliberately pushed it away from him. "For the record, the online reviews said that it was written in Chinese and badly translated into English, which would have been great because I can read Mandarin, but I don't read fucking Korean." That last bit was directed at the half-folded instruction sheet in my hands.

I looked over at the box of trackers. One of them was blinking green. "Hey, Nate. One of those is blinking."

His eyes got big. "Oh, you tricky little bitch." He pulled it out and read a number off the bottom. He grabbed his phone and typed and swiped and cursed a bit more. While he was doing that, the other trackers began to blink one at a time.

"They're all starting to blink." I tipped the box to show him. The last one came to life as I did it.

"Well, that's just special, isn't it?" He took them out of the box and placed them in a line on the table. He checked the numbers against a list on his phone. "Do you have duct tape?"

"Yeah, just a minute." I went into the laundry room and dug around in the cabinet next to the washer. I brought the tape back to him.

"Scissors and a Sharpie would be great too."

I went to retrieve those. Nate cut small rectangles of tape and stuck one on each of the trackers.

"How can I help?"

"Label each one with initials. JS, RS, JA, whatever. Then tell me which number is which name." I read off the first number, which was about twenty million digits. Nate typed the number into his phone. When we were done, he spun the phone so I could see the screen. It was a map centered on my address. Six dots lit up in the center. "Theoretically, each one is nicknamed according to the guy whose car we are going to tag."

"Theoretically?"

"I'm doing my best here. All of this is theoretical."

Good enough for me. "So are we ready to head out?"

"You have the list of residences?"

I held up the list. It was probably more detail than we would need, but I had a feeling this would be a long night. No need to make it worse.

The first on our list was Raymond St. Maris. He was the only one who lived in midtown, so he was the closest. His place was up near the train tracks on C Street. When we got there, I drove past his apartment at a crawl.

"There. The blue building." Nate pointed out the address. "You see his car anywhere?"

We scanned all the cars parked on the street and came up empty.

"I'm going to take the alley. It runs behind here. There might be parking," I said. Nate nodded. As we approached Raymond's building, Nate leaned forward.

"Yep. Parking overhang at the back. You see the Civic? It's third over."

"Yeah. Check the license as we go by."

"Yep. That's the one."

I turned back onto C, drove a block, and parked. Nate picked out the GPS tracker with Raymond's initials. We left the box in the car. Nate watched his phone as we walked.

"See? The signal for RS is moving." He held out the phone so I could look at the screen.

"Your theory is panning out so far."

"Well, I am really smart."

We turned into the alley. It wasn't lit except for a hazy orange light at the opposite block. I scanned windows for movement, but didn't see anything. Nate ducked into the parking area for Raymond's building. I watched the alley. Nothing. We were alone. I glanced back at Nate. He was on the ground with half his torso under the car. A minute later, he scooted back out. I looked at him for confirmation. He nodded. We walked back at a nice, unsuspicious pace.

"That was simple," I said once we were in the car with the doors closed.

"Yeah. Just like I planned."

"Check your phone. Is it transmitting?"

He checked the app. "All systems go."

"All systems go?"

"I wanted to be an astronaut, but my mom said that dreams should be reasonable."

"You'll always be an astronaut to me."

"Aww. You're an asshole," Nate said in a sickly sweet voice.

"Where to next?"

"Aragón and Norris are in Oak Park. We can hit Tran on the way. He's just off Second."

"Street or Avenue?" I asked.

"Avenue. He's in Curtis Park off Freeport."

"Got it."

I took us down 19th until it turned into Freeport. I turned on 2nd and waited for Nate to point out the cross street. Tran's car was easy to spot. He drove a classic Mustang. So unimaginative. And not smart for a drug dealer. If ever anyone interviewed a witness about me, all they would say was that I drove a smaller silver SUV. I did my best to be nondescript when I was breaking the law.

I parked a block away, same as at Raymond's address. The Mustang was in full view of more houses than I liked, but it was just past four in the morning. I doubted anyone was awake. Nate dropped between the curb and the car. Half a second later, he was standing again. We circled the block until we were back at my car. Nate checked his app again. The dot for RT glowed a block from where we were sitting. Perfect.

Aragón and Norris were as uneventful as Tran and the younger St. Maris. Which was good. When planting GPS trackers on rival drug dealers, uneventful is exactly what you hope for. Aragón had thrown us for a brief loop when we couldn't find his truck, but then we checked his girlfriend's apartment ten blocks away and found it there.

Christian Dilsey was the last up for the evening. He lived in Carmichael. With his parents. We weren't sure of that because his file hadn't been specific. But when we pulled into the neighborhood it was clearly a place for nice, middle class types who didn't work for drug dealers. Then again, Jerome's house was an argument against that theory.

Dilsey's address had a two-car garage, but his Mazda was parked on the street. There were discarded kids' toys next to the front door and a handmade sign welcoming us. Everything about the place suggested the Dilseys were standard grandparents with a wayward, law-breaking son.

It was five in the morning, less than an hour until sunrise. The street was still quiet, just like the last four neighborhoods, but a few houses already had lights on inside. Christ, these people got up for work before dawn. This was why I had never bought into the system. I couldn't remember the last time I was awake at this hour, but it had definitely been the result of a long night, not an early morning. We parked two houses down from the Dilsey residence. In all the other neighborhoods we could have made an argument for walking home late at night. Here, people would question that. These people weren't the type to walk.

Nate and I sat in the dark and watched the street. Sixty yards up, a door opened. A kid came out. She was late teens, early twenties, and carrying a green apron.

"As soon as she's gone, we need to move. This neighborhood is too lively for me," I said.

Nate nodded. "A porch light just came on three houses behind us. We need to hurry."

The kid got in her car and took off at a nice, appropriate pace. Watching this was killing me. As her taillights disappeared around the corner, Nate opened his door.

I scanned the houses around us while Nate dropped to the asphalt and wriggled closer to Dilsey's Mazda. I heard the light click of the magnet against the undercarriage. Nate held out a hand and I hauled him up. A light came on in the Dilsey's front room. We froze. A shadow moved behind the curtain. We weren't visible yet. Nate followed me back to my car.

"I didn't like that. Let's go," Nate said.

"Check your phone first." I turned the key but waited to pull out.

"It's live." Nate flashed the screen at me, but his word was enough. We were silent until we got back to the main road, as if that would ensure that no one had seen us.

"So we're done for now, right?" I asked. Jerome's GPS wasn't in place, but we knew that one would take more time.

"Yeah. I'll try to follow Jerome later today, but he will be at home for a while still."

"When you get home, sleep for a while, okay? There's a rush, but it will keep for a few hours." I knew I was planning on sleeping until mid-afternoon. Asking Nate to be sleep deprived on my behalf seemed idiotic.

"You don't need to convince me," Nate said.

"Want to get some breakfast?"

"I'm pretty sure you owe me breakfast. Turn south on Watt Ave. There's a little diner I practically lived at during my first year."

"Do they have good waffles? I need waffles."

"Of course they have good waffles. I'm not a heathen."

CHAPTER EIGHTEEN

We couldn't have chosen a better day to visit Braddock Farm. The temp had gone to three digits at eight in the morning. When I forced myself out of bed at nine, it was over one hundred. It wasn't surprising really. The nighttime low had hovered around ninety so we could only go up from there. When Laurel showed up at my place, I went out and let the car idle long enough for the AC to do some damage. By the time we got on the freeway, the air in the car was breathable. Sacramento summers were brutal.

"Is it weird that I'm so excited?" Laurel asked.

"No. The farm is awesome. Plus, Shelby is really excited to meet you. Well, she's excited that it's Thursday and she's also excited that the sun is shining and that we have been given the gift of life. But you're toward the top of the list."

"If that's not a winning endorsement, I don't know what is."

"Exactly."

"So what do we do when we visit the farm?" Laurel leaned against the window and propped her foot up on the seat.

"Eat stuff, mostly. Clive will give us the latest tour. Shelby will give us food. She's really into the barter system right now. Last time, it was cheese. But she's been working on this woman who bakes amazing bread in town."

"Seriously? She barters?"

"Yeah, she's got her own rules for the world. The advantages of a barter economy are part of it. And she's very convincing."

"So she's going to convince me to participate in the barter system?" Laurel chuckled.

"Laugh now. When we drive home this evening, you're going to be a vehement fan of the barter system."

"I look forward to it." She wasn't convinced, but I decided to let her live in her fantasy world. "So tell me about the farm. Did you grow up there?"

"No. We bought it my last year of college. It had been Clive's dream since forever."

"Why then?"

"I told you he raised me, right?" Laurel nodded. "He took custody of me when I was a toddler, but he was only twenty when that happened."

"He adopted you when he was twenty?" She sounded incredulous. It was valid.

"Yeah, we lived with my grandparents—well, a guesthouse on their land—until he finished his teaching degree. That wasn't his plan, but it was the easiest way for him to support us."

"I'm amazed the state allowed it."

"I think that was a big part of his rush to start teaching. He needed something steady and flexible that would look good to the court."

"This guy sounds amazing."

"He is." I nodded. "Anyway, he sacrificed a lot for me. My senior year in college, we sat down and realized that a farm was feasible. My loans were low. The college fund was long gone, but we hadn't dipped into his savings as much as he anticipated we would need to."

"And you didn't mind helping him start a farm?"

I shrugged. "My dreams were more along the lines of reading poetry and going to art shows. I'm very good at indulging myself and accomplishing nothing."

"I have noticed that. And I totally mean that in a complimentary way." Something in her tone made me believe her. This chick was a keeper. She valued my ability to do nothing.

"Of course, the farm almost failed the first year. The second year was even worse. And then..." And then my high school buddy

Henry called me up and made a very inviting offer. Free drugs. And Clive already had a cover business set up. But I couldn't tell her about Henry. "I got a call about some easy access to prescription drugs. I convinced Clive that it would keep his dream alive."

"So he didn't want you to deal?"

"What parent wants their kid to be a drug dealer?"

"Good point. So that's it? You sell drugs to pay for seeds and shit?"

"And water and farm equipment. Electricity, business permits, greenhouse construction. Farming is like hard."

"I'm getting that."

"We're almost there, by the way. You ever been to Apple Hill?" Apple Hill was a group of apple orchards just north of Braddock Farm. They were the main source of Shelby's bartering. They also made up a large portion of the farming association for the county.

"When I was a kid. My parents used to take us every fall. Isn't that a requirement if you grow up within a hundred miles of here?"

"Yeah, it kind of is. Clive and Shelby are trying to market Braddock to be one of the stops when people come up. He's got big plans for pumpkins this year. And Shelby is working on a line of holiday products. Spices, that sort of thing."

"You're actually into this, aren't you?" She had caught me. Kind of.

"I'm into them succeeding. This is Clive's life. He never had his own kids. His brief marriage failed. But I always got the impression that he didn't really care about the stuff he was supposed to care about. He just wanted a little farm. That was it."

"Cash Braddock, that is a lovely sentiment."

"Yeah, whatever."

I took the turn for the farm. Laurel studied everything out her window with barely concealed enthusiasm. When we pulled up behind the house, she practically vaulted out of the car.

I led the way around the house to the path to the greenhouse. It was the most likely place to find Clive. The door creaked as I pushed it open.

"Cash? That you?" Clive called from somewhere at the back of the greenhouse.

"Yeah, where are you?"

"Walk past the onions, turn right at the flowers, then keep straight."

"You do realize that all of these seedlings look like little green sprouts to me, right?"

I heard him laughing. "Go outside, I'll be there in a minute."

Laurel and I turned in the small space and went back out. "He doesn't generally let people wander in the greenhouse."

"I thought greenhouses were those little wood and glass boxes your grandparents bought you for your birthday when they ran out of ideas. This is not a greenhouse," Laurel said.

"No, this is a real greenhouse. It was a quarter of this size when we started. I told him to build a second one, but I think he likes that it's a labyrinth."

"Why do you need such a big space?"

"Clive starts all his seedlings in there. Every year he adds new plants to the rotation."

"No, every year you make me add new plants to the rotation." We turned and found Clive gently closing the greenhouse door. He was in a skintight T-shirt that was soaked through down his chest. I was hoping it was from a rogue watering can, but then he hugged me. Not water.

"You're covered in sweat, man." I tried to push him back.

"You're just jealous of my natural musk." He half smiled and shoved me away. "And you must be Laurel." Clive put out his hand. "Either that or Cash has finally become a player."

Laurel shook his hand. "I think she's far too lazy to be a player."

"That's my girl. Shaky moral compass with just enough laziness to prevent her from behaving badly." Clive tried to swipe at my hair, but I ducked out of his reach.

"Do you think that would fit on a T-shirt?" Laurel asked.

"I know it does. I already had them printed."

Laurel laughed. Clive laughed. I didn't laugh. I had a moral compass. It wasn't shaky, just had low sensitivity.

"Aww, pouty." Laurel leaned her shoulder into mine. She smelled good. I decided to forgive them.

"So what do you say to a greenhouse tour, Laurel?" Clive asked.

"I'm looking forward to it."

"You coming?" he asked me.

"I guess I can tag along."

Clive led us back into the greenhouse. He explained each of the seedlings to Laurel as we wandered through. I tuned him out. I'd heard the tour before. It changed every time because the plants changed, but the gist of it was the same.

Laurel asked questions. Judging by Clive's reaction, they were good questions. At certain pallets, they leaned over and looked at the sprouts or soil. He made her smell various plants. I mostly just watched her ass every time she bent over. She was wearing slim navy chinos, cut off at the knee. Her legs were tan in a way I'd never been able to achieve. In summer, the best I could hope for was a slightly darker shade of white and a new crop of freckles. Not Laurel. She apparently turned into a sun god of some sort. Her threadbare white tee was a size too big. Whenever she shifted, turned, reached, the cotton would cling and drape in unexpected ways. One moment I'd get a glimpse of tanned skin at her hips, the next the perfect outline of the curve of her breast.

I realized Clive was speaking to me.

"What?"

"Nothing." Clive turned back to Laurel. They both seemed to think my inability to pay attention was funny. "Anyway, that's why we started this last group of plants. Shelby wants us to create products that aren't entirely dependent on the crops following a schedule."

"Where is the famous Shelby? Cash says she's very interesting."

"That's a nice euphemism." Clive clapped his hand on Laurel's shoulder. "She should be here in the next half hour, which, in Shelby time, means an hour ago or three hours from now."

"What a fascinating approach to a schedule."

"I spent too much time trying to mold Shelby to my schedule. She works better on her own." Clive shrugged. "Let's head out. I think we have seen all the highlights in here."

"So do I get to see the fields?" Laurel asked.

Clive lit up. "If you want to. It can be pretty boring to some people." He nodded at me.

"Some people really struggle to notice their environment. You know, they just pay attention to women's asses and miss important details about their own business."

They laughed. Glad they were getting along so well. I had a feeling that their camaraderie was going to be bad for me.

Clive treated Laurel to the short version of walking through the fields. They hit the fun stuff like the berry patches, but skipped the endless rows of lettuce and kale. I learned an important lesson. As long as I brought someone new and shiny to Clive, I wouldn't be subjected to a discussion about squash growth. Sure, I endured the discussion of berry growth, but that involved eating berries so it was a fair trade.

By the time we got back to the house the temp had climbed to the nineties. Hot for this far up the hill, but downright temperate considering the last few days at home. Sure, I had slept through the heat, but my news app seemed to think it was worthy of constant bulletins.

A large umbrella had been erected over the patio table on Clive's deck. I found Shelby stretched out in a lounge chair wearing a pair of forties era sunglasses and drinking iced tea. There were a handful of slim braids and some thread woven into her hair. Her jeans were cuffed to mid-calf and her bare shoulders were turning pink.

"How's it going, kid?" I sat on the edge of her lounger.

"Divine. How was the tour?" She stretched out her feet and poked me in the stomach. "Where's your girl? Did you bring her? I get to meet her, right?"

"Walking with Clive." I nodded in the direction of the small set of stairs leading to the patio. Laurel and Clive were still walking up the hill. They had gotten distracted by a bush with pink flowers. I had seen flowers before.

"Oh, she's so your type." Shelby sat up and watched them intensely. "Look at how confident her walk is. Is my walk confident? Do I need a new walk?"

"You need a chill pill."

"A chill pill?" Shelby flopped back down. "Sometimes I forget you're not my age. And then you say things like 'chill pill.'"

"Yeah, whatever."

"I made iced tea. You want some? I'll go get the pitcher." She swung her legs to the ground. I managed to stand just in time. Shelby had dumped me off the end of many a lounge chair.

"I'll follow you in. You need sunscreen, by the way," I said.

"So do you. Your nose is pink."

"Dammit." I held the door for her.

Shelby went into the kitchen to round up glasses and her pitcher of iced tea. I continued through the house to the bathroom. Clive had ten kinds of sunscreen, but I grabbed the 50 SPF. My face wouldn't survive without protection.

I brought the bottle back into the kitchen. Shelby was about to go outside.

"Hold up. Sunscreen."

"Oh, yeah." She set down her tray.

I waited until she had shifted the straps of her tank top off her shoulders, then spread the lotion across her back. "Move your hair."

She gathered it and held it up out of the way. I rubbed sunscreen onto her neck. "Am I good?"

"Yep." I capped the bottle and washed my hands.

Shelby waited at the door for me to open it. I pulled it open and held the screen. Laurel and Clive were sitting at the table deep in conversation.

"Hey, guys. How was the tour? You must be Laurel." Shelby set her tray down and hugged Laurel. "It's so nice to meet you. You know, Cash really likes you. She won't say it 'cause she's all caveman, but she totally likes you. I made iced tea. Do you want some?" She didn't really give them a choice because she was already pouring and handing them glasses.

Laurel took her glass and looked at me with wide eyes. The look suggested that she hadn't quite believed the speed at which Shelby talked.

"It's great to meet you too. Everyone speaks very highly of you," Laurel said.

Shelby scoffed. "No, they don't. They say I'm crazy and talk too fast and I'm flaky."

Laurel laughed. "That's true. But they also say that you're accomplished and have an uncanny ability to come up with unique, brilliant plans that no one thinks will work. And then you make them work."

For the first time ever, Shelby was speechless. I poked her.

"I think you broke Shelby," I said.

"Oh, Cash." Shelby hugged me. "That's so nice of you to say."

I shook my head. "I didn't tell her all that."

"No, I had to interpret the information I was given. But I think the conclusion is accurate," Laurel said.

Shelby sighed and sat next to Laurel. "Tell me more about me."

"No, you tell me more about you." Laurel was very charming when she chose to be. "Clive said you were at some big meeting."

Shelby squealed. "I was. Oh, Clive, you're going to love this. Love, love this. I was at The Old Firehouse. You know that restaurant on Main?"

"Is it in an old firehouse?" Laurel asked.

"No." Shelby looked at her all deadpan serious. "Why would you think that?"

"Umm." Laurel didn't have a response to that one.

"I'm screwing with you. Of course it's in the old firehouse." Shelby laughed at Laurel's realization that she was being mocked. "They're really getting into this whole local produce kick. And we are their new suppliers." Shelby smacked Clive with the back of her hand.

"You're kidding." Clive was shocked.

"Nope." Shelby was vibrating with excitement.

Clive leaned over and pulled her into a massive hug. "That's amazing. How did you manage that? Are we going to be able to produce enough?"

"Yeah, we won't supply all their produce. Just specific seasonal offerings. Whatever our best crop is that week, that's what we will give them. I negotiated a slightly better price for them in exchange for a line on the menu."

"So we're getting free advertising too?" Clive hadn't looked this happy in a long time.

"Congratulations, guys. This sounds like a big deal," Laurel said.

"It's huge," Clive said.

"Well, I am employee of the month." Shelby grinned at Clive.

"You're my only employee," he said.

"I didn't say the competition was fierce."

As I watched Shelby and Clive pat themselves on the back, I remembered why I was so happy when he hired her. She cared about farming. I cared about the success of the business, but that was an extension of caring about Clive. Shelby was passionate about growing things and making them profitable. Just like Clive. It was a whole earthy thing that I just didn't have. It was good that he had found someone he could share that passion with.

I knew plenty of people found this platonic relationship between a young adult who was barely past twenty and bachelor nearing fifty odd. But those assumptions didn't matter. It worked. That was what mattered.

CHAPTER NINETEEN

Lunch had stretched into an early dinner. The beer was cold, the food was never ending, and the company was good. The sun was beginning to drop when my phone rang. I glanced at the readout. Andy.

"Sorry, guys. I should take this." They nodded. I swiped and stood up. "Hey, tiger. How's it going?"

"Could be worse."

"What's up?"

"The power is out. It's already gone out like ten times. My mom texted. She's probably going to be at the hospital all night. I'm supposed to call you and ask when the power is going to be back on." She didn't sound very concerned. She sounded bored.

"Just a sec. Let me check my phone."

"All right."

I went to my home screen and saw five text messages. One was from Nate telling me that Jerome was tagged. The rest were automated from the power company. The power on our block wasn't going to be turned on for at least another five hours. I clicked back over to Andy. "It looks like there won't be any power tonight."

"I kind of got that impression. Mom said the hospital is crazy busy. And I'm not supposed to go out. The traffic and heat are making people terrible."

"That makes sense. How hot is the house?"

"Hot as fuck. The AC was going on and off with the power, but I don't think it's coming back on anytime soon. I turned off all the AC units."

"Good idea. Will you do me a favor and check on Nickels?"

"Already did. Your windows are open, blinds are closed. Nickels has a million bowls of cool water."

"You're the best. Let me talk to Laurel and your mom and I'll figure out when I'm going to be home."

"Cool. Bye."

"Bye."

I went back to the table. "Laurel, check your phone. Power is out all over midtown."

She only looked mildly concerned. Until she read her texts. "This looks bad." She typed and clicked and frowned.

"Yours is out too?"

"Yeah, but it's not just us. Portions of Oak Park and Land Park, all of Curtis, half of East Sac. It's going to take them hours to sort this out."

"I'm calling Robin. Andy is home alone," I said.

"Yeah, good idea. She works at one of the hospitals, right?" I nodded. "Ask her how the roads are. They are probably getting an influx of injuries if it's as bad as the news says it is."

I clicked Robin's name, but was sent straight to voice mail. "Hey, I just talked to Andy. It looks like power will be out until one, at least. Maybe later than that. Laurel and I are at the farm, but we will get on the road soon. Call me when you can."

"I take it you didn't get her?" Laurel asked.

"Nope. I'm guessing she doesn't have time for phone calls." As I said it, my phone vibrated. It was another text. This time from Robin.

Don't drive. Roads are terrible. I'll call later.

"Should we get going?" Laurel asked. "I'm assuming we shouldn't leave Andy alone."

I showed her the text. "Robin says not to drive."

I texted Robin back. *What about Andy?*

It was five minutes before Robin responded. *She will be fine. Will you text Alejandro's parents and Sophie's mom? One of them should be able to run over if Andy needs someone. You might want to stay up the hill.*

"Robin says we shouldn't drive into midtown tonight," I said.

"So you'll stay here," Clive said. "I have plenty of room."

I glanced at Laurel. I didn't want to commit her to anything she wasn't cool with. She nodded. "It makes sense. If it's as bad as they say it is, we don't want to be driving down there."

"Okay. Give me a minute." I shot off texts to Alejandro's dad and Sophie's mom. They both wrote back immediately. The kid was covered. I swiped to Andy's name and hit call.

"Hey."

"Hey, I talked to your mom. She says we shouldn't drive home tonight."

"Okay. It's not like I haven't been left alone before," Andy said. Which was adorable. She had been left home alone only on nights when I was there. But I realized that Andy didn't know that. Robin and I had always kept it to ourselves so Andy could feel independent, but Robin wouldn't have to worry.

"That's true. But it's an odd situation. Plus, I'm normally close by. I already texted Alejandro's dad and Sophie's mom so they are available if you need help."

"I'll be fine."

"I know you will, but if you need something, call them. What percentage is your phone at?"

"Eighty-five. I plugged it in when the power came back on the first time."

"Smart kid," I said.

"I know."

"And don't waste battery power on Snapchat. Read a book or something."

"Yes, ma'am," she said.

"And don't light a ton of candles. Just a few so you can see."

"Got it," she said.

"And keep a flashlight close."

"Cash, the power is out. It's not the apocalypse." She sounded exasperated.

"Sorry. Keep an eye on Nickels. Have fun, but not too much."

"Bye, Cash."

"Bye." I hung up. "That kid is going to give me a heart attack."

"I love these full circle moments," Clive said.

I found Laurel lying on one of the picnic tables Clive had built last summer. She was stretched out with her ankles crossed and feet hanging over the edge. The flannel shirt she'd borrowed from Clive was spread under her like a blanket.

"Look at this." Laurel stretched out her arms.

I climbed up and sat next to her. "Here." I had two beers and a blanket. I gave her one of the bottles and I rolled the blanket so we could use it as a pillow. "What are we looking at?"

"The stars. Seriously. Have you ever seen so many stars?"

I looked up. There were a ton of stars. "Oh, yeah, there are a lot more visible stars up here."

"No, but really. Lie down. Look at this."

I sighed. A gorgeous woman wanted me to look at the stars with her. Life was tough. "Scoot over." I stretched out next to her.

"You talk to Robin?"

I folded my arms behind my head. "Yeah, she finally called."

"You feel better about leaving Andy now?"

"Yeah. Robin talked to Alejandro's mom before she called me. Andy is covered." I nudged her feet with mine. "What about you? Do you need to call the office and tell them you'll be late?"

Laurel closed her eyes and shook her head. "I texted. It doesn't matter." She exhaled loudly. "If I show up, I'm irresponsible, if I don't, I'm irresponsible." She forced a shrug.

"That bad?"

"Yes. No. I don't know."

"Well, you let me know when you figure it out." That got me half a smile.

"It's not as dramatic as I'm making it seem. I'm just tired of my parents, of their…everything."

"Have you considered not working for your father?" It didn't exactly seem like a barrel of laughs.

"Every day."

I glanced over at her and found that she was studying me. She propped herself up on an elbow. "I'm thirty-two. I shouldn't give the remotest of fucks about what my parents think of me."

"No, probably not."

"Yet, I do. Every time, I think I'll prove them wrong and instead, they prove my assumptions right."

"What do you mean?"

She shook her head again. "It's like every decision I've made in the past fifteen years, they disagreed with. What college to go to, where to live, what to wear, who to date."

"So fuck them." I was missing something here. But then, I'd been told the same thing by countless people. There had been times that Clive was my only advocate. Overalls in elementary school weren't for girls. Baseball shirts in middle school weren't okay. Pretty girls had long hair in high school. But every time, Clive had gone out and bought the overalls and baseball shirts. He continued bringing me to his barber when I asked if I could keep my hair short. He didn't care that my grandparents disagreed with him or that my teachers thought I was too active.

"Yeah, fuck them." Laurel lay back down.

"So what's the issue?"

"It's dumb."

"Seriously? We are in the mountains, watching the stars and drinking beer. It's a warm summer night. What better time is there to talk about the reasons you're angry at your parents? It's either that or philosophy, and Nietzsche was never my favorite."

"What about Foucault? He seems more your speed."

"Yeah, but if we discuss the *History of Sexuality*, we're going to land right back at the reasons you're mad that your parents judge your wardrobe." I made it sound really trying.

"Okay." Laurel laughed. "I'm angry that they disagree with all my decisions, argue passionately against them, and then, when I make said decision, they brag about it. I'm tired of fighting against them to accomplish something, then them taking credit for my having accomplished it."

"That would piss me off."

"And they are so well connected, well respected that I hear about it all the time." Laurel dropped her voice a register, "'Your dad said you graduated cum laude.' 'Your parents are so proud of you.' 'Everyone just loves how unique your style is.'"

I laughed. "Fuck them."

"Yeah, fuck them. I'm proud of myself, dammit."

"Well, yeah, you're super fun and smart and shit."

"Hella smart and shit. And my style isn't fucking unique; they're just all the same."

"Total sheep. It's not your fault they're so heteronormative."

"Yeah, heteronormative." She was quiet for a moment. "Is it weird that I feel way better now?"

"Not really. It's exhausting to have people tell you that you're wrong in some way. We get enough of that everywhere else. Family shouldn't pile it on."

"But they do. Well, I guess yours doesn't. Clive is just as cool as you said he would be."

"He is, but it took us a while to get here. I mean, I was a teenager once."

"No." She sounded incredulous.

"I swear." She chuckled. "Plus, my grandparents tried to help and just made everything harder on us. We got the double whammy of people telling us that there was something wrong with me and something wrong with him for not forcing me to change."

"See? So you totally get it."

"You know what I learned, though?"

Laurel turned on her side to face me. "What? Is it profound? I hope it's profound."

"It's super profound." I shifted and looked at her. "You're allowed to cut people out. Some people will say you're a dick, but it doesn't matter. If someone makes you feel bad and balances it with only a modicum of feeling good, it's not worth it."

"That easy?"

"Well, it's not easy, but it's worth it. It doesn't matter if you're related by blood or marriage or whatever. Why would you maintain a relationship with someone who worked against you feeling happy and healthy?"

"You know, I really don't know. If a friend treated me the way my father does, I wouldn't spend time with them anymore."

"Exactly. So why put up with it? If anything, your family should treat you better than everyone else. Being family isn't an excuse to treat you extra shitty."

"Oh, my God."

"What?"

Laurel did that thing where she pushed her hair out of her eyes. It flopped to the side. "I think you just convinced me that familial obligation is worthless."

"All obligations are worthless."

"And how did you arrive at such a brilliant conclusion?"

"I'm not sure it's brilliant. It's kind of just the way I have always operated."

"Why?"

I thought back on that. It could have been the elementary school kids and teachers. They certainly taught me that working for scraps of respect wasn't worth it. But it seemed more ingrained than that. "I think it has something to do with my mom."

"Do you hate her?"

I pursed my lips and thought some more. I tried to conjure any sort of strong feeling for my mom and came up empty. "No. I don't feel much of anything for her. She doesn't exactly factor in to my daily thoughts."

"Do you love her?"

"Yeah, but I don't respect her. I have no interest in a relationship with her. The decisions she made are her own. I can't judge that. But her decisions did alter the general trajectory of my life. I'm happy Clive raised me instead of her." Laurel reached over and started tracing patterns on the back of my hand. "Of course, it's not hard to keep her out of my life. I don't know where she is. Hell, I don't know if she's alive."

"Yeah, that makes cutting her out easy."

"But I've let go of plenty of people who didn't simply disappear." I turned my hand and held hers.

"How do you do that?"

"I guess you find a balance that you're comfortable with. Like, you probably can't remove your parents entirely. You probably don't even want to," I said. Laurel nodded. "But you can dictate the terms of your relationship. If Mom calls and wants to grab lunch, say no."

"That's it? Say no?"

"Simple. If you hadn't noticed, I'm kind of self-indulgent."

Laurel smiled, then leaned up and kissed me. It started simple, then became indulgent. Her warm mouth moved against mine. There was a dart of tongue that I tried to lift up and chase. She scooted until she was lying half on top of me. Her breast pressed into my arm. Her hands pressed into my stomach. Her weight felt delicious.

I slid my free hand down and cupped her ass. She shifted again so that she was entirely on top of me. Her lips left mine and followed that line across my cheek, down my jaw, then back up my chin to my mouth. The kiss turned deeper. Her open mouth gasped against mine, our tongues vied for dominance. Her fingertips edged up my shirt until they were digging into my bare stomach. I used both hands to rock her into me. She spread her legs enough to let my thigh slip between them. At the pressure, she groaned into my mouth.

She moved her hands from my stomach, planted them on the table, and lifted up to stare at me. "Cash." She was breathing hard. Her tone was serious. I waited. "You're a terrible influence." The tone changed. "You know that, right?"

"Yes." I squeezed her ass.

"As long as you're aware." She dropped back down and continued kissing me. This was torture. The good kind.

She put her hands back under my shirt. Soft, slightly calloused fingers traced my ribs, climbed up my torso, then back down. Her hips shifted against mine. I was going to come in my pants if we didn't slow this down. Or speed it up. I slid my hands onto her back and pushed her shirt up. Her bare stomach pressed against mine. That really didn't help with the whole turned on thing.

I dug my thumbs into the curves of her hips. She rolled her hips against me again. This was ridiculous. I gave in to temptation and popped open the button on her shorts. Laurel groaned and pressed her hips into me. I started in on the zipper, but she grabbed my hand and stilled the motion.

"Okay, we need to slow down," she said.

My breaths were labored, but I managed to nod and say, "Yeah, okay."

"Really?" she asked. She looked nervous. I nodded again. "You don't mind?"

"Well, I had some ideas that were not slowing down, but yeah. If you want to stop, we stop." I grinned at her.

"Sorry."

"Don't apologize." I was very aware that most of her body weight was still pressed against me. It was excruciating. "But if you want to slow down, lying on me is cruel."

Laurel laughed. "I do enjoy being cruel to you." She rocked her hips once more, then rolled off of me.

"I'd complain about the cruelty, but I'm kind of enjoying it."

"Yeah?" She arched her hips and buttoned her shorts.

"Totally."

I tugged my shirt back into place. She did the same. We both were breathing hard. I stared at the stars and enjoyed the rush of aborted hormones coursing through my body. I would have preferred to continue, but this was good too. The high of making out, the way I was hyper aware of how restrictive my clothing felt, the warm gasping woman next to me. I could wait. As long as I could have this anticipation.

Laurel reached over and grasped my hand. This was good.

CHAPTER TWENTY

We had just crossed into Sacramento County when my phone started blowing up. I ignored the first few texts, but then it started ringing. I glanced at the readout. Nate.

"Would you mind answering this?" I handed it to Laurel. I couldn't talk on the phone and drive. I was a law-abiding citizen, after all.

"Sure." She swiped it. "Hey, this is Laurel." I could hear Nate talking, but I couldn't understand what he was saying. "No, we are just passing Citrus Heights. We will be home in about twenty." He talked some more. "Okay, I'll tell her. Just a sec." She pulled the phone away from her ear. "He thinks Jerome is headed to your place. Nate is going over there. He also says Henry is downtown? How does Nate know where Jerome is? Is he following him?"

"Shit. Tell him Andy is still home."

Laurel repeated the message. Nate cursed, which echoed nicely with the curses in my head.

"Okay, just a sec." Laurel moved the phone away from her mouth again. "Nate says he will be there in ten minutes and Henry should already be there. Jerome just drove around your block a few times and now he is going down Nineteenth." Nate said something else to her. "Okay, Jerome just stopped on Nineteenth and R. Henry and Nate are going to wait in case he comes back."

"Tell him to haul ass. I'll be there soon. Tell him to call me if Jerome moves before he gets there. And ask him to tell Henry the same."

Laurel relayed the message and hung up. "What the hell is going on?"

"Jerome is the guy you punched." I moved into the fast lane and held it at eighty. "I kind of broke into his house a few days ago and left him a message."

Laurel grimaced. "And how does Nate know where Jerome is?"

"We planted GPS trackers on his and all of his employees' cars."

She took a couple deep breaths. "Okay, this is a lot of information to take in."

"My life is usually very boring."

"Why did you guys put GPS on their cars?" Her tone was anything but understanding.

"To see if they were moving in on our customers. Of course, I didn't consider the whole tracking his movements thing. I guess it paid off in the early warning." I was trying to stay positive about this whole situation and Laurel was kind of bringing me down.

"You do realize that it's illegal to put a GPS tracker on a vehicle without the owner's consent?"

I took everything in my power to not make a crack about her working for a law firm. "You know, I didn't check. I'm a drug dealer. I tend to pick and choose which laws to follow."

"That's great. So how exactly did you threaten him? I assume this is the wheelchair bound father you and Nate were talking about." She wasn't quite yelling, but she wasn't exactly calm either.

"I took a photo with the old man and gave Jerome a copy."

"I take it you didn't just hand it to him."

"No, I broke in and left copies of the photo. So when he came home he saw that I could have ripped him off, just like I could have hurt his old man, but I didn't. Because I don't operate that way."

"That is so big of you." There was a lot of sarcasm in that sentence.

"You knew I was a drug dealer. What did you expect?"

"I don't know. A little sanity." She stared out the window. "You're not like—you don't act like a normal dealer. You're not arrogant and dangerous."

"You know a lot of dealers?" It seemed like a good question to ask.

"Just my father's clients. You seem more level-headed than they are."

I was pretty sure she meant it as a compliment, but it was massively insulting, and I didn't have the time or inclination right then to examine why.

"I am. This is a fluke." My exit was coming up. I moved over three lanes just in time to hit the 26th Street exit.

"So what if he goes back to your place? What about Andy? Do you realize how much danger you put her in?"

That pissed me off. "Yes, I do. I'll handle it."

She stayed silent until we were two blocks from my place. My phone rang. She picked it up.

"Nate?" His voice rumbled through the line. "We're almost there. Stay put." She hung up the phone. "Jerome is sitting outside your place. Nate and Henry are watching him. Who is Henry?"

"That sheriff buddy of mine. We went to high school together." I turned onto my street. Nate was sitting on my steps glaring. Henry was parked two houses up watching them. Jerome was leaning against his Cadillac. When I pulled into my driveway, Jerome smiled and waved at me. I yanked the keys out of the ignition and walked up to Jerome. He looked relaxed. His grin suggested that he found the whole thing entertaining.

"Hey, Cash. Looks like the gang is all here."

"What are you doing here?"

Jerome put up his hands. "I come in peace. Listen, I got your message. Loud and clear." He chuckled. "I liked the condoms. It was a nice touch." He reached into his car and pulled out a bottle of Scotch. "Truce?" He held the bottle out to me. There was a little white bow tied around the neck.

This was unexpected. "I'd like that." I took the bottle.

"You fucked up. I fucked up. Let's not make it a big deal."

"You'll stay away from my employees? And my customers?" I asked. I didn't trust him, but I could at least take the peace offering and hope it was sincere. If not, I'd deal with it later.

"Yeah, as long as you stay away from mine. And my father."

"Deal." I held out my hand. He shook it.

"You don't come here anymore," Laurel said. I turned and found her standing uncomfortably close to my shoulder.

"I wouldn't dream of it. You've got a great right hook, by the way." Jerome was walking the line between reverence and condescending. He grinned and tipped the scale toward respect. "Enjoy that Scotch. You've earned it."

Jerome climbed back into his car and started the engine. He gave us a cute little wave before pulling away from the curb.

Henry got out of his car and approached. He was still watching the street as if he expected Jerome to come back.

"That was interesting." Nate stepped up to stand next to us.

"What did he say?" Henry asked.

"He wanted to call a truce." I held up the bottle.

Nate and Henry looked as surprised as I felt.

"We haven't met," Laurel said to Henry.

He pulled his gaze from the street for the first time. It took him a moment to find his charm. "You must be the girlfriend. I'm Henry Brewer." He put out his hand.

"Laurel Collins." They shook. It was very civilized. But Henry was scrutinizing her like he had seen her before. The entire interaction felt odd. "How did you get roped into this rescue mission?"

"Nate called and asked how close I was." Henry shrugged. "Couldn't leave Cash without a savior." He lowered his voice. "You know the two of them are pretty soft. Can't make the hard decisions."

Nate opened his mouth, but I shook my head at him. It wasn't noon yet and I was so done with today. I'd been offered a bottle of Scotch and a truce from an enemy, insulted and doubted by a woman I was falling too hard for, and mocked by a friend who treated me like shit and expected me to thank him. I couldn't handle Nate and Henry going at it too.

Laurel grinned at him, but it looked forced. "Then why keep them limping along?"

"Misguided pity, I guess." Henry smacked me on the shoulder.

I couldn't even muster a response so I turned and started up toward the house. Everyone followed me. Their presence felt suffocating. "I'm going to make some coffee. You guys want some?"

"I have to get to school. I'm lecturing undergrads in an hour," Nate said.

I stopped walking. "Thank you."

He shook my hand. "Anytime. I'll be watching GPS when I can today, but you need to keep an eye too."

I nodded. "Will do."

Henry stopped on the walkway too. "I have to get going as well."

"Thanks for getting here so quickly," I said.

"Of course. It was nice to meet you, Laurel."

"You too." They locked eyes for a moment. There was a challenge there.

The guys got in their cars and took off. Laurel sat on the front steps and waited. She pushed her hair up out of her eyes, and I really wished I didn't find it so attractive. We were two minutes from a breakup and I so didn't want to go there.

"You coming in for coffee?" I asked.

"No. I'm going to take off too. I don't think I can…" She picked at a sliver of wood on the steps.

"I get it. The reality of dating a drug dealer is a bit more intense than the idea of it."

Laurel looked up sharply. "No. That's not it." She looked back at the steps. "Okay, yeah, that's part of it. I just need time to wrap my head around it."

"You're not breaking up with me?"

"No, God. No." She grabbed my hand and tugged me down. "I just don't get it. I saw the farm. It's doing well. I don't see why you need to deal."

"It's not that simple." I thought about Henry. Even if the farm did well enough to survive on its own—which it couldn't—I doubted he would let it go so easily. I had Nate to think about. I had customers. It wasn't something I could just step back from. It wasn't something I wanted to step back from. I was good at dealing. The last few weeks notwithstanding.

"You're more than this." Laurel sounded sad. She traced a fingertip over our joined hands.

"That's the thing. I'm not. I am this." I kissed the back of her hand. "You need to decide if you can live with it."

"Yeah, I know." She kissed my cheek and stood. "I'll call you." She sounded like she meant it. I was sure she did. Right then. In the intervening hours, things would shift, change.

I wanted to ask her not to break my heart, but I had a feeling she couldn't control that. It was already broken. She was already walking away.

❖

I started a pot of coffee. The rote movement was comforting. I checked the house for Nickels. She was hiding under my bed. It was already getting hot so I closed all the windows and turned on the AC. I realized that I couldn't hear anything from the Ward side of the house. Andy wasn't usually quiet. That was worrisome. I couldn't handle any more scares today. I pulled out my phone and called Andy.

"Hey, Cash. Shit. I was supposed to call you."

"Where are you?"

"Sophie's mom picked me up. It was like half an hour ago. Mom said it was okay as long as I called you and I forgot. I'm sorry." She had that tone teenagers get when they regret screwing up. It's different from the tone where they screwed up and don't give a fuck.

"No worries. I couldn't hear you moving around and I was a little concerned. Glad you're not broken."

"No, ma'am. Hey, Cash?"

"Yeah?"

"I'm really sorry."

I must have sounded more worried than I wanted to. "Don't be. Have fun with Sophie."

"'Kay. Later."

I hung up the phone and set it on the counter. The coffee pot beeped. I stared at the pot as the remnants dripped from the filter.

Laurel wasn't going to call me. If I cared about her at all, that was probably a good thing. What had she called dealers? Arrogant and dangerous. That was me. Arrogant enough to think I could control the uncontrollable. Arrogant enough to assume the people I loved would be protected. That was the dangerous part.

I took a mug out of the cabinet and set it next to the coffee pot. I needed to pour it next, but my brain's signals didn't seem to be translating into movement.

It was good that Andy hadn't been here. I was glad she hadn't seen anything. Somehow that would have made the shame unbearable. It was bad enough that Laurel had seen the results of my posturing. No, it was bad that she had seen through my posturing.

Pouring the coffee was too difficult. I couldn't figure out how so I sat on the floor instead. I wanted to cry. When I was a kid it made everything okay. But the tears didn't come. I hadn't cried in years. I didn't know why I thought now would be the time. Instead, I sat on the floor tracing the edges of the black and white tiles. They were cool. The ridges were subtle and gritty. I was paralyzed. The AC reached the right temperature and turned off. The silence was pervasive. The air felt tight and close. I was breathing too hard, too fast. There was a lump in my throat.

Laurel had called me level-headed. Too level-headed to be a drug dealer. I hated compliments that claimed that I was better than a piece of my identity. It harkened back to the middle school days when my peers celebrated that I wasn't like a normal lesbian. As if it was a plague I was escaping. It's okay to be a dyke as long as you're not too queer. You don't need to be heteronormative as long as you don't challenge normativity. It's okay to be a dealer as long as you're better than a dealer. Break the rules, but only the right rules to break.

There was one tile slightly askew. The corner tilted up ever so slightly.

Henry thought I was soft. Henry was a dick.

The entire day felt like a karmic bitch slap. Last night, I had told Laurel that people who judged her and treated her shitty weren't worth her time. This morning, she told me my job made me a bad person. Or something. And then she had defended me against Henry. I couldn't understand it. I didn't know how to react to it.

The tiles were shockingly hard. I was tired of sitting on them. I was tired of everything. I stood and poured myself a cup of coffee.

After scanning my shelves, I settled on Plath. She seemed like the best match to my mood. Borderline compulsive examination of loathing. A disappointment in the self as a reflection of society. Yes, *Ariel* was the girl for me. I stretched out on the couch and propped the book on my chest. Nickels jumped up and settled between my feet. Smart cat. I wasn't ready for affection. I wanted to hold to this growing vitriol. I wanted my anger to feel justified. The alternative was admitting that all of them weren't wrong.

CHAPTER TWENTY-ONE

When Andy got home that evening, I felt comfortable turning off my phone. I hadn't looked at the incoming messages or calls except to confirm that it wasn't Robin or Andy. Laurel hadn't contacted me. Not that I was watching for that. The peace of having it off felt like a gift. Of course, then I just sat there wondering if Laurel was trying to call me. After a half hour of rereading the same poem, I turned my phone back on and looked at my messages. Only one stood out. It was from Nate.

Jerome has stopped at 3 of ur customers' houses.

That was not what I wanted to hear. I turned the phone off again.

I realized that I was still wearing yesterday's clothes. They felt grimy. Not just because I'd been wearing them for almost forty hours, but because they seemed to be weighted by the actions of the day. I stripped and got in the shower. The lukewarm water was comforting. When I got out, I put on a threadbare T-shirt and my favorite boxers. Still, I couldn't relax. I climbed in bed with my poetry and reread the same page I'd been trying to finish for hours.

Eventually, I fell asleep. That wasn't surprising considering how draining the day had been. But I kept waking up at the smallest sounds. The roar of the AC was driving me insane. I finally got up and turned it off. Nickels followed me around the house as I opened the windows. I went back to my bed and buried my face in the cool sheets. Nickels jumped up, turned around a couple of times, then dropped off to sleep. The nighttime city sounds were comforting. The breeze coming in the window still carried the heat of the day, but the fresh air was a fair trade.

Outside, people walked by. Their voices were slurred from the bar. Car doors slammed and engines started up. A rogue siren echoed in the distance. Vague strains of jazz reached out from the nightclub two blocks over. A familiar engine rumbled down the street and stopped. The creak and pop of the door opening made me open my eyes. I was imagining it. There wasn't any more sound. I looked at the clock. One in the morning. It was wishful thinking. At one thirty, I heard footsteps coming up the walkway, hesitating and pacing on the stairs. Then, there was a knock.

I waited, barely breathing, convinced I was hearing things. And then she knocked again. I got up to answer the door.

Laurel was sitting on the steps, facing the street. She was wearing another baggy tank that trembled in the warm breeze.

"Hey." I leaned against the doorjamb and studied her. At my voice, she stiffened.

Slowly, she turned. "Hi."

"What are you doing here?"

"I don't know." She stood and came to the door.

"Want to come in?" I stepped aside to give her room. She came in, then stopped in the entrance, waited for me to close the door. I didn't know what to say. I didn't know what to ask her.

"I can't decide if I'm mad at you or if you should be mad at me." She put her hands in her pockets. Doing so stretched her chinos tight across her ass. We were not going to be able to have a rational discussion if she was going to stand there looking all hot and shit.

"Both, probably."

"Yeah, but it doesn't quite work like that, does it?" She shook her head in answer to her own question and walked forward. I followed her. She finally spun to look at me. "I know it's irrational to ask you to quit. I do know that."

"But you're still mad."

"I guess." She stared hard at me. "But I said some terrible things to you too. I should apologize."

"Would you mean it?"

She shook her head. "No."

"Then don't." I shrugged. Insincerity wasn't worth the promise. I wanted to be honestly angry, not unsure of my happiness.

"Where does that leave us?" she asked.

"I'm not sure. At an impasse."

"I want you to quit. You say you can't. But I can't seem to force myself to care about that. I know I should. I have to." She pushed her hair up, and my resolve weakened. Not that it was strong to begin with.

"What do you care about, then?"

"The only thing I can think is that I shouldn't have stopped you. Last night. I don't think I've ever wanted someone as bad as I wanted you."

"Past tense?"

"No."

I knew it was stupid to go to her. But I did it anyway.

Laurel leaned away from me, her shoulders set, as though she was being pulled into me, but trying to break away. Her eyes flicked between mine and my mouth. I rode the edge of her anticipation, unable to stop, unable to move forward. I wanted. Christ, did I want. I pushed up the bottom of her tank top, rested my hands against her back, held her closer to me. Still, she studied my face. Every time that gaze rested on my lips, she tipped her chin up like she was going to kiss me. Almost as if it were involuntary. Yet, something continued to hold her back.

This was ridiculous. I leaned in to kiss her. Her breath hitched. She pressed her palms to my chest.

"Wait."

I did. I couldn't control the way my chest rose and fell on every labored breath though. I couldn't seem to control the way my hands pressed her closer to me or the inability to look away from her full bottom lip. But I could wait.

Laurel slid a hand farther up my chest and cupped my neck. Our kiss felt inevitable, but there was a sliver of fear that it wouldn't happen. She was short of breath just like me, but she seemed nearly in pain.

"Please, Laurel." I asked as much for myself as her.

"I need to tell you something."

"You don't." I shook my head once. "We don't need to talk about it."

"But—"

"Do you want me?" I asked.

She nodded, but even that looked like a struggle. I leaned down and tried to kiss her. At the last second, she tilted her head down, away. Her eyes were almost black. They held an accusation as they bored into mine. It made me stop. I extracted my hands from her shirt, took a step back.

"I'm sorry." I felt despicable. How many times did the woman need to tell me to stop before I listened?

She leaned up and kissed me. And that moment, the one we had been poised on for an eternity, suddenly felt daunting, breakneck. It only took a second for me to forget that it was insane, though. Because her fingertips were tracing my cheek, jaw, neck. They pressed and teased. Like she was playing, molding me.

Her lips felt delicate. She kissed, shifted, kissed again. Each time the breath of air between us, the negative space was a cumbersome promise.

And then the air rushed back into the room. Laurel walked me back, her hands gripped and twisted in my T-shirt. My legs hit the couch and she pushed me to sit down. She followed so she was straddling me. I grabbed her ass and pulled her crotch tight against my stomach. She leaned forward into our kiss. I panted against her open mouth. Her tongue dipped between my lips.

I wanted to turn her beneath me. To strip her down and lick her skin. To feel the clench of her muscles surrounding me. But she had told me to stop, to wait too many times. I had to follow her lead.

So I let her explore my mouth, bite my lips, take my air. She traced my neck, shoulders, dipped under the collar of my shirt and dug her nails into my skin. When she yanked the tank top over her head, I waited to touch her. Her breasts were small. Her nipples were dark, almost pink. She tugged at my shirt and I let her pull it over my head. The weight of her tits pressing into my chest felt oppressive. I wanted to fuck her. I had forgotten how to do anything else.

Laurel dropped her hands back to my shoulders, rubbed down my biceps, gripped my forearms. She lifted my hands to the waistband on her chinos and held them there.

"Are you sure?" I asked.

She nodded. Her eyes had gone wild, desperate. "I won't regret this." It was a command. I didn't know which of us she was commanding. I knew I damn sure wouldn't regret it.

I slid open the hook closure and lowered her zipper. Her breathing sped up. I didn't know how she managed to keep breathing. I couldn't get a full breath. Hadn't had one in thirty hours.

Her boxer briefs were tight and short. The edges rode up against the muscle in her thighs. I pushed her pants lower, but they only moved a few inches. Laurel got impatient and pressed my hand flat against her stomach. I edged my fingertips under the elastic of her underwear.

"I want you. Now. I can't wait." She kissed me again and pushed my hand lower.

Who was I to argue?

She was warm, wet against my fingertips. Cooling moisture clung to my knuckles. Her hips twitched, jerked at the suggestion of my touch. I slid a finger through her wetness, skirted her clit. She moaned into my mouth. It suggested pain and wanting. I swallowed the sound.

I broke our kiss and took a nipple into my mouth. She cupped my head and arched into me. I sucked hard enough to leave a bruise. Her skin tasted like salt and smelled like soap.

Laurel shifted closer. She hooked her thumbs in the waistband of her underwear and shoved them down a few more inches. It was enough for me to cup her properly. I traced her entrance, but didn't press inside. Not yet. I wanted this moment to last. Laurel whimpered and tilted her hips. I dipped a finger inside. She grabbed my wrist and held me still so that she could sink onto me. A groan rumbled in her chest.

"Yes," she said. It was a whisper, but I felt her acquiescence spread through me.

I pressed my face to her chest, kissed her as she began to slowly rock. Her muscles gripped my fingers, rippled with each small movement. She was too close to coming. I wrapped my free arm around her waist and stilled her movement.

"Wait," I said. "Just stay here for a minute."

Laurel looked down at me. Her gaze raked over my mouth again, flicked back up to my eyes. She leaned down and kissed me. I moved my hand, just enough to make her breath catch. Out a fraction, then back in. She tipped her weight forward, tried to angle her hips more sharply. I tightened my grip at her waist and held her still.

"Please."

"Soon."

The grasp on my wrist eased, then she let go. I thrust again, harder this time. She bit my lip and sucked on it. When her hands found my tits, I almost gave up. She pinched and twisted, working me higher. I found a steady rhythm. Her hips moved with me. Each thrust took me deeper. Her tongue was in my mouth, the vibrations of her moans resonated through me. I stopped trying to hold her steady and just let her ride it out.

Right before she came, she gripped my shoulders and arched back. I balanced her with a hand on her ass, kneading as she worked herself higher, higher, until she came. Her cunt clenched around my fingers. She cried out, then slumped forward. Her hips twitched as the orgasm finished working its way out. Her breath was a sharp, wet rasp against my neck.

I started to pull out, but she grabbed my wrist again.

"Slow. You feel so good."

So I pulled away in fractions. She sighed when I was free. Her hands climbed my neck again, searching for purchase against my skin. She leaned back and watched me. She reached up and drew a line over my brow, down my cheek, rested with her hands on the pulse pounding in my throat. And then she was cupping my breasts, her palms scraping my nipples. I lifted my hips without meaning to. She grinned and stood. I started to get up to follow her, but she pushed me back.

Laurel dropped to her knees and gripped the waistband of my boxers. I lifted enough for her to pull them down. She leaned forward and kissed my neck, the bruises she had left on my collarbone. Her hair fell forward and tickled my chest. I struggled to stay still.

She wrapped her lips around one of my nipples, tongued it into a hard point. I curled my hands into fists and tried not to call out. Her hands were at my waist, stomach, thighs. She followed that line with her mouth. Her lips, tongue were damp on my skin. She spread my legs and dipped her head.

I groaned and dug my fingers into her hair. I arched up to meet her and her hands guided me forward. Her mouth was hot. She pressed the flat of her tongue against my clit and held for a moment. I tried to move against her, but she clamped down on my thighs and held me still. Then her tongue started to move. I closed my eyes and let myself feel her. The wet kiss of her lips, the hard edge of her teeth, the smooth stroke of her tongue. I tightened my fingers in her hair and held her fast against me. She laughed and sucked my clit into her mouth.

I wasn't going to last long. I arched my hips and Laurel slid her hands under my ass. She pulled me in and shoved me away. I kept a hand against the back of her head as I fucked her mouth. I was so goddamn close. I wanted to stay there in that moment. I would die if I stayed there. I opened my eyes and watched her. It was the sight of her face buried in my cunt that did me in. She sucked at me slowly, eased me back down.

"I think I might be dead," I said.

"You don't feel dead."

"Well, that's good." I tugged her back up on the couch. She crawled on top of me again. "You're still wearing shorts. You shouldn't be wearing shorts." Words were hard.

"I agree." Laurel stood and dropped the shorts. She pushed down her boxer briefs too. I groaned.

"Bed. Now." I forced myself to stand. Which was difficult because my legs weren't ready.

We stumbled into my bedroom and fell onto the bed. Laurel kissed me again. The woman was a damn expert at kissing. I pulled her against me.

Dawn was creeping in the windows by the time we drifted off. I was exhausted, but I didn't want to sleep. I just wanted to keep touching her.

It could have been my imagination. Or sleep deprivation. But I could have sworn, as I flirted with the edges of sleep, that she whispered that she loved me.

CHAPTER TWENTY-TWO

I woke up hot, naked, and alone. Well, without Laurel. Nickels was pressed against my side. Warm cats and hundred degree days don't mix. Plus, there was the whole naked flesh and fear of claws thing. I rolled away and got tangled in a sheet. I listened for any sound that would suggest that Laurel was still here, but there was nothing.

I looked at the clock. Just after noon. No wonder it was hot in here. I put on a fresh pair of boxer briefs, found a T-shirt on the floor, and went around closing windows and turning on the AC. Coffee was next. I couldn't handle waking up alone without coffee. Next to the coffee machine I found a note.

Had to leave. Sorry. L

Well, that cleared things right up.

I'd managed to get coffee brewing when I heard a knock at the front door. I didn't want to answer it. I still didn't want to face this day. The knocking got louder.

"Cash, you home?" Nate shouted.

I guess that ruled out Jehovah's Witnesses. Last time had been so fun. They called me son and asked if my parents were home.

"I'm coming," I called back. He stopped pounding on the door. I swung it open.

Nate looked in a bit frantically, then shoved past me. "She's not here, right? Are you alone?" Not his usual entrance.

"What? Yeah. Why?"

Nate closed the door and locked it. "You sure?" He dropped a duffel bag by the door.

"Yeah, I think I know when I'm home alone. What is up with you?" The coffee machine beeped. "Never mind." I left him staring at shadows in the entryway and went to pour some coffee.

"Where is your phone? Why isn't it on?" Nate followed me into the kitchen.

I decided to be nice and pour him a cup of coffee too. "I turned it off yesterday. I wasn't feeling contact with the outside world."

"Go get it." Nate took the mug I handed him and sat at the kitchen table.

"I saw your message about Jerome. I assume that's what this is about. I knew that asshole wasn't going to back off." I sat across from him.

"What?" Nate looked confused for a moment. "Oh, yeah. That."

"Why are you freaking out right now?"

"Just go get your phone."

I rolled my eyes and went to get the damn phone. I hit the button to start it up and set it on the table between Nate and me. He stared at the bright white apple and drummed his fingers.

"You need to calm down, man. You're driving me crazy," I said. The phone finished starting. I swiped it. Fourteen voice mails. Nine from Henry. Four from Nate. One from Laurel. Nearly thirty text messages. "Jesus Christ. I suppose I need to listen to all five million of these to figure out what is going on?"

"Yes." Nate nodded and studied the tabletop. "Wait. No. You shouldn't find out like that. I just—Fuck." He took a deep breath. "Okay, Laurel is a cop."

I laughed. It was the most obvious response. "Get your head out of your ass."

"No, Cash. I'm serious. She's a cop. Undercover."

My heart started to pound. "No, she works at her father's law firm. And doesn't like institutions. Law enforcement is an institution." It was so trying to have to explain everything to him.

"That's a cover. She's investigating us. She's investigating you."

"You're wrong." I picked up my phone and scrolled through my contacts to her name. She could explain this. It was a misunderstanding.

Nate grabbed the phone. "I'm sorry. It's true. Henry has been trying to call you since last night. He finally sent me over here."

"Nate, she's not a fucking cop. That's absurd." I was doing my best to remain calm. It wasn't working. "Give me my phone."

"I can't. I'm sorry. This is real."

"Give me my goddamn phone." I held out my hand. Nate shook his head. I tried to grab the phone. Nate stood and held it out of my reach. I jumped on him, reached for his hand, yanked on his bicep, but he didn't budge. "Nate."

"I'm sorry." He wrapped his free arm around me. I don't know if he was trying to hold me back or just comfort me, but it didn't work. When I clawed at him again, he shoved me back. He put the phone in his pocket and wrestled me back into my chair. I attempted to stand, but he caged me in and leaned close so I couldn't move. "Give it up. I'm not going to let you call her."

"She can't be. She can't." I realized I was shaking. "She loves me."

"All I know is that she's an undercover cop." He knelt in front of me, but kept my arms pinned. "Maybe there is an explanation. Maybe Henry is wrong. But we need to take a moment and deal with this. Just in case. Okay?" I nodded. "Take a deep breath." I did what he said. "Good. Now, another."

Last night, I finally felt like I could breathe. Now, the shortness was back. My lungs wouldn't fill. I tried to inhale fully, but it didn't calm the racing of my heart or the trembling in my arms. "He's wrong."

"Hopefully. But right now, we need to strip any paraphernalia. Whatever you have. Drugs, baggies, money, anything that could be evidence. Can you help me?"

I nodded. "Yes."

"Good. I already stripped my place. Where are we going to put everything?"

I had an answer to that, but I didn't like it. "Don't worry about it. I've got a place. Just help me gather shit. How much time do we have?"

"I don't know. I don't think she knows her cover has been blown."

"She doesn't have a cover to blow," I said.

"Yeah, okay." Nate nodded. His tone was placating. I didn't like it.

I went to the pantry and pulled out all of the drugs I had stashed. Nate took them and carried the bags to the table. There was cash in the freezer. That was the little stash. I tossed the cold bag onto the pile of pills and shoved the taquito box back into the freezer. My big stash was in the dining room. I went to the built-in hutch and pulled out all of the bottom drawers. There was a dusty bag in the cavity beneath each of them. I realized belatedly that Nate could have made up the entire story to figure out where I kept everything. But I trusted him. More than I trusted Henry. I didn't know if I trusted him more than Laurel.

It didn't matter. Henry was wrong. When we confirmed it, I'd beat him to a fucking pulp.

When I brought the bags back into the kitchen, Nate was piling everything into the small duffel bag from my closet. I pulled out kitchen drawers and rounded up all of the drug-sized baggies and the labels I rarely used. Nate tossed those into the duffel.

"Anything else?" he asked.

"No."

"Invoices, receipts, phone numbers, anything?"

"No, I don't keep any written records. It's all logged as produce," I said. But then I realized that wasn't true. I went to the study and grabbed the small notebook next to my laptop. It had a list of codes. It wasn't much, but with enough time someone might be able to figure out the translation of prices. "This too." I tucked it into the bag.

"Good. Now, pack a bag for you."

"Give me a minute."

I threw my bag of toiletries into a backpack. When I went to grab clothes, I realized I wasn't wearing any. I pulled on a pair of jeans and kicked into my Converse. Red, because a day this shitty needed red Converse. The same rules applied to shoes as cars. If I had to run, at least it would look like I was going fast.

I knew Nate was waiting impatiently so I took mild pleasure in taking my time brushing my teeth and styling my hair. I leaned over the sink as I tried to get my pompadour to stand up at just the right angle. My T-shirt was loose, and I caught sight of the bruises from Laurel's fingertips spread across my collarbone. Immediately, I got wet. And then hated myself for the visceral reaction. And then hated myself for trusting Henry's word over Laurel's, even for a moment.

I marched out to the living room and threw my backpack at Nate. He caught it and stepped back when he realized I was angry.

"Let's go. I'd really like to punch Henry in the face when he realizes that he's wrong."

"Sure. But we need to stash our shit first." Nate kicked the duffel at his feet.

I glared at him and held out my hand. "I need my phone."

He stared at me hard. After a minute of searching my face, he pulled out the phone and handed it to me. I hit Robin's name and waited.

"Hey, Cash," Andy answered.

"Hey. Is your mom there?"

"She's driving. What's up?"

"I'm going to be out of town tonight. Can you feed Nickels for me?"

"Sure. Do you still need to talk to Mom?"

"Nope. I'll keep you updated."

"Okay. Have fun," she said with all the excitement of a teenager who doesn't know what life will bring and is looking forward to it. "Bye."

"Bye." I slid the phone into my pocket. Nate clenched his hands. "Calm the fuck down. I'm not going to call her."

I went to the kitchen and pulled the keys to the Wards' off the hook. Nate handed me the duffel bag with enough evidence to hang us. I left him pouting and went next door.

It always felt strange to let myself into Robin's place. I owned the damn building, but I felt like an intruder. Today, I was. It didn't matter that she had offered. It was years ago and it was theoretical. Taking her up on it felt like a violation. Probably because I had sworn I would never take advantage of the offer. Yet, here I was, creeping through her home. I took the stepladder from the kitchen and carried it into Robin's bedroom on the far side of the house. Her room smelled faintly of lavender and magnolia and Robin's perfume. It didn't smell like my house.

I opened the closet and set up the stepladder. There was a small hatch above the high shelf. I pushed the panel up and slid it sideways. A faint layer of dust shifted and settled. I shoved the duffel in and closed the panel. I was a dick.

I put the stepladder back, made sure there was no evidence that I had been there, and locked the door behind me.

Nate was still pouting when I came back inside.

"It's done," I said.

He didn't question me, which I appreciated. "Cool. Let's go."

I followed him out to his car. He stashed our bags in the trunk and I climbed in the passenger side.

"Where are we going?" I asked once he got in the car.

"Laurel's place. Henry has been watching her since this morning."

My heart jumped into my throat. "Is she there?"

"Yeah, he said she got home around ten."

Good to know. "What is he hoping to accomplish?"

"I don't know. You can ask him when we get there."

We stayed silent as he navigated through midtown. Laurel lived in the twenties on T Street. At least she hadn't lied to me about that. No, she hadn't lied about anything. She was going to be pissed when she found out how I spent my day.

Nate parked and texted Henry. He got a reply almost immediately. "Come on. Henry is a few cars up."

I looked for the electric blue Mustang, but didn't see it. "Where?"

"He's not driving his car. He rented something more discreet. It's the white Suburban."

I supposed it was technically discreet in that it wasn't electric blue. Henry's head was so far up his ass, it was a miracle he accomplished anything. We were in midtown. So his suburban looking Suburban basically looked like a semi.

I tamped down on my irritation. At this point, if I lost it on anything, I would lose it on everything. Instead, I vaulted into the backseat of the Suburban.

"Finally. I was worried about you guys." Henry was stretched out on the bench seat behind me. This thing had two backseats. It was a monstrosity.

"There's nothing to worry about. You're wrong about her," I said.

Henry looked at Nate. Nate studied the floor. "I'm not," Henry said. "I'm sorry. I know you liked her. But she's a cop."

"Prove it."

Henry shook his head like he was trying to keep calm. "Okay, Nate watch Laurel's apartment. Here." He gave him a camera with a big ass lens on it.

"Which one is hers?"

"The big green Victorian. Her apartment is the top floor. There are two apartments downstairs. Young guy with blond hair just left. Ignore him. Other tenant appears to be out as well."

"Sure, what exactly am I looking for?" Nate asked.

"There is a guy up there with her. Early forties, clean-cut. Gray hair. Almost six feet, about a hundred and sixty pounds. Black jeans, blue T-shirt with a logo on the back. He's driving the black Impala out front. Let me know when he leaves."

Nate lifted the camera to eye level and stared at the building. It was his attempt at giving us privacy.

"Here, Cash." Henry handed me a file folder.

I opened it assuming I would find something definitive, a personnel report or something. Instead, I found printed news stories. "Sacramento judge dismisses…" "Prominent Sacramento attorney…" The headlines went on. I flipped through the articles. Henry had highlighted names. Judge Janice Kallen, Randolf Kallen, Judge Kallen, Sergeant Lance Kallen, Randolf and Logan Kallen.

Whoever this family was, they were in deep with Sacramento's law and order community. I went back to the beginning and skimmed the articles. Judge Kallen had a reputation for going easy on nonviolent offenders. Her husband and son apparently ran a local law firm that did a lot of pro bono work in addition to their work as paid defense attorneys. Randolf had worked in the district attorney's office before starting his own firm in the mid-nineties. Lance Kallen was a police officer with Sacramento PD. He appeared to be the outlier, but he was featured smiling with his parents at a dinner benefitting the police department.

"What the hell am I looking at here? Who are these people?" We were wasting time. This was obviously irrelevant.

"They're your girlfriend's family."

"Except Laurel's last name is Collins, not Kallen."

Henry reached over the seat. He closed the file I was looking at and opened the one underneath it. It had a copy of Laurel's driver's license and car registration. It listed her last name as Kallen. That wasn't good. It wasn't damning entirely, but it wasn't good.

"Okay, so she lied about her last name. She hates her parents. Maybe she just goes by a different last name. She told me she works for her father's law firm. Look." I held up the first file. "He has a law firm."

"Did you read the articles?"

"No, I skimmed."

He took the file I was holding up and riffled through it. "Read this one."

I read the stupid fucking article. It wasn't going to tell me shit. It was a profile of Randolf Kallen from *Sacramento Magazine*. It didn't tell me anything.

"See?" Henry asked when I handed it back to him.

"No. What am I supposed to see?"

"The quote. 'Janice and I truly value the contribution of our local police force. One of our sons just finished at the Sacramento Police Academy. He will join his sister on the force next month.' Blah, blah, whatever."

"So what?"

"His sister is on the fucking police force."

"So you've got the wrong family. I'm telling you, man. This isn't her."

"This is her." He shoved another article into my hands. There was a photo of the entire Kallen clan at a benefit in the late nineties. Only Randolf and Janice were named. Their four children were not. I glanced back at the photos of grown-up Lance and Logan. They were obviously the boys smiling in the photo. Their bone structure was familiar. And Randolf's face clearly reflected what they looked like now. The infant Janice was holding offered no help.

I studied the eldest daughter's face. She was in her early teens. Awkward, but pretty. Long, dark hair covered half her face. But it was the boots that made me stop. It wasn't so much the obviously queer, teenage Dr. Martens as it was the way she was standing in them. Laurel had the exact same stance. She always stood in accidental contrapposto. Once I saw her in the pose, I couldn't stop seeing it. Seeing her. Those were her hands, her cheekbones. That was her brow and jaw. It felt cruel that the body I had pored over last night was now the confirmation of her betrayal.

"I'm sorry, Cash." Henry put his hand on my shoulder. I didn't even have the energy to shrug it off.

"What's your plan?" I asked.

"Right now, we watch. We confirm that it's you she's investigating."

I scoffed. Which was impressive because I wanted to scream. "Is there any doubt? Of course it's me."

"There are a lot of angles to—" He stopped when his phone rang. He checked the screen and swiped it. "Hey, what do you have for me?" I could hear a high, soft voice. She sounded pretty. Henry always went for the pretty ones. "You're sure. Can you get more specific? Is it assigned to anyone?" She said something that made him smile halfway. "Okay, thanks. I owe you." She said something that made him smile all the way. "Deal." He hung up.

"Found a girl?"

Henry waved off my question. "She's gullible as hell. But she's good at following directions."

"So what's the deal?"

"She just told me that the Impala is registered to the local FBI field office." He leaned back in his seat.

"The FBI?" I shouted. This was so bad. Henry was wrong. Not because I had gotten fucked by a pretty girl, but because I was so not a big enough fish for the FBI.

"Calm down. It's not as bad as it sounds." He put his hands up as if that would help me calm down. It didn't help.

"I hope not. Because FBI sounds pretty fucking bad."

"It's totally normal."

"This is not normal," I said.

"It's not good, man," Nate said.

"No, it's fine." Henry leaned forward and put his hand back on my shoulder. "A few years ago, Sac PD shut down a number of their units. Narcotics and Vice, among them. They didn't have funding to keep them going. Most of the officers were reassigned, but a select few consult directly with the FBI field office."

"That doesn't make me feel any better," Nate said.

"Same."

"I'm saying, this is how all the narcotics cases are investigated in Sac. They didn't bring the FBI in just for you. You're not special," Henry said.

"You're saying my mother lied to me?" Nate asked.

I smiled because he was trying to lighten the mood. But it didn't help. This morning I was concerned that the chick I had slept with hadn't stayed the whole night. Now, I was concerned that a Sac PD officer was consulting with the FBI to lock my ass up. Nothing could make me feel better.

CHAPTER TWENTY-THREE

There's movement at the door," Nate said.

I was reading through the articles Henry had given me for the third time. We had been waiting for an hour. The AC was running, but the SUV was hot and rapidly beginning to feel like a tomb.

"Who is leaving?" Henry grabbed the camera and started taking photos.

I watched as the door on the second floor balcony opened. The FBI guy came out first. Laurel followed him. She locked the door, and they started down the stairs running alongside the house.

"What's the plan, Henry?" I asked.

"We need to follow them. Nate, get ready to go back to your car. You stay on him, okay?"

Nate nodded. "Sure. What about you guys?"

"We are going to follow her."

Laurel and her buddy casually scanned the street. We froze even though there was no way they could see past our tinted windows. He went to his car and she followed. When she got in the passenger side, Henry whispered, "Yes."

"What?" I asked.

"New plan. Nate, you follow them. Cash, we're staying here."

"Got it," Nate said.

"We're going to break in. Text us when they are far enough away," Henry said. Nate and I looked at him like he had lost his shit.

"Get your head out of your ass," I said.

"You want to find out how much she has on us? This is the best way." Henry seemed confused.

"You just showed us that she's a cop working with the FBI. How the fuck can you possibly deduce that breaking into her apartment is smart?" I asked.

"Guys, they're leaving. I'm going to follow," Nate said.

"Go," Henry said.

Nate touched my arm. "Don't do anything stupid."

"Don't worry. Get out of here."

He nodded and got out of the SUV. We watched him jog back to his car. They turned the corner as he pulled out onto the street.

"Look, I know you don't want to do this, but it's the only way we will get any information. Why can't you see that?" Henry asked.

"It's colossally stupid."

"Nate is watching her. It's the best chance we will get. Why wouldn't we go in?"

I tried to formulate a response. All I could think of was that it was a violation of her privacy. And considering that she had dated me, slept with me, to build a case against us, the violation argument was kind of null and void. "I don't know. It seems wrong. I don't do this kind of shit."

"You broke into Jerome's house without hesitation," Henry said.

"Yeah, but that was to protect us. I have a responsibility to Nate and Clive and you."

"How is this different?"

And that was it. It wasn't. "Fuck." I texted Nate, *We're going in. Give us a heads-up if she's coming back.*

He wrote back a minute later. *Idiot. I've got u.*

"Ready?" Henry asked.

"Yeah."

Henry climbed over the seats to get to the front. He turned off the Suburban and pocketed the keys. He pulled two sets of latex gloves from the console and handed a pair to me. Then he grabbed a leather case and a small point-and-shoot camera off the passenger seat. I was still trying to figure out what was in the case when he climbed out. He leaned back in and asked, "You coming?"

"Yeah." I followed him out.

We crossed the street as casually as possible. Henry led the way up the stairs. He pulled on his gloves so I followed suit.

"Keep an eye out." Henry dropped to his knees and opened the case. It was a lock picking kit.

"You were planning this all along, weren't you?" The kit and camera had been carefully set out.

"Yes, but I didn't realize the opportunity would be so soon." He wrestled with the lock for what felt like several minutes, then there was a small click as it tumbled open.

I walked in to Laurel's apartment. For the second time that day, I felt like an intruder. But this was much worse than Robin's side of the house. Here, it smelled like cedar and boot oil, soap and salt. The smell invoked a visceral response. I sucked in deep lungfuls of it and hated myself. Laurel's apartment was clearly her sanctuary. It was a bit of a shotgun place. The small front room opened into a center room. The walls were painted in unapologetic, contrasting colors. Blue, olive, mustard. Bookcases lined the wall to my left. The books weren't perfect, rather they were cultivated. Newer volumes were shelved with worn, faded texts. The titles seemed to be arranged according to a system other than the alphabet.

To my right was a desk next to a large window. It was an oak behemoth. Henry went straight to it. He took a photo before he started sorting through papers.

"Make sure you leave it the way you found it," I said.

"I already took a picture for continuity. Do you think I'm a complete idiot?"

I chose not to answer. "I'm going to check the rest of the place."

"Good. Don't forget to pay attention to your phone." He spread out some documents and photographed each of them in succession.

I left him to the desk and continued into the center room. There was a TV and a couch. The couch was stark mid century; the frame was solid wood. The walls were almost bare except for a few choice pieces of art. Her taste was impeccable. Somehow that made it worse. The space was exactly as I would have imagined it. It seemed that she hadn't lied about herself. She was exactly who she had told me she was. The only lie she told was how she felt about me, what her intentions were.

Two doorways led out of the room. One to the kitchen, which led to the back patio. The other was a hallway that ended in her bedroom. I went there first. The bed was made in a half-assed sort of way. There was a pile of books on her bedside table. They were mostly worn books, well loved. Except the top book. It was a new copy of *Nightwood.*

The top of her dresser held a variety of items. A glass bowl with a handful of change, a few collar stays, a silver lighter. Two polished wooden boxes were roughly aligned with the back edge of the dresser. I opened the shorter one and found designer sunglasses. The other box was a valet. It held neatly arranged cuff links and tie clips. I lifted out the velvet insert and found jewelry. It was tossed in like an afterthought. The gold chains were tangled. The jeweled pendants piled haphazardly. A pair of pearl earrings were set in the corner. The back was missing from one of them. I replaced the shelf with the cuff links and closed the valet.

Her drawers mostly held clothing. No surprise there. Half of the top drawer was partitioned off for dozens of slim silk and wool ties. The other half held two empty gun holsters. One was a soft leather shoulder holster. The other was small and looked like it would slide inside a waistband. I shut the drawer.

The clothes she had worn last night were tossed toward the closet, but they hadn't made it all the way. I glanced in the closet. Shoes were lined up along the wall. Her oxfords and boots had been recently shined. That explained the smell of oil when we came in. Her clothes were hung military straight. Suits and pressed dress shirts. Chinos arranged by color. Police uniforms were at the back, still in their dry cleaner plastic. I stood there for an eternity, just staring at the perfect blue polyester. One was clearly a dress uniform of some sort. The tie and belt were meticulously hung with it. Somehow that seemed like the most offensive thing I could have found.

She had told me—convincingly—that her parents were overbearing, controlling, oppressive. Yet, she had joined their beloved police force. Those uniforms were cared for, loved. She wasn't just a cop. She was proud of it.

I stumbled back into the bedroom. I almost tripped on the discarded pile of clothes. There were the shorts I had unbuttoned. There were the perfectly tight underwear that she had left on while I fucked her. I took long, shallow breaths as I tried to erase the memory. It didn't work. I could still feel her moans against my lips. I still felt the soreness of bruises on my shoulders and arms. I could still feel the hot clench of muscles when she asked me to stay inside her.

I had been wrong when I thought breaking in here was a violation. This place was the violation. What she had done to me was a violation. I rushed back to the front of the apartment. Henry had given up on the papers and was rummaging through the drawers.

"Hey, you find anything?" he asked.

"No. I…I don't think I can be in here."

"Whoa, hey. Chill out, okay?"

I'd fallen for a woman who had lied about everything. Nothing. Everything that mattered. And Henry wanted me to chill out?

"I can't. I need to go outside."

"I'll be faster if you help me."

"Believe me, I'll only slow you down. Give me the keys." I held out my hand.

Henry looked annoyed but he handed over the keys. "Watch the street and pay attention to your cell phone."

"Fine. I hope you find what you're looking for."

Nate texted periodic updates on locations. He only sent cross streets so I knew how far away they were. Henry texted every twenty or so to make sure he was in the clear.

I studied the street and saw nothing. The apocalypse could have broken out in front of me and I wouldn't have noticed a damn thing. The smell of her clung to me. I knew it was imaginary, but I couldn't seem to rid myself of it. I glanced at Laurel's windows but didn't see any movement. Henry was a pro. Of course he wasn't visible.

Laurel's vintage truck was parked in front of the building. Once I noticed it, I couldn't look away. I remembered the rumble of the engine and pop of the driver's door opening. It felt so familiar.

As I watched the truck, a terrible idea started to form. Once it was there, it stayed. I gave up fighting after a minute and called Henry.

"Do I need to book it?"

"No. You're still in the clear. They are up off Auburn Boulevard near Carmichael."

"On Orange Grove?"

That was uncanny. "Yeah. You're really good at this game."

"They are at the FBI field office."

I took a deep cleansing breath and didn't feel cleansed at all. "Any chance you have a Slim Jim in here?"

Henry chuckled. "Aren't you the little risk taker?"

"Fuck you."

"Calm down. In the back there are a few bags of gear. The black tool bag should have one. Let me know when you find it and I'll keep an eye on the street until you're in."

"Just a sec." I set down the phone and climbed to the back. The tool bag was on the bottom of Henry's gear pile. I hauled it onto the seat next to me. The Slim Jim was tucked along the side with a crowbar. I pulled it out and tossed the tool bag in the back. When I picked up the phone again, Henry was whistling *Jeopardy!* music. "Got it. Are you watching my back?"

"Yep. Just be cool and make it look like you belong. And open the passenger door so that no one can see you from the street."

I let myself out and jogged across the street. I was sweating and it wasn't from the heat. This was stupid. I glanced up and down the sidewalk. It was empty. This stretch of T Street was residential. Most of the tenants were at work. I pulled on another pair of gloves.

I slid the Slim Jim down the window, wriggled it into place, and failed to catch the lock. It took me three tries to get it, but then the lock popped up. I opened the door and jumped in.

I put the phone back to my ear. "I'm in. You can go back to ransacking."

"There is no ransacking. I'm a goddamn artist." He hung up.

The inside of the truck was pretty spare. The seats and dash were clean. The glove box held the usual contents. Registration for Laurel Kallen. Insurance for Laurel Kallen. Under that was a slim wallet. I opened it and found driver's licenses for Laurel Collins, Laurel Thompson, and Laurel Greensburg. There were passports to match two of the aliases. There was also a bag of what appeared to be cocaine. And another of weed. Fascinating. I snapped cell phone photos of everything.

There was a small bench seat in back. It was littered with clothing that clearly didn't belong to Laurel. There was a backpack that was not her style and a briefcase that looked more her speed. I took photos of the backseat with my phone before touching anything. Then I started in on the briefcase. It was a tragic fucking goldmine. My police file was disturbing in its breadth. The file on Nathan Xiao was sparse in comparison, but damning nonetheless.

I called Henry. "I need your camera."

"Bring whatever you have up here and I'll take photos. You're too exposed."

"Okay. I'll be up in a minute."

He hung up on me again. I glanced in the backpack and found more files. I flipped the first one open. Jerome St. Maris. Great, because I so wanted to be lumped in with that guy. My phone rang again. I swiped without looking.

"I told you, I'm coming up," I said.

"Huh? Never mind. They're heading back toward midtown," Nate said.

"Fuck. How long do we have?"

"Fifteen, twenty minutes. Get your asses out of there."

"On it."

I grabbed the briefcase and the backpack. There wasn't time to finish searching. I vaulted up the stairs two at a time and let myself into Laurel's apartment.

"Cash?" Henry called.

"Yeah. We have fifteen minutes. Give me your camera."

"Dammit." Henry joined me at the desk.

I opened the briefcase and laid open my file. Henry started taking pictures. He cursed at each page. We had finished mine and Nate's files when my phone rang again. It was Nate.

"We're off the freeway. They are definitely headed back to her place. Are you out?"

"Shit. No."

"Get the fuck out."

"Okay." I hung up. "We need to go. Is everything back in its place up here?"

Henry shook his head. "Give me two minutes. Go put that shit back in the truck."

"But we haven't finished."

"We don't have time. Go."

I gathered the files and put them back in the briefcase in the order I'd found them.

Henry went back toward Laurel's bedroom. I let myself out and ran down to the truck. I positioned the bags among the shit in the backseat, then checked my photos to make sure they were in the same spot. I grabbed the Slim Jim, locked and slammed the door closed. Behind me, there was pounding on the stairs as Henry sprinted down them. So much for being unobtrusive.

We climbed in the Suburban and started scanning the street. Three minutes later, we could see the black Impala approaching us. It stopped outside Laurel's apartment. She got out, then leaned back in to say something. When she closed the door, she was smiling at whatever he had said. He waited until she opened her front door and waved at him, then he drove off.

Henry started the SUV and pulled onto the street. "Call Nate. Tell him to stay and watch Kallen's place. If that fed hasn't spotted the tail yet, he will soon. We can follow him."

I did as Henry asked. I really didn't want to be in this car anymore, but I didn't have much of a choice. What I really wanted was to look at those photos and see what was in my file. No, that wasn't right either. I wanted to go home and curl up with my cat and pretend none of this was happening. But that wasn't an option either.

"Did you look in the backpack at all?"

"I glanced. It had a file on Jerome St. Maris. I assume the rest were on his buddies."

"So you're not her only focus?"

"I guess not."

The Impala got back on 99 and headed south. He got off in Elk Grove and turned into a neighborhood. When he turned into a driveway, Henry continued on. I turned and watched him pull into the garage.

"Looks like Mr. FBI is home for the evening," I said.

"Or home for a while at least." Henry parked at the curb far enough away that we wouldn't be obvious, but close enough that we could sort of see what was going on with the help of his big ass camera lens. Henry climbed into the backseat and got comfortable with his camera.

"What's the plan? Just watch him and see if he stays?"

"It's early still. I don't trust that he's going to stay home."

"I'm hungry," I said.

"That sucks."

"Seriously. Do you have any food in here?"

"No. But there's water." Henry pointed at one of his bags.

"You brought latex gloves, two cameras, a bag of tools, a Slim Jim, a lock pick kit, but no food?" Clearly, I picked the wrong guy to be on my team. Nate would have brought snacks.

"Three cameras. And all of my equipment makes perfect sense."

"Food makes sense."

Henry shrugged and continued watching the FBI guy's house.

I pulled out my phone and did a search for restaurants. We were a quarter mile from a strip mall. Suburbia was a fascinating place.

"There's a deli in walking distance. I'm going for sandwiches. You want something?"

"No, you're not. What if he leaves while you're gone?"

"We will figure it out. It's six o'clock. He's probably eating dinner like a normal person. I, however, haven't eaten all day. Do you want a sandwich or not?"

"Veggie, please. Munster or provolone. No mustard or vinegar. And chips. Salt and pepper, if they have them." Veggie sandwich with no mustard? This man had something wrong with him. He may as well have requested a mayo and lettuce on white bread.

"Call me if there's movement." I let myself out and walked in the opposite direction of Mr. FBI's house. I had a strong suspicion that he would recognize me if he saw me.

The neighborhood ended at a big main street. I consulted my phone, then turned right. The strip mall was just around the corner. When I got there, it was hard to miss the deli. It was the only non-corporate business in the entire strip. That had to be a good sign. I went in and got Henry's lame ass sandwich. I felt judged. Then I ordered mine and redeemed myself. I paid in cash, obviously. Then again, I was a drug dealer. I always paid in cash.

When I was walking back, my phone rang. Shit. I glanced at the readout. I was expecting Henry and a shit storm. Instead, I saw Laurel's name and had a mini panic attack. I debated answering it or letting it go to voice mail. I was paralyzed by the decision. It went to voice mail all on its own before I could decide. I picked up the pace. Henry would know what to do.

The Suburban was right where I left it. Not that I was surprised. I climbed in and handed Henry his paper wrapped joke. He set it down without taking his eyes off the house.

"Thanks. No movement while you were gone."

"Laurel called me."

"What?" Henry finally turned away from the house. "Did you answer? What did she say?"

"I didn't answer. She left a voice mail."

"Did you listen to it?"

"No." I pulled out the phone and hit the voice mail.

"Hey, Cash. This is Laurel. Sorry for the note this morning. I had a super awesome, fantastic time with you. I'd love to go out again. I'll be waiting by the phone, hoping your voice mail allows for monologues." She laughed at her joke. "Anyway. Call me."

Time had been limping along until Laurel had shown up on my doorstep the night before. And then it stopped. It was as if I'd been walking through water all day. Fighting to keep moving. I couldn't reconcile the woman I'd been with last night with the woman I'd been investigating all afternoon. But at the sound of her voice, her perfect words, it all coalesced. That voice mail had been tailored to me, to us. That voice mail was bait. Laid to make the taker mad.

Time began to move again. I would not be her prey anymore.

"Well?" Henry asked.

"She wants to meet."

"What do you want to do?"

I tossed the phone onto the seat and picked up my sandwich. "I want to eat my sandwich. Then I'm going to read all her reports on me. Then we're going to find a way to take this bitch down."

"That's my boy."

CHAPTER TWENTY-FOUR

Henry's laptop was frustratingly small. Each photo needed to be enlarged, clicked, dragged to be read properly. We had been sitting outside of Mr. FBI's house for two hours. I'd made my way through three-quarters of Laurel's reports. They were uninteresting. The first few were detailed. It was strange to read about myself in the third person. Some time around our barbecue, the reports shifted. She included less detail. The report after Nate was attacked was rich with information about Jerome, but included almost nothing about me. Nate was only a single line. I wanted to believe it was intentional, but that would be naïve. She didn't care about me. She wasn't protecting me. She had simply found a better target.

Every time my resolve weakened, I replayed the voice mail in my mind. It became a temporary obsession. When my focus wandered, that's where it went. "Super awesome, fantastic…hoping your voice mail allows for monologues."

The final report was from yesterday afternoon. Henry was mentioned by name for the first time. He wasn't going to like that. But everything about him in the report was speculation. It didn't seem that she had made the connection between him and the files Nate had showed her. That was good. Her case against all of us was weak as hell. No wonder she had called me back. No wonder she had fucked me. What better way to gain my trust?

It wasn't a betrayal. It was her intention all along. You couldn't betray someone you didn't care for. She didn't care about me. "Super awesome, fantastic…" It was cultivated.

"You making any headway?" Henry asked.

"I finished reading the reports. She doesn't have much of a case."

"Good. That's good."

"She mentioned your name in the last one, though."

"What?" He seemed pissed.

"Don't worry. She doesn't have shit on you."

"Let me see." Henry rolled over the seat. "You watch for a while."

I climbed into his vacated spot and picked up the camera. Mr. FBI was having a very boring night. Or maybe it just looked that way from outside his very boring house. Every once in a while, someone would walk by one of the windows upstairs. It looked like he had a wife and two kids, maybe three. But that assumption was based purely on the height of the little ones running around upstairs. This was going to be a long night.

It took Henry half the time it took me to read the reports. He was skimming for information about himself. Nice to know he cared about Nate and me. Every so often he would make an angry exclamation, but he mostly kept it quiet.

"You told her about me." Technically, Nate had forced my hand. But I didn't think Henry would care about technically. And there was no way I was going to throw Nate on Henry's mercy.

"I didn't know she was a fucking cop." I couldn't be blamed for that shit.

"But you told her about me."

"Yeah, well you're the one who gave her your name."

He went back to pouting and reading the reports. When he finished, he was barely keeping it together. I would have offered comfort, but I didn't have any.

"Call her."

"And say what?" I asked.

"Tell her you want to meet."

"And then what?" This was clearly not a well thought out plan.

"We're going to kill her."

"What?" I turned and stared at him. That was a leap. He wanted to kill her?

"Listen, I know it's not your style or scene or whatever, but this makes it all go away," he said like it was the most rational course of action.

"No." I couldn't believe we were having this conversation.

"Come on, man. She used you. She's a cop. It's not like any of it was real."

I hated that he was right. About being used, not about killing Laurel. "We don't kill people. That's not how we operate. Hell, we don't even beat people up. We're drug dealers. It doesn't mean we're violent."

"You don't have to be the one to kill her." His tone suggested that I was a timid child who needed to be coached. As if he wasn't discussing murder. "I'll handle it. All you have to do is make the call." Yeah, no big deal. Just a murder call.

"It's not happening. Let it go."

"Cash—"

"No, that's final. It's not up for discussion. It's not on the table. It's not a fucking option. We are not killing anyone. So fucking drop it." That pretty much covered it.

"Fine." He was disgusted. "What do you propose then?"

"I don't know."

"That's fucking helpful."

"This situation is delicate. We can't just fix it. It's not going to easily go away." As if killing someone was easy. Even that plan had holes everywhere. Who did he think the cops were going to look at when Laurel turned up dead? It wasn't going to be perfect Henry, the upstanding sheriff. It was going to be my ass. Actually, he was probably fully aware of that. He didn't want me to make it out unscathed. He wanted me tied up like a loose end. No wonder it was such a perfect plan for him.

He pouted and ruminated. "Okay, what if we offer her Jerome?"

"We don't have Jerome to offer."

"You said yourself that her case against you is weak. But we both read the reports. She talked a lot about Jerome in the later ones. And you said she had his file."

"But we don't know how strong her case against him is." I was playing devil's advocate. The idea had merit.

"That's what you offer. I'm sure you can provide all of the evidence she needs to nail his ass. It's kind of perfect, actually. Two birds and all that. Get Jerome off our asses and redirect the feds."

"So how do we go about it?"

"Call her. Arrange a date. Once you've got her in person, tell her you know she's a cop and you can help her get Jerome." He made it sound simple.

I would need leverage, but I had it. I was sure the Sac PD would frown on her having slept with me. Plus the golden Kallen clan wouldn't appreciate a story that tarnished them. Of course, Henry didn't need to know all that. I picked up my phone. "Okay."

"Whoa. Hold up. Where are you going to meet her? How do I monitor you to make sure you're safe?" If I didn't have fifteen years of experience with the man, I would have thought he cared. Of course, I did have that experience so I knew he just wanted to control the situation.

"I'll pick a restaurant. You'll go in and get a table next to us. No big deal."

"She's met me. Nate too. She'll know something is up if one of us is there."

"True. Suggestions?" I asked.

"I know a little restaurant just north of Mansion Flats. It's a ramen house. Lots of windows. You know up Sixteenth Street?" I nodded. I knew the area. They were gentrifying, but the neighborhood was still a work in progress. "There's a gym I used to go to across the street. I can go in there and watch. You'll keep your phone on speaker so I can hear your conversation." His answer was a little quick for my taste, but that was Henry. He cased any joint he went into. It probably made him a good cop. It definitely made him a good criminal.

"Works for me." I pulled up Laurel's name and hit call before I could change my mind. It also didn't give me time to prepare myself. That was stupid.

"Hey." Laurel's voice was smooth and familiar in all the wrong ways.

"Hey." Even that was a struggle to get out.

"What are you up to?" she asked. My mind went blank. "Cash?" Henry smacked my arm.

"Yeah?"

"What's up?"

"Oh, you know. Living the dream."

She laughed. "What are you up to tonight?"

"Taking you out to dinner?"

"I like where this is going."

"There's a little restaurant up Sixteenth. Ramen house. I've been wanting to check it out."

"Perfect."

"I'll text you the address. Meet me in thirty?"

"I'll be there."

"Cool."

After we hung up, I realized my entire body was shaking. I was tired of Henry seeing my weakness, so I willed it away.

"Good job." Henry nodded approvingly. "I just texted Nate and told him to meet me at the gym. He will have plenty of time to get in place."

"If this goes south, make sure Nate gets out of there."

"Of course," Henry said. He pulled up Yelp and read the address for me to text Laurel. I did.

We climbed back into the front seat and headed back to midtown. This had to be a better plan than sitting in a suburban neighborhood and staking out an FBI agent. As Henry drove, I tried to prepare myself. I tried to come up with the right things to say. Should I out her right away? Or maybe bring up Jerome and some big deal I had with him to entice her? Quickly, I realized there was no way to plan this. I'd just have to wing it and hope for the best. The alternative wasn't an option. It wasn't just my ass. It was Nate's and Clive's. Henry's too, I guessed. This situation was fucked, but I wasn't going to let Henry commit a murder. That was extreme. Henry talked big, but he wasn't great at acknowledging anything beyond fact and logic. But the guilt would break him. I hoped.

Not that Henry's suggestion had endeared him to me. Whatever happened, however this turned out, I wasn't going to be working with him anymore. He had jumped to the fast option too easily. And he had been far too comfortable with suggesting that we kill someone. It was a little frightening.

I wasn't thinking about the fact that it was Laurel he wanted to kill. I was doing my best to not think of Laurel at all. Thinking about her hurt. I didn't want pain or anger to alter my judgment. I had to be cold and manipulative.

We merged onto 50. Henry took the 16th Street exit. We were getting closer. This was wrong. Our entire plan was idiotic. I should have called Nate and gotten his opinion. Murder boy obviously wasn't thinking with a clear head. Maybe Nate would have had a better idea. I definitely should have called Clive. I should have called him hours ago. But I didn't want to worry him, and I didn't want to talk to him until I had something substantial to say. I knew Henry wouldn't want to wait while I called them. Maybe that was why this felt uncomfortable.

I almost told Henry to stop the car. I almost told him twenty times. We worked our way up the alphabet. Each turn we didn't take felt like a missed opportunity. Each time, I lost my nerve. I didn't have a decent reason other than this felt wrong. Henry didn't go in for feelings.

We crossed under the last set of train tracks bordering midtown. The buildings here were gorgeous brick warehouses. They had become obsolete in the last half a century as the train station became larger. Newer, uglier warehouses spread west where real estate was cheaper and hipsters weren't interested in the architecture. Henry turned left at one of the side streets. The warehouses on either side still had loading docks, but the interiors had clearly been gutted. What would this be in a year or five? Pretty boutiques that sold arts and crafts under the guise of art. Something resembling culture, but too cheap to follow through.

We took another turn and the warehouses looked less renovated. Henry's plan was looking less and less thought out. Why had I agreed to it? I realized that I didn't have to follow Henry's plan. I didn't have to tell Laurel anything. Suddenly, it felt easy. I would go in the restaurant, share a meal with the woman, and that was that. I could give Henry multitudes of reasons why I had backed off. It didn't matter. It was a stall tactic.

I stretched out and enjoyed the last few blocks of our drive. I had a plan. A non-murder plan.

CHAPTER TWENTY-FIVE

Henry pulled into a parking lot next to a dark building. I didn't see any restaurant. Or a gym. I saw two abandoned warehouses and asphalt that hadn't been attended in years.

"Where is the restaurant?" I asked. It was a dumb question.

Henry sighed. Then he clocked me. Harder than I'd ever been hit before. It was the kind of blow that takes little pockets of your vision and turns them black and sparkly. I shook my head, but that made things spin. I was still reeling from the blow when he grabbed my hands and shoved them up. He pulled the zip tie closed around my wrists and the grip handle above the door before I figured out that he was restraining me. The zip tie was tight. Cutting off circulation tight.

"I'm sorry. It didn't need to be this way," Henry said.

"What the fuck? Let me go, goddammit." I pulled at the zip tie, but it only dug into my flesh. "What the fuck, man? What are you doing?"

"It's okay. I'm going to take care of it."

I started yelling, which was probably stupid. He clocked me again. I closed my eyes against the beating in my skull and concentrated on not vomiting.

"Don't bother screaming. No one can hear you. And if they do hear you and come running, I'll have to kill you too. So calm the fuck down."

I calmed the fuck down. Or I stopped yelling. Same thing to him, I guess. "Please don't do this."

Henry climbed into the backseat and rummaged through his gear. "I know it sucks. But you'll thank me later. I promise."

"It's not about me, Henry. It's about you. You're my friend. I can't let you become a murderer." It was a lie, but it sounded good. If he let me go, I was going to thoroughly kick his ass.

"It's okay. I can do this for you." How kind of him.

"But I don't want you to do it for me." I tried to pull on the zip tie again, but it got me nowhere.

"That's what you think now. Trust me. This is for the best." He clapped a hand on my shoulder and climbed back in the front seat. "I'll be back. You'll be okay. We will be okay."

And he got out of the car.

I yanked and twisted at my bonds. Henry walked along the side of the building we were parked next to, then disappeared around the corner. He was holding a handgun at his side.

"Fucking douchebag motherfucker. I'm going to kill you," I said. But no one was there to hear me.

What if he came back and decided to kill me for good measure? What if he offed Nate too? Nate could have been walking into a trap. I needed to warn him. And Laurel.

Fucking Laurel. I hated her. And I might have loved her. Even if I did hate her, I couldn't let Henry kill her. Which may or may not have had to do with maybe loving her. I tried to hold on to the hate, which was potent. Maybe it would make our problems go away like Henry said.

No. I couldn't let her die. I could hate her alive just fine.

I needed to get out of here. My wrists were already bloody and the zip tie wasn't giving. Maybe Nate would see the Suburban. Maybe her FBI buddies were following her. But maybe wasn't enough. I needed to call Nate. But that was hard with my hands bound above my head and my phone in my pocket.

Unless I could get my phone to call Nate.

"Hey, Siri, text Nate Xiao." I waited to see if she could hear me. There was a muffled tone of acquiescence.

"Okay. What would you like to say to Nate Xiao?" Siri asked. I fucking loved Siri.

"I'm tied in Henry's car and he's going to kill Laurel. Help me." I tried to speak clearly. Siri wasn't great under ideal circumstances. This was not an ideal circumstance.

"You're saying, 'I'm tried in Henry's carb and his going to kill Laurie. Help me.' Ready to send it?"

Close enough. "Yes."

"Okay, I'll send it."

That was anticlimactic. I looked at my worn wrists. Blood was smeared on the zip tie and the grip handle. I wondered if I could pull the handle out. I tried twisting and pulling. The grip didn't budge, and my wrists screamed in protest.

My phone vibrated. Oh, God. It was Nate. It had to be.

"Hey, Siri, read my text." The tone sounded again.

"Nate sent you two messages. Nate said 'Where are you? I'm going to kick that motherfucker's ass.' Would you like to reply?"

"Yes."

"Okay. Go ahead."

"We are off Sixteenth Street by some abandoned warehouses. It's on the left after you go under the bridge."

Siri repeated the message back to me and sent it. Nate needed to hurry. Henry wouldn't drag this out.

I tried to curl my fingers around the grip and pull, but it didn't give at all. I kicked the underside of the dash. It didn't help with my predicament, but it made me feel better.

I heard the thump of a car door and twisted around. Nate's car was behind me. He frantically tried all of the doors, but didn't get lucky until he hit the driver's side.

"That was fast," I said when he opened the door.

"I was already here. I followed Laurel. Henry told me to go home, but I don't work for him."

"That little bitch told me you were meeting us."

"I'm going to kill him. Metaphorically because I'm not a fucking psycho," Nate said.

"I'll help. Cut me loose."

Nate climbed in and dug through Henry's shit until he found a knife.

"Christ, what did he do to you?" Nate leaned over me and attempted to work the knife between my wrists and the zip tie. He seemed very distracted by the state of my face.

"He hit me because he's an asshole." I didn't have time for this. "I don't care if you cut me. Just get this shit off."

Nate shoved the knife in and pulled up. The tie snapped. "Are you okay?" He tossed the knife on the floor and tried to take my hands. My palm was bleeding from the knife, but I didn't care.

"I will be. I have to go stop him." I took off my seat belt and opened the door.

"Wait. Do you have a weapon? A plan?"

"No. I'm going to kick him in the balls."

"Just hold up a sec." Nate climbed into the backseat. He came back with a crowbar.

I took it. "Thanks. See if you can find another gun. I'm going."

"Cash, wait."

"Nope." I hopped out and took off running in the direction Henry had disappeared in. When I rounded the corner, no one was there. I sprinted to the next corner of the building. Nothing. More abandoned buildings. They could have been anywhere. I stopped and bent over, gasping. Running was hard. I closed my eyes and listened.

"Cash," Nate whisper shouted.

I turned and saw him stopped halfway down the building. He nodded at an alcove. I jogged back. There was a door that had been kicked in. Now that I was listening for it, I could hear voices. I edged closer and looked inside. Henry and Laurel were against a far wall, about twenty feet away. She was on her knees with her hands laced behind her head. She looked pissed. Henry was standing over her with his handgun. He didn't look angry. He looked fucking crazy.

"What do they know? That's all you need to tell me." He put the gun to her temple. "Just tell me what they know." His jaw was clenched, his tone desperate.

Laurel stared into his eyes. "I already told you. It's in the reports you read." She was admirably calm.

Nate and I inched back from the doorway.

"He's totally lost it," Nate said.

"You think?"

"What do you want to do?"

"Distract him. Separate them."

"Solid plan," Nate said. I doubted his sincerity.

"Suggestions?" I asked.

"Not really. I'll try to get on the other side of him and get him to look at me. I can go behind that excuse for a wall." He pointed to a wall perpendicular to the doorway. It had been partially demolished, but enough of it was standing to get him most of the way across the room. "Once I distract him, you get her out of there."

"And what about you?"

Nate shrugged. "I don't know. Hit him in the head with that thing when you get close." He nodded at the crowbar. "I can run."

"Okay." Yep. We so had this. We weren't acting rashly.

Nate crept forward and slid to the other side of the wall. I risked another look. Laurel was staring at the place where Nate had disappeared. She had seen him. Good.

"What are you looking at, bitch? Look at me." Henry grabbed Laurel's chin and forced her to look at his face. She smiled. "What the fuck are you smiling at?"

"Why do you have such trust issues? Did your parents not tell you about Santa until after puberty? Oh, or maybe your prom date stood you up for another boy?"

"Don't get cute with me."

"I've never really been able to nail cute. On occasion, sweet. Maybe pretty when I was a kid. But cute wasn't in my wheelhouse."

Henry punched her in the mouth.

"Fuck." Laurel spit some blood. "Well, now I'll never be cute."

Henry pulled back again.

"Henry, hey, man. Where are you?" Nate called.

"Nate?" Henry spun and held out his gun, but there was nothing to aim at.

"I found Cash, but I left her. She doesn't get what needs to be done. Christ, where the fuck are you? This place is a maze."

Henry looked torn. He wanted, needed to believe Nate. But he couldn't leave Laurel unattended.

"Over here, man," Henry shouted.

"Keep talking."

"I'm right here. Toward the door. How did you get back there?" Henry kept up a running commentary. He seemed to be studying the breaks in the walls, listening to the subtle scuff of Nate's feet.

This was the best chance I'd get. His gun was pointed at the floor. Not Laurel's head. Big plus. I took a few long, cautious strides into the room. Laurel stiffened, but stayed in place. He was watching her. I was about five feet from Henry when he heard me and started to spin. I wasn't close enough so I ran the last few steps. He raised the gun as I swung. His shot went wide and he went down. A crowbar to the head was a good deterrent. Henry's gun slid out of his grasp and skittered along the floor. I went to grab it, but Laurel slammed into me and dragged me toward the door.

"You cunt," Henry screamed. "Stop."

I made the mistake of looking back. He had the gun and was leveling it at us. The door was too far away. We weren't going to make it. Laurel shoved me behind the wall Nate had disappeared behind. Shots echoed through the room, but we were safely behind the wall. It looked like the remnants of a hallway. Nate wasn't there. He must have continued farther into the building.

"We need to move," Laurel said.

Henry was shouting. His footsteps as he approached felt menacing.

"Stay low." I ran to the end of the hallway. The wall was destroyed at the end, which would expose us to Henry. I sprinted across it and hoped he wasn't watching. Laurel was right behind me.

We ended up in a room twice the size of the original. Obsolete machines were set at regular intervals. There was a loft that ran the length of the room and around one side. The walls of the loft ended halfway up to the ceiling and the remainder of the space was glassed in. Or was once glassed in. Now, large sections of the glass were missing.

"Up or stay down?" I whispered.

"Up." Laurel pushed me toward the stairs. They made a fair amount of noise, but Henry was still shouting obscenities as he chased us so I didn't think he could hear.

At the top we hunkered down below the wall. I tried to judge where Henry was based on his footsteps. It sounded like he was running around the machines. He shouted to Nate for help. Good. He still thought Nate was on his side.

Laurel reached over and tapped the cell phone in my pocket. She motioned for me to hand it to her. I was relatively certain that doing so would end with me getting arrested. Or at least detained. I was absolutely certain that without help, Henry would kill us both. I unlocked the phone and gave it to her. She held it awkwardly as she typed. I realized that blood was flowing down her arm, pooling in her elbow, dripping on the floor.

I reached over and tried to get a better look, but she shoved me away. Casual gunshot wound. No big deal. This bitch was crazy.

"We need to move," I whispered.

Laurel shot me a death look for making noise, but I motioned to the abandoned furniture strewn around the room and she started moving. At the back of the loft, a series of doorways led to offices. I glanced in one and found that they had windows overlooking the scenic parking lot. Only three of the offices had doors that were still attached. I closed the one closest to the stairs. Laurel started to move away, but I stopped her and dipped my hand in the blood on her forearm. When I smeared it on the closed door and doorknob, she nodded. We went into one of the offices without a door. It had an overturned oak desk that was easily from the forties. It was gorgeous. Behind that, there were a few massive file cabinets. They were at least five feet tall and just as wide. Two were firmly against the wall, but one had been brought in and abandoned. There was about four feet between it and the wall. I squeezed in and crouched down.

Yeah, this was what badass drug dealers did. They hid.

The phone vibrated. Laurel looked at it and swiped it open. It wouldn't unlock for her. I reached over and pressed my thumb to the home button. She typed again. I glanced at the screen.

How much ammo does he have? We'll go in when he is out, the unnamed contact said.

Those assholes were waiting?

"How long have they been outside?" I asked.

Laurel shot me a look. My look was better, though. "Since I got here. They were tailing me the whole time."

"And they didn't intervene when he had you at gunpoint?"

"Why would they?" She seemed confused by the question.

"Because they're fucking cops. And you're a fucking cop. And generally, cops don't let their buddies get shot."

"And blow the entire operation?" She asked like I was stupid. "I was fine."

"Yeah, that bullet wound looks just fine to me."

"I can handle it," Laurel said.

"Did you tell them you were hit?" Apparently, that was another dumb question. My second grade teacher had definitely lied about the nature of those. "Tell them."

"No."

I reached over and tried to take the phone, but she pulled it away. So I grabbed her upper arm next to the bullet wound and squeezed. Just a little. Laurel gasped. I took the phone.

Laurel has been hit. Gunshot to the upper arm. Take Henry out.

"They can't risk it. We're fine. Tell them we're fine."

The phone vibrated. *Let us speak to Kallen.*

I gave her back the phone. "Here, Kallen." I may have sneered when I said her name. Maybe.

Laurel went back to texting. She was operating pretty well one-handed.

"What do we need to do to get them to come in?" I asked.

"Waste his bullets or flush him out."

That I could do. "Stay here." I backed out of the space.

"No." Laurel tried to grab me, but I pushed her back.

I went back out to the loft proper. Henry had stopped muttering curses. I found a broken section of window and looked down. He was working through the room in a grid. There were two doors leading outside in addition to the one we had come through. The outside doors had boxes and shit stacked in front of them. It looked like the shit had been there a while. No wonder he was still searching. He knew we hadn't left.

I looked around for something to throw. Most of it was furniture, which wouldn't help me. I flipped open a box and found rat droppings. Lovely. I tried another. Same thing. One of the desks had an open drawer. I looked inside. Machine parts of some sort. Each was about the size of my fist. They would do. I grabbed a handful and went back to the window. When Henry was facing away, I chucked one of the pieces of metal at the far wall. Henry spun and pointed his gun, but didn't shoot. Dammit. Why was he being cautious now of all times?

Henry hurried over to where the metal had sounded from. He searched the area again. I threw another piece of metal. Again, he aimed and approached, but didn't fire. The third time, he fired. But not at the noise. He fired twice at the loft. And started running for the stairs. Shit.

I sprinted to the opposite wall, opened the bloody door and closed it loudly, then ran back to the room where Laurel was hiding. I squeezed in and crouched down.

Laurel gave me a very sarcastic thumbs-up and mouthed "good job."

I gave her my most withering look. It accomplished a lot. She shook her head and went back to typing. Henry made quick work of ransacking the decoy room. Then he moved on to the next office. It was right next door to us.

I was pretty sure this was the ideal moment for Laurel's friends to come in. But there was no noise downstairs. No shouts, no indication that they had entered the building. Cops were assholes.

Henry finished the second office and entered ours. Laurel and I went completely still. We heard him shove the desk. He tipped over one, two of the file cabinets.

Laurel waved at me and mimicked pushing the cabinet we were behind. That seemed like a decent idea. I nodded. When we could hear him grunting and the cabinet began to shift, we both pushed hard. The cabinet fell. I didn't look to see where it landed. Laurel vaulted over the cabinet and ran for the door. I followed her.

Henry shouted some more obscenities and squeezed off two more shots. We sprinted down the stairs. We were about halfway down when there was a crash upstairs. He must have pushed the cabinet off himself.

Laurel turned back down the hallway we had come in from. I could see the pale light from the parking lot.

"Wait." I slowed down. "Nate is still in here."

"No, he's outside." Laurel turned back and grabbed my shirt to drag me with her. "Hurry."

The moment we were out, a group of uniformed officers ran in. Another group of officers surrounded us and led us toward a circle of vehicles.

"She's been shot. Help her," I told them. Through the crush of bodies, I caught sight of Nate. He was standing next to a uniformed police officer. Good. I was glad she hadn't lied about that. The officer turned Nate toward one of the police cruisers and I realized that he was in handcuffs. "What the fuck?"

Two of the men walking with me closed in. One of them made sure I wasn't going to run while the other slapped handcuffs on me. I looked over to Laurel. She held my gaze as the officer frisked me. There was something hard in her gaze, a condemnation. One of the officers carefully turned her toward the waiting ambulance. At the last moment, the look turned to pity and then an apology and then she was gone.

CHAPTER TWENTY-SIX

They led me to a patrol car and guided me into it. Sitting in cuffs on a hard plastic seat is not comfortable. In fact, it's a little painful. I was careful to pay my share of taxes. I wondered why a larger share of that didn't go toward better patrol car seats. Then I thought about why the seats were plastic. How many people had vomited or urinated where I was currently sitting?

I tried to see if Nate was still outside or if he had been put in a car too. It was impossible to pick out any detail. Night had finished falling. The sporadic lights in the parking lot did little to counteract the patriotic swirls from the police cars and ambulance and inexplicable fire truck. I found that if I picked a spot and stared, the lights and chaos would fade away and detail would emerge. I stared at the back of the ambulance Laurel had been led to. She was sitting on the gurney. An older guy in a suit was leaning in to talk to her. I couldn't glean anything from their posture.

The building we had been in was filled with cops now. I could see silhouettes and movement inside. They were still searching. I looked up at the loft windows and saw the sweep of flashlights. Someone was moving on the roof. I stared hard at the familiar figure. It was Henry. Those assholes were searching the building and he had climbed to the roof. He sprinted to the edge and jumped. My heart stopped. I didn't know in that moment if I wanted him to fall or to make it. But then he landed hard on the next building. His legs were still hanging over the edge, but then he rolled and collapsed on the roof.

If I was going down, that fucker was too.

"Hey," I shouted at the cops outside the cruiser. "Hey, you assholes. He's gone." They looked at me and turned away. "Brewer is on the fucking roof. Go get him, goddammit." I spent a fruitless five minutes yelling at them. In that time, Henry picked himself up and ran toward the opposite side of the building. He climbed over the side and disappeared from view.

This day just kept getting more awesome.

I lost track of time waiting in the patrol car. It could have been twenty minutes. It could have been an hour. My wrists stung every time I moved. They had scabbed over for the most part, but I could still feel the slow drip of blood cooling in my palm. Good, I really wanted to add my bodily fluids to the multitudes deposited here. The muscles in my arms were sore. My shoulders started to burn from the awkward angle they were held in. My face throbbed with every heartbeat. Good. I was still alive. I would have traded a lot for one of the new ice packs sitting in my freezer.

Finally, a uniformed cop climbed in the front seat. He looked about twelve. I was pretty sure he wasn't old enough to drive, let alone join the police force. I debated telling him Henry had gotten away because they were still searching. But then I decided not to. He was gone. They wouldn't find him anytime soon.

We pulled out of the parking lot. He turned onto 12th Street, then I Street. I was headed to County. Big surprise. When we approached, I was surprised for the first time at how tall the county jail was. Usually, it blended into the other buildings downtown. Of course I hadn't noticed it. The almost white, curved lines were nondescript in every way.

My booking took an hour. They asked me a slew of questions that should have been easy, but weren't. I knew my name and date of birth and gang involvement—none, thank you. I nailed the question about my sexuality. Health was a hot mess. I hadn't been to a doctor since I was in college. But the institution happily provided a medical exam. I was pleased that I had resisted every chance to get a tattoo. With the exception of a few small scars, I had no identifying marks. Fingerprinting was still solidly in the twentieth century. My fingertips were inked and rolled over a piece of actual card stock. I was sure my mug shot was laughable. My hair was still perfect, but I could still feel the thrum of blood turning to bruises. The photos had to be a series of red and purple. I was given my very own orange jumpsuit. Be still, my beating heart. For the first time since I was in middle school, I was wearing women's underwear. That, more than anything, pissed me off.

When the whole show was over, I was given time to call Clive. I was sure Nate would call him too. It's not like Nate could call his mother. Even if she were inclined to post bail instead of kill him, she was too far away.

"Hey, Clive," I said when we were finally connected.

"Why the fuck are you calling me from Sacramento County Jail?"

"It's not for the ambiance, I'll tell you that."

"Goddammit, Cash." He was scared. Not the time for jokes.

"I was arrested. I believe Nate was too. We need a lawyer. I've got one on retainer. Her name is Joan Kent. Her number is in your phone and her card is in the address book on your desk. Call her. Tonight. Right now. I don't think Nate and I can have the same lawyer, so ask Kent for a recommendation for Nate."

"What else can I do?"

"Call Robin and have Andy take care of Nickels this weekend. Andy already thinks I'm out of town. Just tell her I'll be gone longer than expected."

"I can do that."

"And if you see Henry, punch him in the face." If he saw Henry, there were a lot of things I wanted him to do. Tie him up and sit on him so we could use him for bargaining. Turn him in. Of course, Clive was in El Dorado County, which meant the cops were Henry's colleagues. No telling how they would handle the situation.

"Henry?"

"The fucker turned on me." I wanted to give him more detail, but I was hyper aware that our conversation was being recorded, if not listened to. No matter what, Clive needed a warning. This was the best I could do.

"No. You must have misunderstood. Henry is a good guy."

I took a deep breath and tried not to scream. "He's not. Trust me." That good guy had attempted to execute someone. That good guy had hit me and tied me up. That good guy was a fucking menace. If that was good, I didn't want to be it.

"Okay," Clive said. He didn't believe me. "How long until we can get you out?"

"I don't know when we will be arraigned, but I'm sure the lawyer will be better equipped to answer those questions."

"All right. Stay out of trouble."

"You probably should have told me that yesterday."

He chuckled, but it sounded forced. "I love you."

"Yeah."

My cell was shared with three other lovely women. They were all upstanding just like me. Actually, I was probably the worst on a scale of criminal behavior. Two of them had been arrested for prostitution. Neither of them had hit twenty, and they already seemed broken. The other woman had been arrested for drugs—buying, not selling. She trembled constantly. She didn't need County. She needed rehab. And maybe a hug.

And people wondered why I didn't buy into society. This was society.

That night, I got a clear picture of why people preferred darkness and silence while they slept. The cries I heard were painful, scared. The lights were dimmed, but never off. I couldn't sleep. All I could think about was Clive's analysis of Henry, the good guy. And his analysis of me. Shaky moral compass and all. I had worn my wrists raw to try to save a woman I hated. I picked at the bandages all night. They made me look suicidal. I had hit my friend in the head with a crowbar. I could still feel the vibrations running up my arms from the blow. I had run after a maniac to save a cop. The cops had arrested me. My moral compass wasn't shaky. It just pointed in a different direction than everyone else's. I wasn't lazy. I was stupid for thinking other people might see the world the way I did. O'Connor was right. Good men weren't hard to find. They were nonexistent. Maybe I could have been good if someone was there to shoot me my entire life. What excuse did Henry have?

Before dawn, the lights came on. My cellmates didn't seem to find that odd. We shuffled down to a breakfast that I couldn't eat. At the end of the meal, we were shuffled back to our cells. Sometime after dawn, a guard came to retrieve me.

"Braddock, you're being transferred."

I got off my bed. "Where am I going? Am I being arraigned?"

"You're being transferred into the custody of Sac PD." He seemed bored by the process.

"What does that mean?"

"That you're being transferred." He escorted me back downstairs.

I was put back in cuffs. This time the cuffs were attached to a chain around my waist, which was attached to long cuffs at my ankles. It was better than having my hands behind my back, but not exactly an overall improvement. They put me in a patrol car.

We drove out of midtown, down Freeport Boulevard. The city was starting to wake up. The coffee shops and restaurants were rapidly filling. Joggers and bikers clogged the sidewalks. I didn't understand what all of these people were doing out on a Saturday morning, but that was their business.

At the Sacramento Police Department main building, I was escorted through back hallways and brightly lit corridors and deposited in an interrogation room. My cuffs were removed. Ah, freedom. They left me alone for a while. Which was fantastic. The room was bright, but silent. I put my head down and fell asleep.

The sound of the door opening woke me up. It was the guy I had seen talking to Laurel in the ambulance the night before. He was still wearing the same suit, which made me happy. My night had been long, but so had his.

"Ms. Braddock, we will be in to speak with you soon, but Detective Kallen wanted me to bring you this." He set a large cup of Old Soul coffee on the table along with a foil wrapped breakfast sandwich. Then he left.

I was fully planning on ignoring the gesture. That was a fifteen-dollar breakfast. Not remotely standard for interrogations. I wasn't going to take her peace offering.

But the sandwich was still warm and the coffee smelled really good. It wasn't like I had dignity to bank on. I opened the foil and dug in. Of course she remembered what I liked. It could have been the twelve hours of jail still clinging to me, but that meal was the greatest thing I had ever consumed.

I was nursing the dregs in my cup and wondering when I was going to have decent coffee again when the door opened. It was the same detective with Laurel following him this time. She had been granted the luxury of going home to change clothes. She was wearing slim gray chinos and boots. Her shirt sleeves were cuffed to mid-forearm. The burgundy cloth swelled over her bicep from the bandages underneath. Her necktie was dark and held in place by an intricate tie bar. Her eyes were puffy and bloodshot. Apparently, gunshot wounds only extended to fresh clothes, not sleep.

"Hello again, Ms. Braddock. I'm Detective Reyes. You know Detective Kallen." They sat across from me.

"We're well acquainted." I even managed not to smile when I said it.

Detective Reyes opened the interview by reading my rights. He noted time—it was eleven a.m.—and date. I acknowledged that I understood my rights.

"I'm sorry. We tried to keep them from booking you last night, but—" Laurel stopped herself from elaborating.

Reyes smiled without mirth. "Yes, you'll be pleased to know that Mr. Xiao is here as well. We will do our best to make sure you don't need to stay in County."

"That's so kind of you." I wanted to berate Laurel for letting them arrest me in the first place. The only reason they had caught me was because I had kept her alive. But arresting me had been her endgame all along. I wasn't dumb enough to think one good deed would erase all of those stacked against me. That was on me. I could own my decisions.

"Do you know how difficult it was to get a judge to approve your release to us on a Saturday morning?" Laurel lost her cool for a moment.

"What? Your mom was unavailable?" I asked.

She looked shocked, then scared, then angry all over again.

"We're working very hard to resolve the situation," Reyes said.

"Good. Did you catch Brewer yet?"

They both studied the table. Then Laurel looked up. "Wait. How did you know we didn't catch him?"

"I watched him jump from the roof to the next building." Watching their reactions was fun.

"What? Why didn't you tell someone?" Now, she was pissed? "We have been combing midtown all night."

"I did. I shouted at the officers holding me for a solid five minutes. It's not my fault you guys hire incompetent children with superiority complexes."

"Excuse me." Reyes stood and let himself out.

Laurel and I stared at each other. Alone at last. Well, except for the camera I was sure was recording us and the detectives I was sure were watching us.

"I'm sorry," she said again.

"You should be. You're despicable." I felt that I was being civil as hell. I could have elaborated. Fucking the drug dealer you were supposed to be investigating was sure to be a black mark on her record. But it would also get her pulled off the case. As much as I hated to admit it, I needed her. The guilt she was feeling would improve whatever deal they offered me. Right now, she was my best advocate.

"I wish I could defend myself, but I can't."

"Good. Don't bother."

We sat in silence until Detective Reyes came back. Laurel was working hard to stay angry at me, but she was failing.

"Sorry for the interruption. Thank you for the information." He was being way too nice. I hadn't given them shit yet.

"Cash—" Laurel started.

I cut her off. "I don't think we're on a first name basis, Detective." Okay, I was hurt. Why not be petty too?

Laurel took a deep breath. "Ms. Braddock, this is a mess, but I think we can come to an agreement that will benefit all of us."

"That's super. As soon as my lawyer gets here, I'm sure she can help us work that out." Maybe it was too soon to play the lawyer card. Maybe I should have played it right away.

"Of course. I believe she has already contacted us. I'll go let them know you would like her here," Laurel said. Both detectives stood.

I thought I would feel better when they left me alone. I didn't.

By the time the door opened again, I had given up on sleep. I was hungry again. And I had to pee. My lawyer was the only one who entered. I had only met her a handful of times. She was pocket-sized and everything about her screamed dyke. The sight of her severe haircut and double-breasted suit gave me hope. Joan Kent was formidable.

"Cash, sorry it took so long for me to get here." Kent sat across from me and set a notepad and pen down.

"Not a problem. I appreciate you giving up your Saturday."

"The recording devices have been turned off. We can speak freely."

"Are you representing Nate as well? Do you know how he is doing?"

"I'm not, but I recommended a former colleague to your uncle. I saw her in the lobby. I believe she is meeting with Mr. Xiao right now," Kent said.

"Good. So what can you tell me?"

"They want to offer you a deal."

"That's good, right?"

"Yes. It's actually a great deal." She didn't look like she wanted to tell me what the deal was. What did it mean when your lawyer didn't want to tell you the details of a great deal?

"What is it?"

"I believe we can get them to release you without charges, but they want you to work as an informant," she said. I didn't know how to react to that. "Cash?"

"What would that entail?"

"I'm still working out those details."

"I don't need a commitment ceremony. Just give me an idea."

"You would continue running your business, but you would regularly pass on information to a detective. At times, you might be asked to develop a relationship with someone in order to gain information about their business dealings or an associate's business dealings." Kent still looked uncomfortable. "The agreement is open-ended."

"All of that sounds really good. Why don't you seem happy?"

"I understand that Detective Kallen was investigating you."

"Investigating is a nice word." I didn't want to get into it. I needed time to sort out my anger. Kent waited. "We were dating. That's how she investigated me."

She nodded. "That was the impression I got. Sergeant Ionescu— he is Kallen's superior—would like her to continue as lead on the case. He believes that the relationship you have publicly built will function as a good cover."

"Well, that is just absolutely fantastic. What an amazing fucking plan."

"This is the best deal you're going to get. They are afraid we will sue, which, frankly, they should be. But our case against them isn't strong enough. And their case against you leaks all over the place."

"So can't we call it a draw and walk away?"

"No. Because their case will only get stronger. It won't take them long to link Braddock Farm to your business. They already suspect that you're laundering money. How difficult do you think it will be for them to connect the credit card transactions of your customers to Braddock's bank accounts?"

"Fuck." I was glad I had hired a competent lawyer. I was glad I had given her background information when I put her on retainer. I just really didn't like what she was telling me.

"You sign this deal, they stop investigating you. More importantly, they stop investigating your uncle and his farm. They will leave Mr. Xiao alone."

"Fine." I felt all my fight leave as I succumbed.

"That's wise. Now, they will send you back to County for the weekend. I can spend time fighting that decision or I can spend time working to get you a better deal. Preferably one where you don't need to work with Detective Kallen. It is your call."

What a fun dilemma. "I can handle a weekend in County."

"You will be fine." Kent tapped her pen until I looked at her. "You'll be out by Monday." I nodded. "Good." She opened her notepad. "I'd like you to tell me everything you can about this case. While we are doing that, I'm going to tell them we are still making a decision and have one of my associates bring lunch. What's your pleasure?"

In any other situation, a hot dyke in a power suit asking that question would have been exquisite. In this one, all I could manage to say was, "Chinese?"

CHAPTER TWENTY-SEVEN

I was processed for another transfer sometime after noon on Monday. The jumpsuit and cuffs seemed unnecessary considering I was on my way to the district attorney's office to sign whatever deal Kent had secured for me. But who was I to judge procedure? It was obviously super effective.

Another junior officer drove me the four and a half blocks to the DA's office. He escorted me upstairs and into a secure room. We were only there for a minute before Joan Kent joined us. The rookie stepped outside to give us privacy. Kent sat across from me.

"I couldn't get Sergeant Ionescu and the DA to agree to a different handler," she said as soon as the door closed. "Reyes will act as backup in the event that Kallen is unavailable, but you will be instructed not to contact him unless it is an emergency."

"You couldn't soften that blow? Maybe tell me how jail soap is doing wonderful things for my hair?"

"Jail soap is doing nothing for your hair. We don't have a lot of time. Do you still want the deal?" I suppose her candor was a good thing considering she was paid by the hour and was a beast.

"Did you guys get Nate included in the deal?"

"Yes. He is meeting with his lawyer right now. You and Xiao will be working together. The deal treats the two of you as a single entity, essentially."

"Then let's do it."

Kent nodded. "You are going to be escorted to a conference room. I'll be there, as will Xiao and his lawyer. Sergeant Ionescu and Detectives Kallen and Reyes will be there as well. Ionescu is displeased with a number of aspects of this deal, so try not to piss him off. The deputy district attorney, Brian Walton, has been very charitable, so try not to piss him off either."

"So shut up and sign the documents."

"Basically, yes."

"I think I can follow those rules."

Kent nodded and knocked on the door. The rookie opened it and let her walk out. He retrieved me—dangerous criminal that I was—and took me to the conference room. It was packed, just like Kent had described. Nate was already there. He gave me a small smile and a nod. Good enough. We sat across from him and his lawyer. When the detectives came in two minutes later, they sat on the same side of the table as Kent and me.

I could easily pick out Sergeant Ionescu and Deputy DA Walton across from the detectives. Ionescu looked weathered and tanned. He was slim, but built. The sleeves of his dress shirt were taut against his muscled arms. His sun bleached hair was military close. The guy looked like he belonged on a boat or a farm or blowing up a third world country. Or whatever it was that good ol' boys did. He should have been anywhere but a conference room in the district attorney's office. Walton was obese and flamboyant. It was already over one hundred outside, but he was wearing a forest green sweater vest, a faintly pink dress shirt, and a beige suit. Ionescu managed to look calm, restrained. Walton looked bored.

I was careful to not look at the detectives. Reyes had finally gone home for a shower. His hair was artfully combed back. His fresh suit was less disheveled and a lot cleaner. Laurel had also changed her clothes and combed back her hair. I wondered if either of them ever noticed that they had the same haircut. Probably not.

Walton handed out copies of the agreement we were about to sign. He walked us through it page by page and outlined the specifics of the deal. It was the very long version of what Kent had already told me. The lawyers nodded respectfully. The detectives took notes. Ionescu stared longingly out the window. When Walton was finished, he asked if there were any questions. Laurel put up a finger, but finished writing a note before she spoke.

"Yes, Laurie?" Walton asked.

Laurel gave him a look that could have killed. If he was looking at her. He wasn't. I watched Reyes reach under the table and squeeze Laurel's leg just above the knee. She took a deep breath and schooled her expression into one of reverence.

"There is the matter of Henry Brewer. He is still at large and we can reasonably assume that Ms. Braddock will be a target," Laurel said.

"You're not concerned about Mr. Xiao?"

"Less so. Brewer likely still believes that Xiao was trying to help him." Reyes squeezed again. "Sir," she added.

"What do you propose, sweetheart?"

I thought the first look was bad. This look was enough to make a normal person cry. This look was a death wish. Reyes wasn't even squeezing anymore. He had a vice grip on her leg. Laurel put her hand on Reyes's wrist and forced a smile.

"I believe it would be wise to divert part of our team to help track down Brewer," Laurel said.

"I think it would be a waste of time and department resources," Ionescu spoke for the first time. His voice was deep and masculine and condescending and everything I expected it would be. "Brewer will turn up quickly. He has ties to the community. We have also been in extensive contact with the El Dorado Sheriff's Department. He makes them look bad so they are being cooperative. Sheriff Tolson is personally invested in seeing Brewer brought in."

I bet he was. If I remembered correctly, Henry's grandmother was friends with Tolson's wife. They had a knitting group. Henry's behavior didn't look good for anyone.

Reyes jumped in. "While that may be, we are still responsible for Braddock's safety. Kallen and I think that patrols should be increased around her house."

"Which would potentially jeopardize the investigation," Ionescu said.

I glanced at Kent, but she gave a quick shake of her head so I didn't speak. Which was fine. I enjoyed being discussed while I was sitting five feet away.

"What do you think should be done?" Walton asked Ionescu.

"Kallen's cover makes it reasonable to spend time at Braddock's house. Having a detective inside would be far superior to a noticeable police presence in the neighborhood."

Walton closed his notebook. "That settles it, then."

I don't know who was more unhappy about that resolution. Me or Laurel.

Rookie boy brought me back to County so I could be released. When my clothing and possessions had been returned to me, I was allowed to walk out into the blinding heat of downtown. My phone was dead. I was a solid twenty blocks away from home. This was going to be a long walk. I put on my sunglasses, thankful they had been in my pocket instead of Henry's rental. I had only taken two steps before I saw the large, baby blue truck double-parked at the curb. I turned the other direction. Laurel got out of the truck and came toward me.

"Don't," I said and kept walking.

"Just let me give you a ride home." She grabbed my arm.

"I'd rather walk."

"That will take you an hour. Longer in this heat. We don't need to talk. Just let me drive you."

If I let her drive me, I could be home and drunk a lot faster. Except I didn't get drunk. And I didn't think poetry was going to make me feel better. But at least I could see my cat. Fucking unconditional love, that was what I needed. I turned toward the truck, disgusted with myself.

The door cracked and popped like it always did. The noise was an affront. Laurel climbed behind the wheel and pulled into traffic.

"I'm sorry," Laurel said.

"You said we didn't need to talk."

Laurel nodded and concentrated on driving. I hated watching her drive. I hated watching her. She was everything I was attracted to. On top on that, she had conviction and a killer right hook. Then again, all of that was probably a lie. I wondered how much of what I had fallen for was specifically engineered to make me attracted to her. Was this her normal haircut or did she cut it to fit a profile? Was this her usual wardrobe, or had some pencil pusher at Sac PD designed it to make her more my type? What if she wasn't even gay?

I was trying to piss myself off. I had literally dug through the woman's closet. Everything in her apartment showed that she was exactly who she said she was. Plus, that photo of her as a teen definitely suggested she was a lesbian. Not to mention the hot sex. Okay, she was gay.

We went three blocks before I broke my own rule.

"What's the deal with Walton?"

"He's an old friend of my mother's."

"And he's known you since you were an infant?" That much was obvious.

"Basically, yes. I avoid him like the plague because he treats me like shit."

"How did he land my case?"

"I asked him."

I nodded. That sounded like a stupid idea to me. "Why?"

"I knew he would give me special treatment."

"Smooth. Make sure the deputy DA is in your pocket. That way, if anyone finds out you were fucking the person you were investigating, he will look the other way." I settled into my subject, into my anger. "This is why I don't buy into the system. You wanted to know. This right here is why. As long as your mommy is friends with the deputy DA, you can do whatever the hell you want. Nice moral code, Kallen. Really. I'm so glad the system has been kind to you."

"Fuck you."

"Fuck me?"

"Yeah, fuck you. I'm sorry life was tough for you. But I would trade my parents' disinterest for your uncle's love any day." She took the next turn at a brutal speed. "You want to know why I asked Brian to take the case? I knew he would cut a better deal for you and Nate. I called him at six a.m. on a Saturday. I interrupted his tee time." Was that golf? Well, gosh if she had interrupted his tee time, it must have been a big deal. "I'm going to be indebted to that piece of shit excuse for a human. For your ass. To keep your ass out of jail."

"You got my ass put in jail," I shouted.

"No, you did. You're a drug dealer. That was your decision, not mine. Stop blaming other people when things don't go your way."

"I don't."

"Yes, you do. You claim some sort of enlightenment as if you're better because you chose not to buy into the system. As if choosing the people around you is easy. Everyone else is weak because they do what is expected out of normal fucking human beings."

"They are weak. You're weak." This wasn't the time for pulled punches.

"No. Sometimes, strength is making the hard decision and making it work."

"Christ, now you're going to tell me that you're changing the system from within instead of rejecting it, right, Stevo?"

"No. I'm just saying that you can't reject every institution. Some of them are broken, some can be fixed, and some of them you just don't understand. But it's childish to claim that you reject them all." Her arrogance was astounding.

"I never claimed that."

"You're right. You pick and choose. That's not how adulthood works."

"You're seriously lecturing me on adulthood? Thanks, I think Sacramento County Jail already gave me the extended version of that lecture."

Laurel sighed. "This isn't productive."

"No shit," I said. "We disagree on basically everything. You just lied and told me that you agreed."

"That's the thing, though. I don't disagree with you." Her tone made me believe her. Which was just insulting. She had proven pretty well that her tone was a tool of manipulation.

"Yeah, that rant was pretty indicative of agreement."

"I'm angry at you," she said.

"Good."

"But the only thing I lied about was my job."

"And that I was your job." That was an important detail.

"And I'm sorry for that. I really am."

"Look, I'm stuck with you. I don't see any way out of that right now."

"Neither do I. You're going to have to trust me again."

"I can't." How could she ever imagine that I would trust her?

"What can I do?"

"You can't do shit. You targeted me. It was a planned betrayal."

The anger seemed to drain out of her. "I didn't know you." Her tone was pleading, desperate.

"And you still don't. Don't go soft on me now just because you feel bad for fucking me to get ahead, Detective." I spit the title at her.

"I didn't fuck you. I lo—"

"Pull over. Let me out."

"What?"

"Let me out of the truck. I'd rather walk." Laurel slowed, but didn't pull over. "Pull the fucking truck over." I opened my door and she slammed on the brakes.

"What the hell are you doing?"

"Walking." I got out and slammed the door behind me. If the only truth she had told me was that she loved me, I didn't want to hear it.

"Cash, please." I made the mistake of looking back. Her forearms were braced on the wheel. She looked young and small. "I didn't know." Her voice cracked.

I believed her. And I hated myself for it. But believing her wasn't enough for redemption. So I walked away. I needed to go home. Feed my cat. Read poetry. Do something other than look at Laurel Kallen.

Everything I'd built was in pieces. A part of me knew that I was to blame. Hell, a part of me had always expected that it would fall apart. Selling drugs didn't exactly engender a feeling of security. I didn't fault her for that. But she had held up a mirror to me. I didn't like what I'd seen.

The slow rumble of her engine followed me until I reached the corner of a one-way street. I turned so she couldn't follow me. She idled for a long time before the hum of her engine faded as she drove away. I loathed the part of me that wanted her to come back.

I'd find a way to make this work. I'd feed pieces of information to the police in exchange for my freedom. I'd build protective walls between my dealing and the farm. I'd make enough for the mortgage and Nate's tuition. But I couldn't forgive her because I couldn't forgive myself.

I was broken, but I lied and told myself it didn't matter because none of us are whole.

About the Author

Ashley Bartlett was born and raised in California. Her life consists of reading, writing, and editing. Most of the time Ashley engages in these pursuits while sitting in front of a coffee shop with her wife.

It's a glamorous life.

She is an obnoxious, sarcastic, punk-ass, but her friends don't hold that against her. She lives in Sacramento, but you can find her at ashbartlett.com.

Books Available from Bold Strokes Books

18 Months by Samantha Boyette. Alissa Reeves has only had two girlfriends and they've both gone missing. Now it's up to her to find out why. (978-1-62639-804-7)

Arrested Hearts by Holly Stratimore. A reckless cop with a secret death wish and a health nut who is afraid to die might be a perfect combination for love. (978-1-62639-809-2)

Capturing Jessica by Jane Hardee. Hyperrealist sculptor Michael tries desperately to conceal the love she holds for best friend, Jess, unaware Jess's feelings for her are changing. (978-1-62639-836-8)

Counting to Zero by AJ Quinn. NSA agent Emma Thorpe and computer hacker Paxton James must learn to trust each other as they work to stop a threat clock that's rapidly counting down to zero. (978-1-62639-783-5)

Courageous Love by KC Richardson. Two women fight a devastating disease, and their own demons, while trying to fall in love. (978-1-62639-797-2)

Pathogen by Jessica L. Webb. Can Dr. Kate Morrison navigate a deadly virus and the threat of bioterrorism, as well as her new relationship with Sergeant Andy Wyles and her own troubled past? (978-1-62639-833-7)

Rainbow Gap by Lee Lynch. Jaudon Vickers and Berry Garland, polar opposites, dream and love in this tale of lesbian lives set in Central Florida against the tapestry of societal change and the Vietnam War. (978-1-62639-799-6)

Steel and Promise by Alexa Black. Lady Nivrai's cruel desires and modified body make most of the galaxy fear her, but courtesan Cailyn Derys soon discovers the real monsters are the ones without the claws. (978-1-62639-805-4)

Swelter by D. Jackson Leigh. Teal Giovanni's mistake shines an unwanted spotlight on a small Texas ranch where August Reese is secluded until she can testify against a powerful drug kingpin. (978-1-62639-795-8)

Without Justice by Carsen Taite. Cade Kelly and Emily Sinclair must battle each other in the pursuit of justice, but can they fight their undeniable attraction outside the walls of the courtroom? (978-1-62639-560-2)

21 Questions by Mason Dixon. To find love, start by asking the right questions. (978-1-62639-724-8)

A Palette for Love by Charlotte Greene. When newly minted Ph.D. Chloé Devereaux returns to New Orleans, she doesn't expect her new job, and her powerful employer—Amelia Winters—to be so appealing. (978-1-62639-758-3)

By the Dark of Her Eyes by Cameron MacElvee. When Brenna Taylor inherits a decrepit property haunted by tormented ghosts, Alejandra Santana must not only restore Brenna's house and property but also save her soul. (978-1-62639-834-4)

Cash Braddock by Ashley Bartlett. Cash Braddock just wants to hang with her cat, fall in love, and deal drugs. What's the problem with that? (978-1-62639-706-4)

Gravity by Juliann Rich. How can Ellie Engebretsen, Olympic ski jumping hopeful with her eye on the gold, soar through the air when all she feels like doing is falling hard for Kate Moreau, her greatest competitor and the girl of her dreams? (978-1-62639-483-4)

Lone Ranger by VK Powell. Reporter Emma Ferguson stirs up a thirty-year-old mystery that threatens Park Ranger Carter West's family and jeopardizes any hope for a relationship between the two women. (978-1-62639-767-5)

Love on Call by Radclyffe. Ex-Army medic Glenn Archer and recent LA transplant Mariana Mateo fight their mutual desire in the face of past losses as they work together in the Rivers Community Hospital ER. (978-1-62639-843-6)

Never Enough by Robyn Nyx. Can two women put aside their pasts to find love before it's too late? (978-1-62639-629-6)

Two Souls by Kathleen Knowles. Can love blossom in the wake of tragedy? (978-1-62639-641-8)

Camp Rewind by Meghan O'Brien. A summer camp for grown-ups becomes the site of an unlikely romance between a shy, introverted divorcee and one of the Internet's most infamous cultural critics— who attends undercover. (978-1-62639-793-4)

Cross Purposes by Gina L. Dartt. In pursuit of a lost Acadian treasure, three women must not only work out the clues, but also the complicated tangle of emotion and attraction developing between them. (978-1-62639-713-2)

Imperfect Truth by C.A. Popovich. Can an imperfect truth stand in the way of love? (978-1-62639-787-3)

Life in Death by M. Ullrich. Sometimes the devastating end is your only chance for a new beginning. (978-1-62639-773-6)

Love on Liberty by MJ Williamz. Hearts collide when politics clash. (978-1-62639-639-5)

Serious Potential by Maggie Cummings. Pro golfer Tracy Allen plans to forget her ex during a visit to Bay West, a lesbian condo community in NYC, but when she meets Dr. Jennifer Betsy, she gets more than she bargained for. (978-1-62639-633-3)

Taste by Kris Bryant. Accomplished chef Taryn has walked away from her promising career in the city's top restaurant to devote her life to her five-year-old daughter and is content until Ki Blake comes along. (978-1-62639-718-7)

The Second Wave by Jean Copeland. Can star-crossed lovers have a second chance after decades apart, or does the love of a lifetime only happen once? (978-1-62639-830-6)

Valley of Fire by Missouri Vaun. Taken captive in a desert outpost after their small aircraft is hijacked, Ava and her captivating passenger discover things about each other and themselves that will change them both forever. (978-1-62639-496-4)

Basic Training of the Heart by Jaycie Morrison. In 1944, socialite Elizabeth Carlton joins the Women's Army Corps to escape family expectations and love's disappointments. Can Sergeant Gale Rains get her through Basic Training with their hearts intact? (978-1-62639-818-4)

Before by KE Payne. When Tally falls in love with her band's new recruit, she has a tough decision to make. What does she want more—Alex or the band? (978-1-62639-677-7)

Believing in Blue by Maggie Morton. Growing up gay in a small town has been hard, but it can't compare to the next challenge Wren—with her new, sky-blue wings—faces: saving two entire worlds. (978-1-62639-691-3)

Coils by Barbara Ann Wright. A modern young woman follows her aunt into the Greek Underworld and makes a pact with Medusa to win her freedom by killing a hero of legend. (978-1-62639-598-5)

Courting the Countess by Jenny Frame. When relationship-phobic Lady Henrietta Knight starts to care about housekeeper Annie Brannigan and her daughter, can she overcome her fears and promise Annie the forever that she demands? (978-1-62639-785-9)

For Money or Love by Heather Blackmore. Jessica Spaulding must choose between ignoring the truth to keep everything she has, and doing the right thing only to lose it all—including the woman she loves. (978-1-62639-756-9)

Hooked by Jaime Maddox. With the help of sexy Detective Mac Calabrese, Dr. Jessica Benson is working hard to overcome her past, but it may not be enough to stop a murderer. (978-1-62639-689-0)

Lands End by Jackie D. Public relations superstar Amy Kline is dealing with a media nightmare, and the last thing she expects is for restaurateur Lena Michaels to change everything, but she will. (978-1-62639-739-2)

Lysistrata Cove by Dena Hankins. Jack and Eve navigate the maelstrom of their darkest desires and find love by transgressing gender, dominance, submission, and the law on the crystal blue Caribbean Sea. (978-1-62639-821-4)

Twisted Screams by Sheri Lewis Wohl. Reluctant psychic Lorna Dutton doesn't want to forgive, but if she doesn't do just that an innocent woman will die. (978-1-62639-647-0)